THE GREEK WARRIOR
(A Giles Courtenay Adventure)

by

BRIAN WITHECOMBE

B.J.R. Withecombe
Badgers Holt,
16 Weybridge Walk,
North Shoebury,
Essex SS3 8YJ
01702 216435
01702 221522 (Office)
07809768474(Mobile)

Also by the same Author and available on Kindle

Courtenay Adventures

The Seagull and LeCorsair
Aphrodite's Quest
Amazon at the Nile
The Winged Avenger
HMS Pegasus

Chris Metcalfe Stories

CID Algarve – Metcalfe's Challenge

ONE

The large two-decked ship edged very slowly through the mist which covered the narrow channel between the rocky coastline and the off-shore island. The sails hung wetly against their masts as the ship, with barely enough wind behind her to give her steerage, gingerly moved eerily through the darkness.

In the bows men watched anxiously ahead and abeam, and on his platform, the leadsman was casting his lead and line again, feeling the tell-tale markers on the line with his hand, recognising the different ways the depth was shown. The man felt the latest marker, turned and spoke to his mate, and the depth was passed by word of mouth quietly along the deck to the broad quarterdeck where a number of officers were also watching the progress of the stately ship of the line with a certain amount of unease.

If the Captain of this ship was concerned, he was not showing it. He stood near the larboard side of the quarterdeck, hands behind his back, apparently at ease with the situation. Another man, dressed in a cox'n's uniform, stood beside him. Behind them was the great double wheel and a cluster of figures mostly in blue and white. A very tall man was next to the wheel, looking at the sails flapping above, just the topsails set at present, and then listening for the messages from the man with the lead and line. He knew the chart for this area like the back of his hand. He ought to, and he knew that if he did not, his Captain would have had him out of the   ship as soon as he took command.

For the past few weeks, since the new Captain had taken command, this ship, His Britannic Majesty's ship *Hercules,* had been on blockade duty. This was July 1801, just a few short months after the Battle of Copenhagen, and the Royal Navy was still intent on bottling up the French in their ports.

Hercules was a 74-gun ship of the line, originally of French construction, and called the *Hercule.* She was a prize, taken the previous year and re-fitted as a King's ship. Now she was under the command of Captain Sir Giles Courtenay, and part of the Inshore Squadron blockading this part of the French coast. As his cox'n, Alex Trafford, looked on, Courtenay glanced to one side as he heard the message from the leadsman in the chains being passed back. The tall man near the wheel gave his Captain an anxious glance, or at least, as anxious as he dared. Jacob Wetherby had been at sea for more years than he cared to recall, and he had seen everything, served in almost every kind of ship.

Courtenay smiled to himself. He could almost feel his Sailing Master's eyes boring into his back. He turned.

"Very well, Mr Wetherby, bring her up a point, if you please."

"Aye sir."

The hands had been waiting for the word, because they knew they would shortly have to alter course to stay in the channel, and as the wheel moved slightly to bring the ship's head round a degree to starboard, they tailed onto the braces and adjusted the sails so that none of the slight wind was lost.

Courtenay shifted his gaze from the sight of the Master visibly relaxing as the chant came back they were in slightly deeper water as he heard feet on the starboard ladder to the gangway and the cocked hat of his First-Lieutenant appeared.

The man, who had a grave face for quite a young man, came to him and touched his hat which was covered in moisture from the mist.

"All ready sir. Hands all mustered."

"Thank you Mr Cressy. I trust that the hands selected were all *volunteers?*"

Simon Cressy allowed himself a slight smile. "Yes sir. Your instructions were most explicit on that point."

"Good. Well, if my memory of the chart serves me correctly a few more moments and we will be in position. Then you may leave. I wish to be as close to the mouth of the river as I can be. That will save the men a long hard pull."

"Aye sir."

At least the men in the two boats which were going on this mission would have the darkness and the mist on their side, Courtenay thought. Provided they did not get lost!

Trafford shifted his feet and looked sideways at his Captain. He sensed Cressy was scrutinising him but cared nothing for that. He was unreachable.

Courtenay looked at him. "And what ails you, Alex? Do you wish you were going with the First-Lieutenant?"

"No Sir Giles, it ain't that. I just don't like being this close to the Frogs on a dark and dismal night and with land on both sides!'

Courtenay smiled. "Never fear. The Island to our left ends shortly, and as it does so we will be near the entrance to the River, although I think that whoever named it a river was being incredibly optimistic. It is little more than a large creek!'

"Bit like some of the places back home then, sir?"

"Aye there are quite a few around the coastline just like it!" He turned back to Cressy. "The Commodore has received intelligence as you know, that invasion craft are

5

being not only stored, but built up this, er river. Do not take any chances Mr Cressy. Get into the river, have a careful look around, and then return. If you see anything, we will then report back and await instructions."

The tall Master called quietly. "By my reckoning sir, the Island on our larboard side ought to be ending in a few moments. We will then be in position."

"Thank you Mr Wetherby. Very well Mr Cressy, I suggest you go and take command of your men. Good luck to you, and remember, no chances!"

"Aye sir."

Cressy touched his hat and hurried down the starboard ladder.

The Master coughed politely.

Giles Courtenay smiled. "Very well Mr Wetherby, heave-to if you please."

Without any shouted commands, it seemed like a ghost ship which slowly drifted to a halt as its sails were loosely furled up. Courtenay walked to the starboard side of his quarterdeck and watched as the two boats were lowered. His thoughts turned inward as he watched them without really seeing them at all.

The First-Lieutenant watched critically as the men filed quietly down into the boats, and before he went through the entry port he turned and looked up at the quarterdeck. Courtenay lifted a hand and Cressy touched his hat by way of reply. Then he was gone and the boats were pushing off from *Hercules'* side.

Trafford was watching with professional interest as the boats moved away, noting the way one or two of the oarsmen had not picked up the stroke properly, and he could imagine the hoarse commands and threats which were being issued to the men responsible. He gave a sigh and Courtenay turned to smile.

"Not up to our standard yet Alex, but we will endure, never fear!"

The tall, languid figure of his aristocratic Second Lieutenant loomed by the wheel, checking the bearings and glancing at the ramrod helmsmen. Courtenay had not had time as yet to get to know all his officers well, although that would change, but John St Clair, despite his haughty manner and seemingly impeccable manners was someone he had already decided he was going to have to watch. Trafford saw his Captain looking at the man and grimaced inwardly. He had already heard tales about that one!

He expression changed to a smile as a familiar figure appeared. The fifth Lieutenant, Percy Wedderburn, had been detailed to go with the boats, and the Fourth Lieutenant, a friend of his, was coming to watch him leave. He leaned over the side and waved to his friend, then turned and saw Courtenay watching him.

"I am most terribly sorry sir. I did not realise you were there."

"That is perfectly all right Mr Jeffrey. I know you and Mr Wedderburn are friendly. It is good to have friends."

Courtenay smiled. "Walk with me. The exercise is good for both us, I fear!"

Trafford looked on as the Captain and Fourth Lieutenant strode up and down the quarterdeck whilst the boats disappeared into the gloom. He looked at the straight back of the young officer and it was not difficult at all to see the Midshipman.

It was scarcely any time at all from the Battle of Copenhagen, when Vice-Admiral Lord Nelson had led the Fleet into the attack against the Danish defences in what can only be described as bully-boy tactics on the part of the British Government to break up the so-called Armed Neutrality of the North between Denmark, Sweden and Russia which was threatening to prevent the Royal Navy searching neutral ships to make sure they were not trying to run the Blockade off the coast of France.

Trafford recalled the Battle only too clearly. He and Giles Courtenay were in the *Pegasus* at that time, a fine 74, but slightly smaller than the *Hercules.* The battle had had the desired effect, even though there had been a terrible loss of men, worse so on the Danish side.

On return home, Courtenay had been given some leave, but it had ended all too soon, and although his wife Jessica had done her very best to hide it, she was heartbroken he was required to return to sea so quickly. His old mentor, Admiral Lord Crompton, had been very apologetic, but he wanted Courtenay in command of a new ship, and back where he could be of most use. He also knew a Peace Treaty was planned, and he was determined to make sure the blockading ships forced as much discomfort on the French as possible so as to extract the best possible terms.

And so Captain Sir Giles Courtenay had had to leave the *Pegasus,* a ship he loved, to begin again somewhere else. However, as Trafford well knew, Courtenay was very pleased with his new command. Although she was slightly larger than *Pegasus, Hercules* drew less, which meant she was ideal for what she was doing now.

She had sneaked in between an island off the French coast and a battery on a headland guarding the entrance to what was really little more than a creek, but a deep one at that. It was literally just like a slash in the French coastline, but perfect for the task Napoleon Bonaparte had set his Generals and Admirals. The construction of invasion craft. Courtenay had chosen a misty night, with no moon to perform the task which the Commanding Officer of his Squadron had given him.

Commodore Hugh Griffiths had been until a short while ago the Captain of the *Hercules,* and well knew what she was capable of. When he had been unexpectedly advanced to Commodore, he had relinquished command to Courtenay and flown his

Broad Pendant in the largest of the line of battle ships present off the French coast, as he had been ordered to do by the Admiralty. He had known however, his was to be a short appointment, at least at sea. He was ordered to return home when relieved by the Vice-admiral who was to take command of this Inshore Squadron.

He had also known Courtenay's record. He had had no qualms about seeing him in command, and giving him the task of sneaking into Boney's back yard.

That had been three days ago. Courtenay had been forced to wait in frustration for the right weather conditions, and this night they had arrived. Just in case, the French Tricolour was bent on to the halliards and the Signals Midshipman, a very ernest young man called McMasters, stood ready to haul the flag up to the mizzen gaff if necessary.

Trafford looked over the side at the dark water and then realised that Courtenay was at his side.

"It will be a while before Mr Cressy returns Alex, so I think I will go below and enjoy a mug of Kingston's excellent coffee. I am sure you can find something to amuse you?" Courtenay turned to Jeffrey, smiled, and walked to the doors under the poop which led to his spacious cabin. Trafford grinned at the young Lieutenant, who patted his arm as he walked past to take up position at the rail.

The time seemed to drag. Courtenay, sitting with a coffee mug in his hands, knew that very little time had actually passed, but it was always the same. He knew he would rather have been with the boat party, but he had to accept he had to allow those beneath him to show what they could do. To him, the entire ship's company were still strangers, but it must be even worse for the crew. The man who could hang every single last one of them if he could come up with sufficient excuses, and they knew not what he was like. That would change of course, but he had to gain their trust.

The Sailing Master, Jacob Wetherby, was looking anxiously around, and he paced across the quarterdeck and back, his hands behind his tall figure, and trying to hide his concern.

Jeffrey turned to him in the end and smiled shortly. "Goodness, Mr Wetherby, you are all of a quiver! In the time I have been in the ship, I have never seen you so concerned?"

Wetherby turned on the young officer, a reply forming on his lips. Even the Fourth Lieutenant was not immune to an occasional respectful blast from the Master, but he realised Steven Jeffrey was not being conceited or sarcastic, just concerned. His face softened.

"I do feel a mite concerned Mr Jeffrey, I have to admit. If that mist goes we will be seen by the battery on the headland, and we have reason to believe there is one on the island as well!"

Jeffrey smiled again. "The Captain has the French flag ready to show, Mr Wetherby, we are in a French-built ship, and whilst I accept the only thing we do not have at the moment is the recognition code, if we have to we can be well away before those lazy Frogs can ram ball and powder. Although," he added, I doubt the Captain will abandon Mr Cressy and the Fifth Lieutenant!"

Wetherby turned a doubtful look on his face which young Jeffrey correctly interpreted.

'Rest assured Mr Wetherby, Sir Giles is not the sort of Captain to abandon his men to save his own skin."

"I forgot, Mr Jeffrey, you are the only person in the ship who has ever sailed with him before."

"I have a feeling one or two of the hands have been with him, but I had the honour to serve with the Captain in two of his commands."

"In that case Mr Jeffrey, I am sure we can accept your word!"

Jeffrey took the polite smile off his face and replaced it with a scowl as the person who spoke the words came into view. It was the haughty Second Lieutenant, St Clair.

Jeffrey coloured slightly, touched his hat and walked away. St Clair turned his face towards Wetherby, but he was making a show of checking the compass card. His scowl became deeper as he walked back to the other side of the wheel.

Two hours later, with Courtenay back on the quarterdeck and tapping his foot on the pale planking in agitation, there was a hushed call from the waist of the ship.

'Boats' comin' back, sir!' That was Jeremiah Smith, the Bosun. Courtenay had been to pains to ensure he knew who that person was. With a very young wardroom, he knew he would have to rely even more than he had done in the past on his backbone of senior warrant officers, and the Bosun was the most senior of those in the ship, save the Sailing Master.

Courtenay did not know how the man knew the boats were returning, because when he looked over the side he could see nothing, but then there was the slight swish of oars. Men were lining the side with muskets, just in case, and various of the deadly swivel guns were also manned, packed with a full charge of grape. There was no need for worry. Out of the gloom, the two boats appeared, and came alongside with a slight bump.

Courtenay paced this way and that, impatiently waiting for his First-Lieutenant to report to the quarterdeck. He heard steps on the starboard ladder and turned.

Cressy stood in front of him, touching his hat.

The man suddenly smiled broadly and Courtenay realised it was the first time since he had taken command he had actually seen his senior do anything than wear a stern expression.

"They are there alright, sir. Construction has been going on a-pace if you ask me. There are all kinds of invasion craft there, and some gunboats. Flat-bottoms, chase-maries, everything. Oh, and a frigate, 32 guns by the look of her, and a corvette."

"So the Commodore was right then." commented Wetherby. "may I suggest we set some sail and move out to sea, sir?"

Courtenay looked at him and nodded. "Yes Mr Wetherby, make sail and let us return to the open sea. Mr Cressy, come below after seeing to your men and we will discuss what you have found. I would suggest a large tot for each man."

Cressy went back to his stern expression. "Won't go down well with the Purser, sir!"

Courtenay was exasperated. "My God Mr Cressy, when did anything at all ever meet with a Purser's approval unless it was lining his pocket? Just tell him I said so and I will not hear of any arguments, do I make myself clear?"

Without a further word Courtenay turned on his heel, and with a final look as the topsails were dropped and sheeted home, went to stand near the wheel. Cressy looked at the Master and went to shrug his shoulders. "I think I asked you to look after your men, Mr Cressy" Courtenay said quietly.

"Aye sir. Immediately." Cressy left. Trafford, still near the side, moved away and gave a small shiver. He walked towards the other side of the ship, and then leaned back to watch the sails as, sheeted home, and with the hands tailing onto the braces, they started to fill with what wind there was. *Hercules* moved slowly, easily, with the leadsman in the chains once more, and silently, almost eerily, down the channel to the open sea.

Later, with the ship on the larboard tack and a gentle nor-easterly pushing them along, Cressy reported to Courtenay in the cabin. Kingston padded in with a tray and some glasses, and Courtenay gestured for Cressy to be seated. The First-Lieutenant took a glass of brandy gratefully.

"Well sir. As the Commodore supposed there are plenty of invasion craft there, and only two men o'war to guard them. I had a leadsman in my boat as you know, and he was taking soundings as we went in. The mist was quite thick in places and we managed to get quite close without being seen."

"How deep is the channel?"

Cressy smiled again because he knew what his Captain was thinking. It was what any man of action would be considering. "Deep enough for us sir, and some to spare."

Courtenay stood and opened the chart. He traced a line into the inlet. "Is there room to wear ship?"

"Yes sir, I believe there is. May I ask what you intend, sir?"

"You may. I will tell you now and then before we execute the plan, everyone else will also know. I intend that *Hercules* will enter the inlet, rake the men o'war before they know what is happening and then sink or damage as many of those damned invasion craft as possible."

"When sir?"

"When the tide and the wind is right, so that we can both get in and out."

"Even at night sir, at this time of the year, if there is a moon we will be seen by the batteries and engaged sir. We will not get anywhere near the ships."

"I know that Mr Cressy." Courtenay was calm. Trafford, standing near the door, was conscious of the fact his Captain was about to order this two-decker into an enclosed inlet on the French coast, and he was as calm as if they were taking part in a fleet review. He smiled. Normal service, then!

"You will surely remember this was a French ship? Build in the Brest yards? She will be recognised as such."

"We have no recognition signals sir."

"Then, dammit Mr Cressy, we will improvise!" Courtenay, Trafford could see, was becoming agitated. Even Kingston poked his head around the door of his pantry with a questioning look on his face.

"I am sorry sir, but I am the senior in this ship, and it is my duty to....."

"Yes Mr Cressy, I am aware of your duty. I too have been a First-Lieutenant, although my service in that regard was in a sloop-of-war. However, I have *my* duty and that is to execute the Commodore's orders, is that clear?"

"Of course sir."

Courtenay paused for a moment and instead of Cressy's serious countenance, saw the face of James Fenwick, until recently his First-Lieutenant and close friend. After Copenhagen, in line with tradition all the First-Lieutenants of the ships in the battle were promoted to Commander. Fenwick had been secured a command by Lord Crompton. He was Captain of an 18-gun sloop. Tim Spellman's face appeared for a moment, too. He had been his senior in the sloop *Seagull*. He dragged his mind back.

'We will tarry a while off the coast and out of sight of land. There is very likely to be a fisherman. He will know the recognition codes. All we need is enough to get in. I have reason to believe the battery on the island faces the sea only, so we will have the one on the headland, and any that are on shore. However, what I intend is that whilst we are entering the inlet, with the aid of the Tricolour, some of Captain Merilees' men will be landing at the bottom of the headland, and arranging to take the battery there. I am sure he will be most grateful for some employment for his men, would you not agree?'

Cressy allowed himself a small smile. Jason Merilees was their dashing Captain of Marines. He was always boasting about his men. Time to make him put his men where his mouth was!

"I am certain that you are right sir. Will give them something to do, after all."

"Even if we are able to secure the recognition code, we still need to get out, because the game will be up once we fire our first broadside!"

"Yes sir."

"Very well Mr Cressy, you may carry on."

Cressy stood up, replaced his hat and moved to the door. Trafford closed it after him.

"He ain't much like the others sir, is he?"

"Now now, Alex, give him a chance. But you are right, he is not. However, he is clearly a most competent officer and very experienced. Still, I would rather….."

"Aye sir. I know. Mr Fenwick or Mr Wyvern, they would have known what you intended before you knew yourself!"

"Perhaps, Alex, perhaps. Join me for a tot?"

"Aye sir, reckon I will!"

The following morning found them cruising along the French coast on the larboard tack, with a fine wind coming in over the larboard quarter, and all sails drawing well. The sun was strong, and the hands had turned to with a will. This had in fact been one of the best days for weather since Courtenay had taken command, and many a seaman turned whilst they were carrying out their duties to watch their new Captain pace up and down his quarterdeck dressed only in shirt and breeches. They were used to officers who always appeared in full uniform, and they were unused to the relaxed mode of dress their Captain preferred. The Bosun, Jeremiah Smith, soon put a stop to their speculating with a few sharp commands, but even he was forced to take in the picture of his new Lord and Master standing with a foot on a bollard, holding onto a ratline and looking at the sea creaming down the side, with his longish hair loose and blowing in the wind. He had heard plenty of tales about this man, how he fought like a tiger, but he kept his own counsel and wanted to wait until they were in action together before forming an opinion.

He could not fault the Captain on his seamanship, that was certain. Even the Master, Wetherby, had been forced to admit that Captain Sir Giles Courtenay knew his way around when it came to ship-handling.

Courtenay could sense the scrutiny, but was impervious to it. He knew what the men were thinking, and he knew also things would change once he had taken them into combat. That was something which was going to happen very soon.

He heard six bells of the forenoon watch strike. The Officer of the Watch was the Third Lieutenant, a pleasant young man called Alan Frobisher whose father was a Vice-admiral. Fortunately, as yet, he had not exhibited, at least not in front of Courtenay, any of the traits which his father had. As a Captain, Frobisher senior had something of a reputation for flogging his crew for the slightest aberration.

"Mr Frobisher, pass the word for the First-Lieutenant, if you please."

"Aye sir." Frobisher turned and spoke quietly to the Midshipman of the Watch, Mallory, and he disappeared down the companion to the Wardroom. Three minutes later, Cressy arrived on deck, not a hair out of place, and dressed as if he was undergoing an Admiral's inspection. If he was surprised at his Captain's attire, he tried not to show it, although not very well. Trafford, watching from near the Poop, saw the senior's expression and smiled slightly. He would learn a lot more shortly!

"Mr Cressy. In a moment we will come about and head back to that creek. I have timed it so that we will approach again during the night, and so that we will be in position to attack at dawn. I wish to have a conference with my officers during the afternoon watch at six bells. Senior Warrant Officers as well of course, and the Midshipman, aside from those on watch."

'Senior Warrants sir?'

"Do I have to repeat myself Mr Cressy?" said Courtenay mildly.

"No, of course not sir, it is just that…."

"It is just that….nothing. It is important everyone taking part in this operation knows precisely what is expected of them Mr Cressy. The Warrant Officers are the backbone of my command a fact which you ought to be sensible of. They are to be kept as informed as my officers."

"Of course sir. I will make the arrangements."

"Good. Very well Mr Cressy, carry on. I know you are off watch at present, and rest is always precious."

Cressy touched his hat and turned away, frowning. He saw Trafford studying him and was momentarily quite angry. Then he was going down the companion and Trafford was forgotten.

"Gentlemen, gather round the map if you will." Courtenay was in the cabin, with all this officers, Warrant Officers and Midshipmen who were not on watch. He had the chart open on his desk, and everyone had crowded around it. Courtenay himself strolled to the stern windows. The sun had gone, and there was now thick cloud. The Master had predicted this would remain. Courtenay had clapped him on the arm and said "Excellent. We need no shining moon for what we are about tonight!"

"You can see the Island. Intelligence tells us there is a battery on it, probably with 12 pounders. Look at the headland. There is a battery on the headland, and they have 24 pounders. That we know for a fact."

"How is that sir, may I ask?" this from the Fifth Lieutenant, Jeffrey's friend Wedderburn. He coloured as Courtenay turned to look at him.

"Of course you may ask Mr Wedderburn. Any officer may ask me anything he chooses if he is uncertain as to something. What is it?"

"How do we know there are 24 pounders, sir?"

Courtenay smiled. "From the same source of intelligence which told us about the invasion craft. There is an agent working ashore, passing on this information to us."

"Can he be trusted sir?" Cressy looked worried.

"I understand from the Commodore the Agent has the Admiralty's confidence, Mr Cressy. I am sure we can share that confidence?"

Cressy said nothing, just bent further over the chart.

"You will notice gentlemen, that both batteries face out to sea as usual, so that when we are in the creek, although perhaps it is unfair to call it that, there is no protection from them. However, they do cover the entrance, and that is something which could be very disadvantageous to us. Which is why, gentlemen, our Marines are going to come to our rescue!"

All eyes turned, as Courtenay knew they would, to the two marine Officers, Captain Merrilees and his Lieutenant, Pemberton.

"Very well, " Courtenay continued, "this is what we will do. We will approach the land again under cover of dark. We will enter the channel again, and we will be flying French colours, just in case. If we are challenged, we will have to try and persuade the battery we are going about our lawful occasions! Using that darkness, and the Master assures me that there will be thick cloud tonight, Captain Merrilees will take his men ashore, land on the small beach below the headland, climb the same, and take the battery. He will destroy the guns, retire to the beach in what I am sure will be an orderly fashion, and be ready to re-join us. In the meantime, gentlemen, at dawn, we will force the entrance, sail up the creek, rake the frigate and the corvette and sink as many of the invasion craft as we can. We will wear ship, and give the starboard batteries a chance to cause more damage before we leave. Simple, gentlemen, but effective!"

Trafford had to smile. The Captain made it sound simple, but there could be problems, especially if someone woke up to the fact there was a ship of the line slipping through the channel between the island and the headland. And suppose the battery had more men than the Marines had?

Kingston appeared with a laden tray and Trafford went into the pantry to collect the other one the cabin servant had prepared. This one had glasses of rum on it. The Captain knew that as soon as the briefing was over, the Warrant Officers would slip away. That was not Courtenay's way at all.

Kingston circulated with his tray until all the glasses had gone and Courtenay was standing in the centre of the group.

He saw the Warrant Officers move to open the cabin door and slide away, then Trafford appeared next to them with the rum. He also saw the surprised look on their faces. They took their glasses and turned back to the cabin.

"Gentlemen, it's an old one, but tried and tested. Death to the French!"

"And confusion to our enemies!" came the roared reply.

TWO

Hercules was once again in the channel between the Island and the headland. It was pitch black. No moon, and thick cloud as Wetherby had predicted. There was a flap from above the quarterdeck and the Midshipman in charge of signals, McMasters, looked up to see the French Tricolour. He looked down and checked the other halliard. That was the one with their own colours bent on. The ship was moving very slowly, and he knew from what the Captain had said that the ship would very shortly be hove-to, whilst the Marines manned their boats. It was four bells of the hated middlewatch, 2am. The Marines would be leaving soon, to allow time to be rowed ashore and then for them to get into position.

Courtenay was on the quarterdeck, pacing slowly up and down with Trafford watching from near the poop. Trafford knew his Captain better than to think he had doubts about the forthcoming attack. What Courtenay was doing was going over his orders again in his head to make sure he had not forgotten anything.

Cressy however, standing by the rail and keeping his eyes on everything, was thinking that perhaps Courtenay was nervous about what he was about to do. He glanced at Trafford, and saw him watching Courtenay. As if there was some sixth sense, Trafford felt the scrutiny and looked directly at the First-Lieutenant. He touched his hat, and went back to watching his Captain.

Wetherby coughed politely. "Time in my view, sir."

Courtenay smiled. "Aye, I agree. Heave-to Mr Wetherby, if you please. Mr Cressy? It is time the Marines left us, I believe."

"Aye sir. Captain Merrilees will know, from the ship heaving-to."

"Maybe. But you will take him a message from me before he and his men leave. My compliments to him and his men, and I wish them all good luck."

"Aye sir." Cressy left the quarterdeck.

Courtenay walked to the rail and ran his hand along its polished surface, still warm from the day's sunshine. He walked across to the starboard side and stood, hands behind him, as he watched the Marines climbing down into the boats which would take ashore. He saw the Marine Lieutenant, Arthur Pemberton, go through the entry port, and then Merrilees stepped up. He turned and looked directly up at Courtenay and raised his hat. Then he was gone, down into the boats with his men, and the boats were shoving off from the side. They were soon lost in the gloom.

It appeared oddly quiet after they had gone, not that they had made any kind of noise. Silence was at a premium.

"Mr Wetherby, are we snug here?"

"Aye sir. As long as I can keep some kind of eye on how she might be swinging."

"Then anchor. We are out of sight of the battery for now. We will weigh before first light and proceed to the entrance of the anchorage. I wish to enter the same as dawn breaks."

"Them Frogs ought to be well and truly asleep by then, sir!"

"Precisely so, Mr Wetherby."

Courtenay went below, not because he wanted to, but because he knew that he had to show the Ship's company that he trusted their officers. He slumped down on the bench seat in the cabin, and gratefully took a mug of coffee which Kingston had made for him. Trafford came in, and took down Courtenay's sword from its rack to clean it, not that he thought it would be needed later. He knew the plan of attack. In, sink or severely damage as much as possible, and back out again, hopefully with the guns of the headland battery silenced.

"Why don't you get some sleep, Trafford. Nothing is going to happen until dawn."

"Perhaps, Sir Giles, you ought to take some of your own advice? Some sleep would do you good!"

Courtenay smiled. "My God Alex, you have been listening too much to that wife of mine! I could hear her say that!"

"Plenty o' sense, Miss….Lady Courtenay."

"You know she does not like that title to be used among the family and friends, Alex. To you, and quite a few other shipmates, she will always be Miss Jessica."

"Aye sir. True enough. You sure you won't get some sleep?"

"No, I want to be awake in case anything goes awry."

"In which case sir, I'll see if Kingston has any of that coffee left!"

In the last moments before dawn, the eastern horizon was lit with a subtle saffron glow, tinged with pink, announcing the sun on this new morning. All the hands had been called an hour before and had had breakfast. The decks had been cleaned, and the ship was cleared for action.

Wetherby was by the wheel, next to three quartermasters who stood ready to translate his orders into actions. He sniffed the air. There had been no sounds from the headland, but Courtenay had expected none. However, there would be soon, if Merrilees stuck to the plan.

Courtenay said over his shoulder, "Get the ship under way, Mr Wetherby.'

"Aye sir." At a signal from the Bosun, Smith, the topmen rushed aloft and set the topsails. Men swarmed out onto the bowsprit and set the jibs'ls. The anchor had been hove short earlier by the men on the capstan, dragging the ship very slowly and very quietly up to its hook. The anchor now came up quickly, the sails filled and the ship started to move. He looked up and saw the French Flag. A glance at McMasters told him that the ensign was ready to go up to the gaff in its place.

The sky was getting lighter, then as they surged level with the headland and the anchorage opened up in front of the starboard bows, a bugle could be heard from the battery. Almost as if that had been the signal, there was a sudden burst of firing, followed by cheering, and Courtenay could almost see the Marines moving into the attack, led by their officers, swords in their hands. More firing and more cheering.

"Alter course to weather the headland, Mr Wetherby!"

"Helm over you men, come on, *move!*" The helm went hard over, the men on the braces dug their toes into the deck and pulled the yards round, then *Hercules* was round and charging into the anchorage. The guns on the battery opened fire, but by the time they had the range, *Hercules* was through. There was the constant crackle of musketry from the battery as *Hercules* moved deeper into the anchorage, then Courtenay forgot all about them as the first ships came into view.

Cressy had been looking at them through his telescope.

"One frigate sir, one corvette and a whole host of invasion craft sir. Just as I reported."

"Yes Mr Cressy, you did well the other night. Do not concern yourself, it all went into my report."

"Sir, I did not….."

"I know you did not. You may open the larboard ports and run out. We will rake the men o'war as we pass, and then concentrate our gunnery on the invasion craft. I believe the carronades should be busy today. We will then wear, and the starboard battery can have what I hope will be target practice!"

He turned to the Signals Midshipman. "Strike that flag, Mr McMasters and run up the Colours!"

There was a cheer as the Tricolour disappeared to be replaced with their own Ensign.

"Upper batteries at the frigate and corvette, Mr Cressy!"

As *Hercules* surged level with the first ship, and a bugle could be heard blaring from it, the 18 pounders of *Hercules'* upper batteries poked through their ports. At a blast from the Second Lieutenant, St Clair on his whistle, every gun fired at the same moment, and smoke funnelled in over the side. There was the sound of splintering wood, and some screams, then she was past and headed for the much smaller corvette, which in the Royal Navy would have been classed as a sloop of war.

Courtenay noticed she had run up her colours and her larboard ports were opening. Her Captain was either brave or a total fool. The whistle shrilled again and the upper deck guns threw themselves back on their tackles. When the smoke cleared, the corvette was a dismasted wreck, listing heavily to larboard. Her flag had gone, blasted away.

Courtenay looked at the invasion craft which were now appearing. As they came in range, the larboard carronade blasted its 32 pound ball at the first group. There were a few people on them, but they were blasted away by the contents of that large ball, hundreds of smaller lead balls. Two of the invasion craft turned turtle, and then the whole of *Hercules'* larboard battery fired controlled broadsides. There was devastation among the small invasion craft, many flat-bottomed.

With the leadsman on the other side of the ship calling out depths, Wetherby started to cast an anxious eye at his Captain.

"I agree Mr Wetherby. Wear ship if you please. Mr Cressy, standby with the starboard batteries."

Cressy touched his hat and turned to the Midshipman who was his messenger. He was the most junior, a twelve year old called Harvey Cook. Quite what he was thinking about this was hard to imagine. He had joined the ship just before Courtenay. This was his first action.

The starboard batteries blasted away more invasion craft, and then fell silent as they passed out of range. The corvette was sinking and the frigate, although badly damaged, had most of her guns run out and her colours flying.

Courtenay shook his head. He looked on with a stone face as the upper deck blasted their 18 pounder balls at the unfortunate frigate. The fore went over the side, closely followed by the mainmast. The side was pitted with shot holes and there were more screams.

'Cease firing Mr Cressy!' called Courtenay above the noise.

The guns fell silent, then there was a cheer from the men on the larboard side of the ship. As Courtenay looked towards the headland, he could see in the sun from the new morning that the Union flag was at the top of the flagstaff at the battery. He lowered his head, wondering how many men had died to run that flag up to where he and his men could see it. How many brave men had perished.

Smith was yelling at the hands to make them be quiet, but he was also watching his Captain.

"Mr Wetherby, we will heave-to at the entrance to the anchorage and await Captain Merrilees and his men. Then, we will return to the Squadron!"

"Aye aye, sir!"

Hercules was lifting her fat shoulder into an offshore roller, all sails drawing well as her Sailing Master took her to where he judged the Squadron ought to be. He would be the first to admit it was not a difficult guess to make. The Inshore Squadron beat up and down the stretch of coast assigned to it in all weathers, keeping the French locked up in their harbours, and ships from outside getting in.

There was a hail from the mainmast look-out.

"*Deck there!* Sails ahead. It be the Squadron, sir!"

Wetherby turned to the Midshipman of the Watch, the second most senior one named Arthur Fulford. He was sixteen.

"Get yourself below, Mr Fulford. My compliments to the Captain, and we have sighted the Squadron."

Courtenay heard the hail from the masthead, but chose to remain seated at his desk, completing his report for the Commodore, and drinking a last mug of Kingston's coffee. Trafford was looking through the stern windows, dappled with spray and covered in salt rime, and half-turned, expecting his Captain to be heading for the cabin door. He frowned slightly. This was not like Giles Courtenay at all. There was a rap at the door, and the roar from the Marine sentry.

"Midshipman o' the watch, *sir!"*

The door opened and young Fulford entered, taking off his hat and standing in front of his Captain.

"The Master's compliments sir, and the Squadron has been sighted."

"Thank you Mr Fulford. You may inform Mr Wetherby I shall be on deck in a moment."

The Midshipman disappeared.

Courtenay looked at his cox'n. "Is something troubling you, Alex?"

Trafford smiled. "What ever gives you that idea Sir Giles?"

"I can tell. There is something not right, something you do not approve of, am I right?"

"Nothing that won't be fixed sir, once you've had this lot in and out of the usual amount of fights you have a knack of getting into!"

"Yes, it takes a lot of getting used to, does it not? We were quite a while in *Pegasus*. Never fear, we shall come to know everyone, by and by. Very well, I think I had best go on deck."

Courtenay strode out from under the poop and walked to the wheel. Wetherby stiffened very slightly, and the officer of the Watch, Frobisher, Third Lieutenant, straightened his coat a little.

Wetherby touched his hat. "Squadron in sight sir, running towards us on the larboard tack, course roughly sou'west."

Courtenay nodded, took a glass from Fulford and walked to the starboard side. He levelled the telescope on the approaching ships, then turned back to the middle of the quarterdeck. Cressy had appeared, silently.

"It would seem the Commodore has left us, gentlemen. There is now a Vice-admiral's Flag at the fore on *Agincourt.*" That was the Flagship.

"Do we know who the Vice-admiral is, sir?" asked Cressy.

"Yes. Lord Cairns."

Cressy looked at Courtenay's face for a moment. He thought he saw something there, for just a moment.

"Do you know him, sir may I ask?"

Courtenay smiled, a trifle bitterly. "Of course you may ask Mr Cressy, and yes, I do know him. I have served with him before. I will be honest and say that we do not get along together!"

"I see sir."

"No Mr Cressy you do not, but it does not matter....for the present." He added the last three words quietly, but not so quietly Cressy did not hear them over the wind thrumming through the rigging, and the hiss of the sea along the side.

"Very well. Mr Wetherby, shorten sail. We will allow the Squadron to run down on us and await instructions from the Flag."

Trafford wandered over to the larboard side of the quarterdeck to leave the signals party plenty of room because he suspected once they were well within signalling distance, they would be busy. Much to his surprise they were not. Cairns only hoisted one signal, which was for the *Hercules* to take station astern of the other ships.

As the Squadron approached, Courtenay ran his eyes along the battered and streaked hulls of their compatriots. There were three other seventy-fours and in addition they had two frigates, and two sloops. None of these were in sight, but he knew one of them. *Amazon,* a forty-gun frigate, had been his command at the Battle of the Nile in 1798. In her he had a number of adventures, and had rescued his wife to be from her Spanish jailers. It was strange how small the Navy was. In command of his old frigate was David Van der Saar, whom he had met when he was a Flag-Lieutenant when he, Courtenay, had been in command of the frigate *Aphrodite.* Van der Saar was now a post-Captain and a good one.

He rapped out his orders as the last ship in the line, *Sirrus,* approached, and *Hercules* neatly tacked and took up position astern of her.

"Sir, Flag is signalling!" called McMasters. "*Flag to Hercules. Send Report aboard immediately*"

"Mr Cressy. Call away a boat's crew if you please. I suggest you send the cutter. I have my report ready." He turned, but Trafford had beaten him to it. The cox'n was holding the envelope for him.

"Thank you Trafford. Mr Frobisher. Take my report to the Flagship, if you please. I wish you to ensure that it is given either to the Flag-Captain or the Admiral himself. Do you understand?"

"Aye aye sir. Captain Jarvis or Lord Cairns." he stopped. "What about the Admiral's Flag-Lieutenant, sir?"

"Just follow my instructions Mr Frobisher, if you please."

"Shall I go with the Third Lieutenant, sir?" asked Trafford.

Courtenay smiled. Trafford was ahead of the game as well. He would make sure Frobisher did as he was bid. He nodded. Frobisher opened his mouth as if to protest, saw the look on Trafford's face and changed his mind.

The boat dropped onto the next swell and its crew ran smartly down into it, followed by Trafford, and last of all Lieutenant Frobisher.

Courtenay watched it shove off and then turned to Cressy.

"I am going to my cabin Mr Cressy. Let me know if there are any more instructions."

"Aye aye sir."

There were none. The boat returned and Trafford confirmed Frobisher had passed the envelope safely into the hands of the Flag-Captain, Henry Jarvis. The Admiral's Flag-Lieutenant had been there and had tried to snatch the envelope away from Jarvis, but the Captain was too old and wily to stand for that, and he gave the Flag-Lieutenant a withering look as he strode off to see the Admiral. The Flag-Lieutenant was left seething.

Marmaduke Spencer-White never did like being snubbed. He considered that as the Vice-admiral's Flag-Lieutenant he was entitled to do as he pleased, talk even to his seniors as he wished, and generally mistreat everyone below him. He had already run foul of Giles Courtenay on a number of occasions. He had tried (although Courtenay could never prove it) to have Giles' wife Jessica kidnapped when she was pregnant, had tried to attack the home of his Uncle's estranged wife and although, again Courtenay could not prove it, had been shot in the process but had managed to get away, and later claimed that he had been wounded by a footpad.

The Flag-Lieutenant was an able assistant in his family's long running feud with Giles Courtenay, whom they blamed for the death of one of their own, an idiot called Prankash, who had been killed when he was commanding a sloop-of-war, a ship which Courtenay had been given command of. Spencer-White had succeeded to the role after the last encumbent, Harding, a professional assassin had been killed by Courtenay at La Mancha, on the Spanish Main.

Courtenay would not give him the time of day let alone any of his reports or despatches!

He would not have been surprised to be summoned to the Flagship to be cross-examined about his report, because he was fairly certain that the Admiral would not believe the damage which *Hercules* had wrought in the anchorage. As they had cleared the same, the corvette had turned turtle and sunk although she had not gone down far, because of the shallows. The frigate had been listing badly, with all its masts overboard, although in time she could be repaired. When she had been, Courtenay was minded to return, if ever duty permitted, and cut her out.

Instead, peace and quiet ruled. The Admiral appeared content the Squadron should sail up and down on its allotted station blockading the French ports and catching the odd fishing boat which tried to sneak out and catch something to sell. Whenever this happened, the Admiral generally took the catch for himself, sunk the boat, keeping back a rowing boat or dinghy and sent the fisherman home in it.

Several days after *Hercules'* foray into the anchorage, a sloop could be seen closing the Squadron. It was one of their 'eyes', the *Dove.* She did not stay long. Her Captain had been rowed over to the Flagship and within half an hour was on his way back. Within ten minutes, the lithe 18-gun sloop was setting its sails and disappearing to the north.

Three days later she rejoined. She sailed jauntily to the head of the slow-moving ships, and the Admiral ordered the Squadron to hove-to.

Courtenay took a glass from the rack and opened it, aiming at the sloop. Memories flooded back, although she was smaller than his old *Seagull,* which had been more like a small frigate, with 22 guns. There was a slight noise beside him and he turned to see the Officer of the Watch, Steven Jeffrey.

"Fine sloop, sir."

"Yes Mr Jeffrey, as you say. Wonder what she is in a hurry for? Her Captain is going over to the Flagship although I saw no signal."

"Commander Dennis, sir."

"I beg your pardon Mr Jeffrey?"

"Her Captain, sir. Commander Alexander Dennis, or should I say, The Honourable Alexander Dennis."

Courtenay smiled as he watched Dennis being rowed to *Agincourt.* "Do I gather you have little time for the Commander?"

"Well sir, I….perhaps I should not say anything further sir."

Courtenay looked around. The other officers were engrossed in watching the other ships and the Flag for signals. Trafford was a couple of paces away, watching both of them.

"Now Steven, you know me well enough to know if there is something which troubles you, you are free to share it with me?"

Jeffrey smiled slightly at the easy use of his first name.

"You know Commander Dennis, is that it?"

"I do not know him well sir, but I have met him ashore when we were collecting stores. He was with the Admiral's Flag-Lieutenant. A friend of mine was at the same school as the Commander, sir. He and Mr Spencer-White are, I understand, good friends."

"Is that all Mr Jeffrey?"

"I think it just as well that you know sir. The rumour I heard was that Commander Dennis got the *Dove* through Lord Cairns' patronage."

"That does not surprise me in the slightest!" He nodded to Jeffrey and replaced the glass in its rack. Trafford turned and followed him as he walked beneath the poop.

Half an hour passed and then the Senior Midshipman, in charge of signals, suddenly stiffened. "Flag is signalling sir! *Flag to Hercules. Captain to repair on board forthwith"*

Cressy was there, as always. "Acknowledge." He snapped. "Mr Mallory. My compliments to the Captain and he is required aboard the Flagship immediately."

The small Midshipman disappeared towards the cabin and a few moments later Trafford came back with him, hurrying towards the boat tier and yelling for the barge's crew. Courtenay himself came onto the quarterdeck five minutes later, wearing his usual sea-going coat.

Moments later the barge was in the water, riding up and down against *Hercules'* side, and Courtenay was passing through the entry port.

"Ship is yours Mr Cressy. I doubt I shall be long."

"Aye aye sir." Cressy looked a little doubtful as he replied. He was becoming used to the way Courtenay did things, like his favourite manner of dressing when out of sight of the Flagship and the way he actually encouraged his officers to ask him if they were concerned over something. He had even seen him conversing with some of the men and the warrant officers. He was more than a little worried. He had heard about bad blood between Cairns' family and Courtenay and he had also heard that whippersnapper Dennis was very friendly with the Flag-Lieutenant. As the Captain was rowed away in his barge, with Trafford at the tiller, he rubbed his chin thoughtfully.

An hour later Courtenay had still not returned.

A few moments after the hour Cressy heard the Bosun call out the usual challenge as a small boat approached.

"Boat ahoy?"

"A friend." was the reply which floated up. A man climbed the stairs and came through the entry port just as Cressy arrived at the same spot.

"Permission to come aboard sir? I wish to speak with your Captain."

Cressy stood his ground and looked the man up and down. He was not dressed in any kind of uniform, and instead was clad in loose fitting clothing of the type worn by French workers.

"And who might you be?" Cressy asked.

"I might be anyone I wish to be, but my name is Tandy. Colonel Piers Tandy."

"You do not have the appearance of an officer, let alone any kind of military person I have ever seen." Cressy said. Tandy did not take too kindly the slightly offensive attitude he was taking.

"In my profession, er, who *exactly* do I have the dubious honour of addressing?"

"My name is Cressy. I am the Senior Lieutenant."

"Well then *Mr* Cressy, as I was saying, in my profession is not a good idea to stride around in uniform."

"And what kind of profession is that *Mr* Tandy?"

"Enough of all this. I must speak with your Captain!"

"You are not speaking to my Captain, or indeed anyone else on this ship until I am satisfied as to your credentials, and so far I am not! I have a mind to clap you in irons first and then continue my questioning!"

"Why……"

"Colonel Tandy sir!"

They both turned as Steven Jeffrey hurried along the gangway.

"Do you *know* this, ah, gentlemen, Mr Jeffrey?" asked Cressy, taken off guard.

"I do indeed sir. He was Major Tandy when I met him in Ceylon. He did a lot to help me recover from my injuries when I was in *Aphrodite* with Captain Courtenay."

"Steven Jeffrey!" exclaimed Tandy. "How are you sir? How is the wound?"

They shook hands warmly.

"Hardly notice it all these days Colonel. The Captain will be so pleased to see you again!"

Cressy was looking more than a little awkward but he took Jeffrey's arm and turned him away, speaking to him quietly.

"You know this fellow Steven?"

"Yes Simon, of course I do. I told you. I met him in Ceylon and then again when we rescued Lady Courtenay from a Spanish island when we were in *Amazon*. He is an Intelligence Officer. He is who he says he is and the Captain will not be best pleased if he finds out he has been ill-treated!"

Cressy nodded and turned back. "My apologies Colonel. Mr Jeffrey here has confirmed your credentials. You are very welcome aboard *Hercules*. There is one thing however. I gather you are in intelligence and have been in France?" Tandy nodded. "Then how did you know that Sir Giles was commanding this ship? He has not been in command for very long and I would have thought that perhaps you would not have had access to intelligence packs where you were?"

"I watched your attack on the invasion craft the other day. I saw Giles Courtenay as he walked up and down the quarterdeck directing the attack. Good enough?"

Cressy nodded and smiled briefly. "I am afraid you have had a wasted trip, Colonel. The Captain is not here. He had an appointment in the Flagship."

"When?"

"An hour or more ago."

"Is Lord Cairns now in command?"

"Yes......how did you know about that?"

"Because I am a bloody intelligence officer! I was told of his appointment before I left England." He stopped and looked at Steven Jeffrey, and the young officer was disturbed by the look on his face. "I hear one of your sloops took a fishing boat the other night. She is over there but I see no sign of the fishing boat. Shame, would have been very useful to me. Who commands her?"

"The Honourable Alexander Dennis." put in Jeffrey.

"Hell's teeth!" exclaimed Tandy. "Mr Cressy, I have need a boat. Now!"

"Well, Colonel, I do not...."

Jeffrey cut in. He knew Tandy of old. "Sir, I think the Captain would want you to let the Colonel have whatever he wants."

Cressy looked at him and saw the ernest expression on his young face. Jeffrey was a damn fine officer, and if he felt that way.....

"Very well. You may have the gig."

"I am off duty sir, so I will accompany the Colonel." said Jeffrey firmly.

Cressy allowed himself a small smile. "Take care Steven." He said very quietly. He nodded and strode away.

The Bosun, Smith, had been trying hard not to hear but he acted too quickly, even for him, when Jeffrey turned with the order to call away the gig's crew on his lips.

"Gig's crew sir? Right away sir!"

Ten minutes later the gig was pushing off from *Hercules* with Jeffrey at the tiller.

"Give way lads. Fast as you like!"

The gig fairly flew across the water.

Tandy swarmed up the side of the Flagship and was through the entry port before anyone could stop him. Trafford had seen him approach in the gig and as Tandy went up the stairs, he looked at Jeffrey. The Lieutenant turned the gig so that it was next to the stern of the barge.

"Looks like trouble Trafford. Do you know what is going on aboard?"

"Nary a word Mr Jeffrey. What did Colonel Tandy want?"

"I think he smells trouble. He saw the attack on the invasion craft."

"I think we should try to get aboard sir. The Captain might need help."

"Yes. I will go aboard and you will come with me."

Jeffrey climbed swiftly up the stairs in time to hear Tandy, in a no-nonsense voice demand to see the Admiral. The officer of the watch, who was no Simon Cressy, fled and Tandy followed him. Jeffrey climbed through the entry port and Trafford stopped beside him.

Meantime in the Admiral's quarters, Courtenay had been fuming at the fact he had been kept waiting for forty-five minutes before being ushered into the presence.

Cairns was holding Court, with his nephew standing next to him, smirking.

"Now, Sir Giles," started Cairns, "I have it from a reliable source that when you attacked the French shipping the other day, you did so whilst still flying French colours." In fact Cairns did not believe one word of it. The damned feud was going nowhere, it was just causing more and more ill-feeling and even getting to the ears of the Admiralty. If it got to Lord St Vincent, the First Sea Lord, he fancied there would be more than a small amount of trouble. He knew very well that an officer of Courtenay's calibre did not make the mistake of fighting under enemy colours but he had been told by his nephew that this was exactly what Courtenay had done and he was duty bound to investigate the allegations. Cairns watched Courtenay. "If that is so it is a despicable thing to do, and not the actions of a King's Officer and a gentleman."

Spencer-White could not resist the jibe. "I do not believe Captain Courtenay *is* a gentleman Uncle, and if this is true I doubt he will be a King's Officer for much longer!"

Cairns turned and looked at his nephew and Spencer-White almost shrank away.

"I will conduct this investigation dammit!" He turned back to Courtenay. "Well, Sir Giles?"

"It is all in my report my Lord. I entered the anchorage flying French colours but that is perfectly allowable. However, as noted in the log, before any gun opened fire the colours were struck and we raised our own!"

Spencer-White stepped forward, colour returning to his face. "That is not what I have learnt! I have been told by a King's Officer that he has questioned a French fisherman who saw the attack and *Hercules* fought under French colours!"

Courtenay broke in. "Which King's Officer?"

Cairns beat his nephew to it. "Commander Dennis of the *Dove.*"

"Is that the *Honourable* Alexander Dennis Mr Spencer-White, the one you are very friendly with?"

Spencer-White went purple with rage. "What are you suggesting sir!"

Courtenay grinned. "Nothing. I was merely asking."

There was an altercation outside and the doors burst open.

Cairns was on his feet. "What the devil is going on! Oh. its you Colonel Tandy. I am very sorry, but whatever it is you wish to speak to be about will have to wait."

Tandy walked to the Admiral's desk. "It is about what you are discussing with Captain Courtenay here that I wish to speak." He turned to Courtenay. "Hello Giles, it is good to see you again. What are they suggesting this time?"

Out of the corner of his eye, Courtenay saw Spencer-White about to draw his sword but Cairns put out a hand and stopped him. If he drew a sword against either Courtenay or Tandy, even his Uncle would not have been able to save him.

Courtenay smiled grimly. "Hello Piers. Apparently the Captain of one of our sloops, *Dove,* spoke to a French fisherman who says that when I attacked some French shipping a few days ago I fought under the Tricolour."

Tandy threw back his head and laughed. "Are we talking Lord Cairns, about *Hercules* attacking a few days ago a frigate, a corvette and a lot of invasion craft at their anchorage?"

"Yes."

"Yes, I thought perhaps we were. Do you know from where the Commodore who authorised the attack gained his intelligence?"

Cairns closed his eyes. He knew what was coming next and he knew that this was another half-baked plan that his nephew had come up with to try and discredit Giles Courtenay.

"No, but I am sure you are going to tell me?"

"Yes. It came from me. I sat and watched the attack. I saw *Hercules* enter the anchorage. I saw her disable the frigate and the corvette, which by the way sunk, and the frigate nearly followed her. I watched from a small cave in the hillside overlooking the anchorage. By the way Giles, your Marines did a good job on that battery." He turned back to the Admiral "Not a shot was fired from the *Hercules* until that damned Tricolour was struck and the Ensign was at the mizzen gaff."

"Well, you would say that!" exploded Spencer-White. The Admiral had had enough. He had not asked for this appointment. He did not want the appointment. He wanted a nice safe job in Admiralty where there was no possibility of a cannon ball separating his head from his shoulders. However, he was not popular enough to have the influence he needed.

"Be quiet! If that is what Colonel Tandy here says, then that is what happened. Commander Dennis must have been wrong to believe a pack of lies from some Frenchman! I will have words with him later." He looked up at Courtenay.

"I think an apology is owed to you Sir Giles. You may return to your ship. The Squadron will resume course."

"Aye, aye sir."

THREE

After the Admiral's cabin it was a relief for Courtenay and Tandy to stand on the almost deserted quarterdeck. Although it was a warm evening, the breeze over the larboard quarter was somehow cooling and cleansing.

Tandy looked at Courtenay but said nothing, simply taking him by the arm and walking to the starboard ladder. Unseen by either of them, Lieutenant Spencer-White slipped out from under the poop and then went down the larboard ladder before dropping down a companion.

Trafford was standing by the entry port, and Steven Jeffrey was speaking quietly to *Agincourt's* officer of the watch.

"I do not know how to thank you Piers." Courtenay was saying as they walked towards the entry port. "How did you know I was here?"

"Your Senior told me when I went aboard *Hercules* to find you. When I heard you had been summonsed aboard the Flagship and I knew that Cairns had arrived, two and two seemed to add up to four, my friend." The officer of the watch melted away as they approached. Jeffrey smiled his relief at seeing his Captain and touched his hat. "But it was young Mr Jeffrey here you have to thank. I believe had he not been one of your officers Giles, I would not have been allowed aboard your ship!"

Courtenay smiled his thanks at the officer. He motioned Trafford to go down into the barge, but something in his cox'n's attitude stopped him. "What is…..?"

Trafford suddenly lunged forward and started to push Tandy, who staggered backwards. There was a flash of moonlight on something shiny and a grunt from the intelligence man.

"Damnation!" he uttered as he sank to his knees. There was a seaman's knife protruding from his arm, just by his shoulder.

There was another yell from the maindeck. "There he goes! Stop that man!"

They all turned, apart from Tandy to see a startled seaman first of all stand as if rooted to the spot then suddenly turn and run for the side. He clambered up onto the gangway, but even as he did there was a pistol shot, and the man cried out sharply and fell backwards. He struck the decking hard but he would not have felt it because the ball had taken him in the back of the head.

Spencer-White strode forward with a pistol in his hand, a thin stream of smoke whisping from the barrel.

"By God, did you see what that swine did?" he yelled. "Good job I was here! Was anyone hurt?"

Courtenay turned a more than jaundiced eye on him and said nothing. Trafford was already kneeling next to Tandy, who was trying to stand.

"My God, Colonel Tandy has been injured!" Spencer-White cried. "We must get him to the surgeon at once."

Tandy opened his mouth to say something but Courtenay beat him to it.

"I will take the Colonel to *my ship,* where he will see *my* surgeon. I think it would not a wise move to trust anyone in the Flagship. Who was that man Mr Spencer-White?"

Marmaduke Spencer-White was all smarm again. "I really have no idea Sir Giles. Just another common seaman."

"Then why would he want to harm the Colonel? He probably did not even know who he was!"

Spencer-White spread his hands. "Then I do not know the answer Sir Giles. The man is dead now, in any event."

"How do we know it was him?"

Spencer-White lost some of his confidence but Courtenay had already turned to Trafford.

"What did you see Alex?"

"More a feeling than seeing anything sir. Just caught a glimpse of what looked like someone about to throw a knife."

"Well, Alex Trafford, you certainly saved my life!" said Tandy. He had removed the knife and was holding a none-too clean handkerchief over the wound.

"Come along Piers, " said Courtenay, "let's get you back to my ship and have that wound attended to."

Trafford went down into the barge and between them, Jeffrey and Courtenay got Tandy down into it.

Steven Jeffrey was chuckling to himself as he settled in the sternsheets.

Courtenay turned to him. "What do you find so amusing Mr Jeffrey?"

Jeffrey dropped the smile. "I am sorry sir, but I think that Flags is less than happy. He had a face like a thundercloud just now."

"H'mm. Well, I shall send word to the Flag-Captain that I require a full explanation. That was attempted murder."

Tandy was taken to *Hercules'* sick-bay where the Surgeon, Henry Batholomew, was soon tending to him.

"Leave the Colonel with me sir," Bartholomew was saying, " he will be fine. We have to keep a close watch for infection, especially since I have noticed that the, er, *rag* he has been using is far from clean. However I am sure he will make a full recovery."

As Courtenay and Trafford left the sick-bay, a tall thin figure was seen hurrying along, almost bent double because of the lack of below decks' headroom. The Reverend Samuel Perkins had obviously heard that someone might be in need of his services.

Courtenay almost groaned aloud. Trafford grinned broadly and said quietly, "Reckon the sin bosun will get no thanks from the Colonel sir!"

Courtenay climbed the companion in silence thinking the same thing. He had never had a Clergyman on board any ship he had served in, not even when he was a Midshipman in the old *Claymore* and he was not very happy about it. He had become used to taking Sunday services when duty permitted it, but with the Clergy on board Perkins did it. At the head of the companion Cressy was standing, awaiting instructions.

"Orders sir?"

"Follow the Admiral. He has no other orders for the present. At least, when I was there he had none."

"Aye aye sir." Cressy looked worried. "I could not but help that notice the Colonel appears to have been injured sir. What happened?"

"Come aft Mr Cressy and I will tell you. I am sure Mr Frobisher can manage without either of us." He walked beneath the poop and the Marine sentry snapped to attention and slammed the butt of his Brown Bess on the decking. Kingston opened the screen door and stood to one side as Courtenay entered.

"Some cognac Mr Cressy?" Courtenay asked as he threw his hat on the desk.

"That's very kind of you sir."

Courtenay wandered over to the stern seat near the sloping windows and looked at the wake, as straight as a die. Kingston placed a goblet of brandy on his desk, gave one to the First-Lieutenant and then withdrew. Trafford entered the cabin without a sound and followed Kingston. Courtenay turned, picked up the glass from the desk and took a sip.

"Someone on the Flagship tried to murder Colonel Tandy."

"What? Why, for God's sake?"

"It is like this Mr Cressy. According to the Captain of the *Dove,* when we attacked those invasion craft a few days ago, we did so under French colours."

"But that......"

"Is not true. I know that and now so does the Admiral, but up to when Piers Tandy came aboard the Admiral was willing to accept the word of Commander Dennis, and my accuser, our Flag-Lieutenant." Courtenay looked at Cressy and saw the man was gradually growing more and more angry. It was not only a slur against Courtenay, it was against the whole ship.

"My God sir, that lying vermin. I'll call......"

"No Simon, you will not." Cressy did not even notice the use of his first name. "I forbid it. Nothing would please that family more than a duel. Cairns would employ a professional duellist. Don't think you would be facing any of them. Did you ever hear of a Matthias Harding?"

A twisted smile appeared on Cressy's handsome face. "Oh yes sir, a lot of us have heard of that person and that he met his end down on the Main."

"Yes. I killed him when he attacked me. That man was an assassin and that was about all you could call him. Well, that is the way the Spencer-White family settles its little problems."

"I, er, I did hear about the feud before you joined."

"Really? I am surprised it is getting common knowledge. I would have imagined the Spencer-White family would want to keep that quiet."

"It is not common knowledge sir. James Fenwick is a friend of mine."

Courtenay raised his eyebrows. "Did you see him before we sailed? I did not get a chance to congratulate him on his appointment before he took command of his brig and sailed."

"Aye sir. We supped together the evening before he left. He felt since I was going to be your senior there were things I ought to know but he charged me with keeping it a close secret sir, and that I have done. No-one aboard knows. You have my word." He sipped his drink.

"Apart from Steven Jeffrey of course."

"Sir?"

"He was with me in *Aphrodite* remember, and again in *Amazon*. He is far from being stupid. He has put two and two together, believe you me."

Cressy smiled. "I am certain he has sir."

"How is he doing, by the way?"

"Mr Jeffrey is performing his duties to my entire satisfaction sir. I have high hopes for his future, if...."

"If he can stay in one piece, is that it?"

"Aye sir."

"Well Simon, that applies to all of us!"

"Thank you for taking me into your confidence sir."

"You are my Senior, Mr Cressy, and a lot depends on you. It is right that you should know our enemies."

Tandy was not the sort of person to be kept down and it was not long before he was up and about, his arm heavily encased in a bandage and a sling. The first day he made his appearance on the quarterdeck he strolled past the helmsmen and the Master, nodding amiably towards them, and sniffed the fresh sea air. The Second Lieutenant, St Clair, had the watch, and he turned as he heard the footsteps and touched his hat, his eyes curious.

"Good morning Mr St. Clair. Where are we, pray?"

"Good morning Colonel. We are on the starboard tack heading on the downward leg of our patrol. No sign of the French coming out of their little hideyhole!"

Tandy grunted. "Not surprised Mr St. Clair."

There were more footsteps on the dry planking and they both turned to see Courtenay come out from beneath the poop. St Clair looked a little irritated and Tandy saw the look and correctly interpreted it. It was usual for a polite warning to come from someone on deck to warn the officer of the watch that the Captain was on deck. It was a measure of St Clair's popularity that no-one bothered to warn him.

Courtney nodded to Weatherby, smiled at Tandy and motioned for him to follow to the lee side of the quarterdeck.

"Good to see you up and about again Piers. How is the arm?"

"Good be better, but I'll live, thanks to that cox'n of yours. I gather we are still more or less where we were when I first came aboard?"

"You gather right. As usual we are beating up and down getting nowhere. That is blockade. It is important, we all know that of course, but....."

"But your independent spirit says you need to get away from here and do something more important?"

"Perhaps."

Their conversation was cut short by the Second Lieutenant formally reporting that their Admiral had ordered the reversal of course which would take them back from where they had just come.

"Join me for breakfast Piers?"

"Delighted."

St Clair was relieved when both officers walked from the quarterdeck and Weatherby simply shifted his pipe from one side of his mouth to the other. He looked sideways at his men, then at the set of the sails and waited for the orders to come which would mean them coming about.

The following day found the Squadron to the north of their blockade area, near Belle Isle and north of St Nazaire. Courtenay was at the quarterdeck rail, looking over at the French coast and waiting for the orders from the Admiral which would mean turning and running down to the south. This was an area he knew well as he had served in these waters on a number of occasions in the past.

He looked up as the look-out peeled down that *Amazon* was in sight to the south, having been sent further away to investigate some anchorages south of their area. He gave a small smile as he thought of his old frigate now in the capable hands of Captain David Van der Saar. Then came an odd signal.

The signal Midshipman, McMasters, looked at the hoist on the Flagship and turned to his Captain hesitatingly.

Steven Jeffrey was the officer of the watch and he saw the youngster's expression before Courtenay did.

"What is it Mr McMasters? Do you not understand the signal?"

"Sorry sir. Yes of course I do. The Admiral has ordered us and *Amazon* to return to the south whilst the Squadron remains on station here."

"What was that Mr McMasters?" interrupted Courtenay.

Jeffrey turned and touched his hat. "An odd signal from the Admiral in view of our orders sir?"

Courtenay smiled. "Yes Mr Jeffrey, so it would seem. No doubt the Admiral has his reasons for sending us back to wait off St Nazaire whilst he remains here."

Jeffrey persisted. "But there are no French ships hereabouts sir. Not even any invasion craft!"

Courtenay's smile disappeared. "Perhaps that is why he has decided to tarry a while here Steven." he said very quietly. Aloud, he said. "Very well Mr Jeffrey, call the hands and standby to alter course to the south. When we are on our new course, signal *Amazon* to scout ahead."

"Aye aye sir." He hesitated. "Still remember serving aboard her sir. She was a good ship."

"Aye, and she still is. Very well Mr Jeffrey, carry on if you please."

A day later *Hercules* was heading along the coast, the wind coming in from the west. The sails were drawing well and a satisfying bow-wave was being washed back from her stem as she pushed through the blue sea.

The foc's'le bell chimed eight bells of the forenoon watch as the Second Lieutenant climbed the companion to the quarterdeck and walked to the wheel where Steven Jeffrey was standing. Jeffrey touched his hat to his senior and cocked his head at the sky.

"It would appear we are in for a blow Mr St Clair."

The Second Lieutenant looked skywards. All he saw were some fleecy white clouds in what was otherwise a blue sky.

"Rot, man! Look you. It is a beautiful day, but a few clouds in the sky and the sea is calm. Where the blazes do you get the idea from we are in for a blow?"

"Look at the clouds Mr St Clair, if you please," said Jeffrey patiently. "they are bad weather clouds. I am sure the Master's Mate will bear me out?" He turned to the man standing next to the helmsmen. "What say you Mr Poole?"

Fred Poole looked more than a little uneasy. The last thing he wanted, not having been long appointed to his position, was to be in between two officers! Secretly he agreed with the young Fourth Lieutenant. Aloud, he said, "Couldn't rightly say sir!"

Steven Jeffrey smiled. St Clair scowled. "Rubbish I tell you! Anyway, I relieve you Mr Jeffrey. Lunch is about to be served I gather. Still some good cheese left. Bread is as stale as leather, though!"

Jeffrey touched his hat and said nothing. As he was running down the companion, Weatherby was going the other way.

"You aren't on watch are you Jacob?" he said quietly.

"No Mr Jeffrey, but I feel a change in the weather coming on. Didn't you notice it when you were on watch?"

"You mean the bad weather clouds and the slight change in the swell?"

Wetherby grinned. "Then you did notice it."

"Yes Jacob, but Mr St Clair did not believe me."

Wetherby grunted and climbed to the deck above. Jeffrey smiled and continued down to the wardroom, whistling gently to himself.

In the next hour or so the wind veered from west, through north-west to north and grew in strength. St Clair stood like a ramrod at the rail, hands clasped beneath his coat-tails, oblivious to the glares being aimed in his direction by Wetherby and his mates. Even the helmsmen were looking at the increasing cloud and noting the strengthening wind.

Wetherby stepped up beside the officer. "Beggin' your pardon sir, but we ought to be takin' in a reef or two I reckon. That wind is growing all the time and it is still veering. Shall I call the Captain?"

St Clair went to reply then there was a quiet cough and Wetherby turned to see Courtenay by the wheel. Giles looked sidelong at the Master's Mate who had suddenly found it necessary to cough and smiled slightly.

"Now then Mr St Clair. I seem to be under the impression that the wind has changed direction considerably and is a lot stronger. I do not care for the look of those clouds and the sea is getting up."

"I have had the sails trimmed sir, and they are pulling well."

"Yes Mr St Clair, but do you not think we ought to take in a reef? Or were you planning to see the masts go by the board?"

St Clair looked him in the eye. "I was just about to give the order sir, when you came on deck."

Courtenay looked at Wetherby, his face expressionless. "Then you had best give your orders Mr St Clair." He turned and strolled to the windward side whilst the officer rapped out his orders.

When he had finished Courtenay motioned for him to join him at the side. "I detected a difference in the weather when the watch changed. Did Mr Jeffrey not say anything to you?"

"Aye sir. He said the clouds were bad weather ones and we were in for a blow. He has the makings sir, but he lacks experience."

"He has gained that experience, Mr St Clair, in far more oceans than you and under the expert guidance of a very experienced Sailing Master. He judges the weather very well."

"He does appear to have been right this time sir."

"Yes. Before the men come down have them take in another reef. That wind still grows, and it is still veering."

Wetherby touched his hat. "Wind is passing through nor,nor east sir, and I reckon it will go further than that." He looked thoughtful. "If it gets any stronger sir, we won't be able to keep a close eye on the Frogs."

"No, but they'll have the perfect chance to slip out with the wind under their coat-tails!"

"Wind could turn back sir."

"That isn't our kind of luck Mr Wetherby. Weather is closing in even further. Make sure that *Amazon* stays in sight."

They had barely reached St Nazaire when the full force of the storm hit them, with a strong gale from the nor-east which forced them out to sea and out of sight of the port, but not before the mainmast look-out, Lees, who had served in the *Seagull* with Courtenay, had counted three ships of the line and two frigates at anchor in the port.

As his ship took the gale, and rode it out with tired dignity, Courtenay stood hatless and coatless on his quarterdeck watching his men as they battled the elements. He was pleased to see that none of their boats carried away and no blocks suddenly came crashing to the deck. The helmsmen slipped and slithered on the wet planking as they struggled to hold the wheel and their course. Courtenay himself took a trick on the wheel at one stage when a man slipped away, leaning back and looking up at the mainmast pendant to check the wind direction, and the set of what there was of the topsails still set.

During the night the storm blew itself out and the wind, always perverse, went back to the west.

As the watch changed for the forenoon watch the Third Lieutenant climbed onto the quarterdeck and was somewhat surprised to see his Captain in a wet and dirty shirt, longish hair plastered to his face and head, but smiling.

"The storm appears to have blown itself out Mr Frobisher. I want to get back on station as quickly as possible. You will signal our frigate to go on ahead and report back."

Frobisher touched his hat, conscious of his clean appearance. "Aye aye sir."

Courtenay smiled at the relieved helmsmen as they left to go below, and walked beneath the poop. Piers Tandy was in the cabin enjoying a cup of coffee.

"You look as though you have been up all night Giles." commented the intelligence man.

"He has." said Trafford, just as wet as Courtenay. "I had to be there with him, just to make sure he was alright!"

Tandy smiled. "Better have some of your coffee then."

Kingston came out of his pantry with two steaming mugs and winked at Trafford. One sniff told him the reason for the wink. There was more than one tot in the coffee!

Courtenay took the mug, nodded at Kingston and walked to the stern windows, throwing himself down on the bench seat. Kingston was just able to catch the mug before Courtenay fell asleep. Tandy just smiled and held his cup out for a refill.

"*Amazon* is in signalling distance sir!" reported Midshipman Fulford. He lifted his glass. "*One ship of the line and smaller craft*"

Cressy was dismayed. "So some of them took advantage of the wind and sailed, sir."

"Aye. Two ships of the line and what else?" Courtenay thought for a moment then turned to the Fifth Lieutenant, who had the watch. "My compliments to the Master, Mr Wedderburn, and ask that he joins me in the chartroom."

Two minutes later the Sailing Master was in the chartroom and he, Courtenay, and Cressy were looking at the chart.

"How is the wind Mr Wetherby? I fancy it is almost back to where it was yesterday?"

"I agree sir."

"So those frogs may not have got too far, would you say?"

"If I know the French sir, they would have seized the chance to get out of port and then, with the wind goin' against them would have found a nice quiet bay to settle down in and wait for a favourable wind."

"Is there such a bay near here, say to the south?"

Wetherby looked at the chart and placed his finger on it. "There sir. Fine bay, good shelter."

"Very well, lay off a course for it."

"Aye sir." Wetherby left.

"But sir, will the Admiral not expect us to report to him and at least keep the remaining liner in port?" asked Cressy.

"I think it would be a far better idea to take the time to see if those Frogs are still nearby, and if they are we will account for them. I am sure the Admiral will not complain in the circumstances. Perhaps we can even take one of them as a prize." As he walked out onto the quarterdeck, Trafford heard him mutter. 'If of course there is anything which pleases that man!'

With the frigate *Amazon* following her larger consort, *Hercules* altered course to run down the coast towards the bay which Wetherby thought might be the place where the French ships were hiding. Courtenay spent a lot of time looking at the chart of the area and from time to time asked Wetherby for his opinion. The bay did in fact give very good shelter. It had a headland which would shelter some ships from the worst of northerly winds. It was about two miles across, but the entrance was a mile in width and there was a shoal in the centre. The deeper channel was to the headland side of the bay. There was another channel the other side, but Wetherby had been doubtful as to whether in fact a ship of the line could get through there. The frigate, drawing substantially less, would get through with no problems depending on a fair wind. All in all, Courtenay decided, drinking a mug of coffee as he stood over the chart, it was not actually somewhere he would decide to anchor in a hurry.

It was a run of just a few hours to find the bay. Courtenay pressed his ship hard and was rewarded with the log streaming ten knots. When Lees, the maintop look-out peeled down that he could sight land again, Courtenay knew it was their destination.

Cressy was beside him on the quarterdeck when Lees hailed.

'They'll like enough have a look-out on that headland, sir.'

'They should have, I agree with you there, but remember, Mr Cressy, they entered that bay probably in the teeth of bad weather, when it was almost certainly very dark, and one would imagine the last thing on their minds was posting a look-out. We will soon see, in any event.'

'Are you going to signal Captain Van der Saar to scout ahead, sir?'

'No. If there is no look-out, we will have them stone cold. If I send in our frigate, that will tell them that at least one ship is about. Let us get closer and we will then evaluate the situation. The first thing to ascertain is if they are actually there!'

'Aye sir, there is that!'

The two ships gradually grew closer to the bay and Courtenay grew a little anxious in case they were not actually there.

Cressy was just about to suggest sending one of the Midshipman aloft with a glass to see if he could see any masts, because although there was a headland, a ship of the line's topmasts would still show above it when there was a hail from aloft.

'Deck there!

Courtenay cupped his hands to call back

'What do you see?'

'Two ships of the line, sir! At anchor!'

'How the devil would he know how they were at anchor, sir?' questioned Cressy. 'All he can see is their topmasts, surely?'

'If all he can see is masts and spars, then no sails are set. If no sails are set, well, would you have a ship of the line in a bay, no sails set and not lay out your anchors?'

Cressy coloured a little, despite his tan.

'No, Mr Cressy, I did not think you would! I bet they are anchored fore and aft. I am going aloft myself to have a look. Mr Fulford, a glass if you please?' The Midshipman handed him a closed telescope and to the amazement of some of the crew, Courtenay started the climb to the maintop where Lees was sitting, leaning against the mast.

Trafford watched the crew, and Courtenay and smiled. They were not yet used to a Captain of a two-decker running aloft. You just wait until they all got into a real fight, he was thinking.

Courtenay climbed out and over and settled down next to Lees, opening the glass.

'Morning Lees. Are you well?'

'Aye, I'm fine sir. I reckon them there ships are anchored fore and aft, sir, and they look as if they will be broadside onto the entrance to the bay. Can't see no look-out on th' headland, either. Lazy bastards!'

'I believe you, Lees, but I needed to have a look myself. We aren't quite as agile as the old *Seagull,* after all.'

'Good days, sir.'

Courtenay shot him a glance and smiled. 'Yes, they were.' He closed the glass and sighed. 'You are right of course. Anchored fore and aft and broadside on to the entrance. And I couldn't see anyone on that headland. It's completely bare of any kind of cover. Well done, Lees. Need anything?'

'No sir. Plenty of baccy to keep me company!'

'Take care when the iron starts to fly. I need those eyes of yours!'

A few moments later, courtesy of a backstay, he was on his quarterdeck.

'They are there Mr Cressy, and well anchored. Broadside onto the entrance, and by the look of it, anchored in a neat little line. Couldn't see the topmasts of the frigate. They are probably hidden by the headland. No look-out. That headland is completely devoid of any kind of cover. Very well. Clear for action.'

He turned to the Senior Midshipman, Robert McMasters. 'Signal *Amazon, Enemy in Sight. Prepare for battle.* When they have acknowledged, you will send this signal. *I will enter bay first. Amazon will not, repeat, not engage until instructed.*'

'Aye aye sir!' McMasters scampered over to his signals party, barking orders.

FOUR

'Cleared for action, sir!' reported Cressy with a slight smile. He knew he had beaten his own record and allowed himself a little pleasure at doing so.

'Very well, Mr Cressy.' Courtenay turned to Wetherby, ready and waiting by the double wheel. 'Come about, Mr Weatherby, hard a larboard!'

Wetherby yelled orders to his helmsmen, whilst Cressy cupped his hands at roared at the hands on deck to let go the sheets, then stood and watched as *Hercules* swung neatly and headed for the entrance. In a trice the yards were secured again. They all heard the blare of a trumpet. Cressy turned with a sour grin.

'Awake at last then sir!'

Courtenay nodded, but he was looking for the frigate, and there she was, smaller than his old *Amazon,* perhaps more the size of *Aphrodite,* away from the heavier ships and no doubt in a position where she would be able to head straight for the sea. Even as Courtenay brought his glass up, he could see that she was cutting her cables, and sails were dropping from her yards.

'Frigate's alive, at least. She'll take that other channel and get out.'

'In which case sir,' said Cressy,' she will come face to face with Captain Van der Saar!'

'As you say, Mr Cressy. Mr McMasters, signal *Amazon, Engage the enemy frigate'*

'Aye, aye sir!'

Hercules swept into the bay, running out her larboard batteries. The guns had been double-shotted for that first clawing broadside.

'Maximum elevation, Mr Cressy,' said Courtenay quietly. 'I want masts and spars from that first one.'

Cressy stepped up to the rail, issuing his orders. Midshipman Cook, the most junior aboard at twelve years old, waited at the top of the companion to the lower deck for his orders and then disappeared below to pass them onto the officers in charge of that gundeck, who were Frobisher and Ralston. Courtenay watched as the elevation of the guns was raised and saw the first French ship approaching.

Trafford stepped up to his side. 'Second frog is cutting her cables, sir.'

'I expected that, Alex. I want to disable this one first and then shut the door on the other one getting out.'

'Frigate is leaving by the other channel, sir!' called McMasters.

'Very well.'

'Looks like a 36, sir.' commented Trafford professionally. 'Look at her paint job. Not very good, considering she's been cooped up in port!'

Courtenay grunted. 'Well, I am sure Captain Van der Saar will make short work of her.' He looked again at the French ship and saw there were some guns appearing, and men alive on the masts. 'Division by division, Mr Cressy, if you please. Then reload and give her a broadside as we pass!'

Cressy touched his hat and went back to supervising the guns.

As the bows of the British 74 swept past the bows of the French ship, the first guns opened fire and in the relatively confined space, with the headland behind them, the noise was worse than deafening. Division by division, the British guns fired as *Hercules* sailed along the length of the French ship. What sails had been dropped were blasted away in the onslaught and by the time the rearmost guns had added to the noise, the foremost guns were reloaded. There was just time for all the guns to erupt together, throwing *Hercules* over to starboard, then they were past.

The smoke was gradually clearing, aided by a strengthening wind even in the bay, and when Courtenay could see what damage his guns had done, he was not displeased.

The mizzenmast had gone completely, together with most of the foremast, and the maintop. The French ship's sails were rags and she was crippled. She was going nowhere for the time being.

'The other ones's trying to slip away, sir!' called Wetherby, peering ahead. The second French ship was indeed under way, having hurriedly cut her cables, but all she could do was to try to cut across the bay, away from *Hercules* and slip out through the other channel.....if there was enough water.

'Hard a' starboard, Mr Wetherby! Time to slam the door!'

With Wetherby and Cressy yelling orders, *Hercules* swung to starboard until she was parallel with the French ship. Even as they settled on their new course, the gunports on the French ship, now flying a defiant huge Tricolour, opened and some of the guns trundled out. Cressy was ready, however, and in addition to double-shotting the guns again had added grape. His sword sliced down and the broadside rippled along *Hercules'* side. This time there was no maximum elevation and Trafford, watching the French ship carefully, swore later that she staggered under the impact. He looked at the other side of the bay, which was very rocky, and again at the French ship. There was nowhere she could go. She could not turn to larboard, because she would then be too close in to shore and she could not turn to starboard because the British ship was there.

Courtenay touched Cressy's arm. 'Avast firing for the moment Mr Cressy. I think the rocks may save us some powder and shot!'

He looked again at the ship and then at Wetherby. 'Keep her thus for a little longer, Mr Wetherby, then you may wear ship.'

'Aye sir. According to the charts it gets quite shallow over there, as well as rocky.'

'I know.'

Wetherby gave a sudden, and rare, smile. he realised that this was exactly what Courtenay had been planning. Then he remembered something young Lieutenant Jeffrey had told him about the way in which Courtenay had destroyed a Spanish frigate in the East Indies.

'Wear ship, Mr Wetherby.'

'Frog's aground, sir!' yelled Cressy from the larboard nettings.

The French ship, unable to go anywhere else, had ploughed into the shallows and the driven hard onto the rocks. The noise of her breaking up was deafening, but sad. It was never good to see a ship die. The masts went by the board in short order, and she tilted over onto her starboard side, a huge rent in her bilges.

'What is the other Frenchman doing, Trafford?'

'Got his guns run out, sir, but I don't know what he intends, since he ain't got anything to sail with!'

'Standby to come about, Mr Wetherby, we will give the starboard batteries a chance, but no need to get too close, eh?'

As he spoke the words, there was a blast from the French ship, but no waterspouts appeared, no balls struck the British ship. As the smoke cleared, Courtenay watched the Tricolour come down and a white flag was run up instead.

'What the.......' said Cressy.

Courtenay smiled. 'I am surprised you have not seen that before Mr Cressy. the French call it *pour honneur de pavilion.*'

'I have heard of it, but never seen it. What a bunch of cowards!'

'Self- preservation does seem high on the Captain's agenda, but in truth he had little option. We would have blown him to bits with him unable to do anything about it, and he knew it.'

In the sudden quiet there was the sound of smaller pieces as *Amazon* got to grips with the French frigate.

Courtenay smiled at Cressy. 'I think a full boarding party for that ship, Simon, to make her our prize, and we will see what the other one's crew intends. If they don't fire her, we will. I am sure the Gunner will be only too willing to prepare some charges!'

He cocked his head as the firing outside the bay ceased and McMasters turned to him with as much as a grin as he would allow himself when speaking to his Lord and Master.

'*Amazon* is signalling, sir. She has taken the French ship.'

'Acknowledge if you please and say *Well done. Report when prize secure and ready to proceed*'

McMasters bounded back to his men, yelling for the right bunting to be got out of its lockers.

Courtenay turned to the Master. ' Anchor, Mr Wetherby. Best to lay out both anchors to stop her swinging but we will have a spring as well, just in case we need to fire into the other ship.

'Amazon is signalling, sir' called McMasters. '*Prize secured. Await instructions.*'

'Signal her, *Maintain station.*'

Courtenay strode to the larboard side to watch what was happening with the beached ship, whilst there was the clamour of boats being loaded to head for the other ship and taker her as a prize. He turned and sought out Cressy. 'Take some Marines, Mr Cressy, just in case. Two squads ought to be enough.'

'Aye sir. I will leave now.'

Courtenay nodded. He walked to the rail and looked down onto the gundeck. The guns were loaded, and run out, ready to fire if necessary.

'Mr Frobisher!' he called 'Lay aft if you please.'

Frobisher ran lightly up the larboard ladder to the quarterdeck, and looked questioningly at his Captain.

'Mr Frobisher, yonder French ship on the rocks needs to be destroyed. I can see that her crew are abandoning her, and when I deem it safe to do so, you will take fifty men, and the gunner, and set fire to it. I want it gutted. I am sure the Gunner will be only too pleased to burn it to the keel!'

Courtenay had seen the crew of the once stately 74 going over the side nearest the shore, taking anything valuable with them, but there could still be some men on board, just waiting for an unwary boarding by some of Courtenay's men.

Hercules also had her starboard batteries still run out, just in case the other French ship reneged on the white flag. It had happened before and, Courtenay reflected sadly, it would probably happen again. Where was honour?

The boats led by Cressy, with Captain Merrilees of the Marines with him, reached the side and were soon on board. Courtenay raised a telescope and watched, smiling gently, as the French Captain, with no pomp at all, more or less threw his sword at Cressy. The Senior's reply was to nod to Merrilees who gave the French Captain a none too gentle push in the back to guide him below.

'Mr Cressy seems to have the situation there under control, Trafford.' commented Courtenay. 'Let us see what the other ship is doing.'

He crossed to the other side. The Frenchmen were still abandoning their ship, but there were only a few left.

'Mr Frobisher. You may select your men and go to the other French ship. It may be a forlorn hope, but search for any confidential papers and then assist the Gunner in firing the ship. Do you understand your orders?'

'Yes sir. Thank you sir.' He turned and ran down the ladder.

Courtenay could see that the Second Lieutenant, St Clair, was not too happy.

'Something wrong, Mr St Clair?'

'I could have performed that duty, sir!'

Courtenay remained calm, although Trafford, standing next to him, knew that he was very close to losing his temper. 'It is my choice as to who performs which duty, Mr St. Clair, but ask yourself this. What would happen if suddenly a superior French force appeared, and before I could recover the men sent to the French ships in this bay, I had to give fight.?' St Clair's face was blank. 'I would be without both my Senior officers, Mr

St Clair. Never fear, you will have your chance when the opportunity presents itself.'

As Frobisher was about to leave, Courtenay appeared at the entry port. Frobisher

turned and touched his hat. 'Sir?'

'If they show any resistance, Mr Frobisher, you are to stand off. As you can see,

Mr Smith has rigged a spring. We will give the remaining Frenchies a broadside or two

and see if that dampens their ardour!'

'Aye aye sir!' Frobisher climbed down into the boat and in a few moments, he

was away from the ship's side and heading strongly for the shattered French liner.

There was no resistance, and after about half an hour, during which time Cressy

signalled that he needed assistance to rig some jury masts, fires were set in various places

in the remains of the ship. As Frobisher and his men left, the flames were taking hold.

Courtenay was anxious about being caught where he was, but the last thing he

wanted was to move outside the bay and give the French crew aboard their prize the

chance to try to retake their ship. He signalled *Amazon* to patrol outside the entrance to

the bay, but always within visual distance of their own prize.

At last, Cressy signalled he was ready to proceed, and with the wind kind for a

change, *Hercules* moved slowly out of the bay, with the French prize, which was called

Racconteur following. *Amazon,* with her prize, stayed to seaward and slightly ahead, and

the small squadron sailed back to meet up with Vice Admiral Cairns' ships.

It was almost as if there had never been the attack in the bay. Courtenay stood in the Vice-admiral's cabin, with a smirking Spencer-White to one side, although what he was smirking about, Courtenay could not understand. Two days ago, he had returned to the Squadron with two good French prizes. The 74 had not suffered a lot of damage, aside to masts spars and sails, because Courtenay had wanted her crippled. The frigate had suffered far more damage, but no shots had hit her under the water line and the rest was damage which could easily be put to rights. He had gained two good ships for the Royal Navy.

'So once again, Captain Courtenay, you were off station. When I returned here I could not believe that you were not making sure that the remaining French were bottled up. Instead I find that you had been off on a jaunt of your own again.'

'I conferred with my sailing Master sir, and decided that, having regard to the weather, there was a very good possibility that the French ships which had broken out where sheltering nearby. That proved to be correct sir. You have my report as to the action I took. There were no casualties to my men sir. Captain Van der Saar tells me he lost three men and had about twelve wounded in his fight with the French frigate.'

'H'mm. Well, I suppose they may be of assistance to the Navy. I will select prize crews from the Squadron and send them in. Portsmouth, I think. You may take your men back, including your officers. I will select the prize-masters.'

'Aye aye sir. May I return to my ship, sir?'

'Yes, yes. Until we meet again Captain.'

Courtenay walked to the door and Spencer-White followed him.

'I believe I can find my own way out, Mr Spencer-White' he said, cuttingly.

Marmaduke Spencer-White coloured, but said nothing.

The wearisome task of blockade continued through the next two or three months. Shops were sent back to harbour to reprovision, apart from *Hercules* and she was not given the opportunity, much to the crew's disgust. They were beginning to run short of drinking water, but Courtenay had made sure they had plenty of all other supplies before they had joined the Squadron, and, unknown to the Vice-admiral, he had sent the Purser into the French liner *Racconteur* and the man had cleaned the ship out of all the provisions he could find. There had been many pigs and chickens on board, and they had been transferred to *Hercules* during the short voyage back to their station. With a large supply of fresh coffee, there had been many cheeses, and the wardroom now sported a rich selection of fine French wines and brandy.

The crew thought for some reason they were being punished for what they had done. Courtenay of course knew why the Admiral was doing what he was. What he planned did not come off. He hoped the crew would turn against their Captain. Lees, however, told the men exactly what their Captain was capable of, and they appreciated that when they attacked the French ships in the bay, he took no unnecessary risks with their safety.

In early October however, Courtenay was becoming worried about the water situation. He had had to start rationing, which was ridiculous when they were not that far away from Tor Bay, to where they could have repaired to stock up on water and other supplies. He was to find it would not be necessary.

One drab morning, a courier brig was seen heading for the squadron. It did not seem to be in a hurry, which was most unusual. Courtenay watched as the signal for the brig to have-to was made and then the Admiral made a General Signal for the whole Squadron to heave-to as well.

Suddenly, there was a roar of cheering from the Flagship, although it did not last for long. Cairns was not the sort of man who would allow a crew any enjoyment such as that. The brig's commander returned to his ship, and soon the sails were set again and it drew away. The Admiral made no signal to get under way again. For two hours, they sat there, swinging with the tide, then, one of the Flagship's Lieutenants came in a boat with a written message for Courtenay.

He was in the cabin, drinking some of the remaining French coffee when the officer arrived. He handed over the note, and then left. He looked curiously disappointed with something, Cressy said later.

Courtenay opened the note, then banged his fist on his desk, which brought Kingston and Trafford running into the cabin.

'What is it, Sir Giles?' asked Trafford. 'Is it Miss Jessica?'

'No, no, nothing like that, Alex. It would seem we are at peace. The Peace of Amiens. It was signed on 1st October. The Squadron is to return to Plymouth forthwith.'

'Are we paying off, sir?'

'I have no idea, Alex. Let us return home first, and no doubt we will find more then. Pass the word for the First-Lieutenant, and I want this news passed to all hands.'

'Aye sir. Her ladyship will be pleased.'

'Yes, but I will be happier when I find out more about this so called 'Peace of Amiens' I do not trust Boney any more than I could pick the man up and throw him!'

'I agree with you entirely, Giles.' Sir Geoffrey, Jessica's father, was pacing up and down in his study at the big London House he used when he was home from his travels. Giles sat in a very comfortable armchair looking out over the square, sipping from a large goblet of brandy.

'The man is not to be trusted at all.' he was continuing. 'We all know that he is merely using this so-called peace to re-stock his army, and to get ready for the next round. I just hope that those fools in the Admiralty and Horse Guards do not fall into the trap of believing him. My God, we are already having to hand back many territories which we took with the blood of thousands of our brave men! If the Admiralty and Horse Guards *do* believe him, he will be at our throats in no time at all. Do you know what lies in store for you at the moment? I mean, are you.....'

Courtenay smiled. 'No, I am not on the beach yet. My orders when I returned to Portsmouth were to leave my ship with my senior and travel to London. I was told to make sure that my crew stayed on board and to re-provision. That suggests to me that their Lordships have something in mind for *Hercules* although whether I remain in command is another matter.'

'You have not been in command long, my boy. I would have thought it unlikely to remove you so quickly, and in any case, you have the ear of Lord Crompton. He would never allow such a thing!'

'His Lordship has superiors, remember, Geoffrey.' Sir Geoffrey smiled at his son-in-law's easy use of his first name. He was very fond of him, and he had proved himself over and over to be a good officer and more importantly to him, a fine husband to his daughter.

Just then, there was a short knock on the study door and they both turned as Jessica came in, holding the hand of their son Edward who was now walking. A maid was behind them with a tray bearing a silver coffee pot and some large cups.

'Excuse me for butting in, father, but Edwards here wanted to see his father, and so did I! You can continue your chatting some other time!'

Geoffrey kissed his daughter on the cheek, and picked Edward up to cuddle him.

'Of course. The coffee will be welcome. And how are you, young man?'

Edwards gave his grandfather a smile and wriggled to get down. When he did, he went straight to Giles.

'It is heartwarming to see that Edward remembers you' he said. 'He was still very young when you last went to sea. He is growing up too fast.'

Courtenay picked up his son and put him on his knee.

There was the sound of the door knocker on the large double doors at the front of the house, and a few moments later the butler appeared, with an apologetic look on his face.

'I am most terribly sorry to disturb you, Sir Geoffrey, but there is an Admiralty messenger to see Sir Giles.'

Jessice's hand went to her mouth. 'Not already, Giles. You've only been home a few days!'

The messenger was shown in.

'Captain Sir Giles Courtenay?'

'That is me.'

'This is from Admiral Lord Crompton sir. He said I was to be certain that you were to receive it from me. Would you sign this receipt?'

The messenger proffered a receipt book, and Courtenay signed for the letter. The messenger gave a short bow and left.

Geoffrey passed a paper knife from his desk and Courtenay slit open the usual canvas envelope.

'It's alright, darling, Crompton wants to see me in two days' time. He says it is nothing urgent, he wants to discuss something with me.'

'Such as?' she asked.

'I will know in two days' time.' he said. 'I am sure however that there is nothing which requires me to be sent off to sea just yet. We are supposed to be at peace, are we not? Perhaps he wants to let me know gently that I am being put on the beach.'

'And what does that mean?'

'It means being put on half-pay because there is nothing for me to command, my love. When we are at peace, we do not need the ships at sea. When we do not need the ships at sea, we need less Captains. Someone more senior than I will probably be given my ship until someone realises what Boney is really up to!'

Jessica passed her husband a cup of coffee and gave him one of her I-hear-what-you-say-but-I-do-not-believe-you looks.

'Don't look like that, Jess. It isn't my fault!'

'Look like what darling?' she said sweetly. Geoffrey raised his eyes to the ceiling. Just like her late mother!

There was a roaring fire in the Admiral's office and Courtenay fancied he could feel the heat even as the double doors were opened and Crompton's Secretary announced him. Crompton got up from his desk and walked round it to greet him, hand outstretched. He limped slightly, but it didn't seem too bad. Courtenay smiled slightly.

'Ah, Courtenay me dear fellah! Good to see you again. Do I find you in good health?'

'You do, my Lord.'

'And Lady Jessica?'

'I am pleased to say she is in rude good health, sir.'

'Good. Let's sit by the fire. Might only be October, but the cold gets to my bones these days. Comes of not having to be at sea in all kinds of weathers! Fetch the decanter and the glasses, Giles, there's a good fellow.'

Courtenay picked up the fine cut-glass decanter on the desk with two matching glasses and took them over to the fire. There was a small table set between two comfortable chairs.

Courtenay raised an eyebrow and Crompton smiled and nodded. It was one of their little rituals. Courtenay always poured the drinks.

'Now, I am most damnably sorry to drag you away from your lady wife, but I have need of your good services.' Crompton looked at him over the rim of his glass.

'I would have thought there would be little need for my services now, my Lord? We are supposed to be at peace with France, Spain and Holland. Who is there left to fight?' Courtenay smiled slightly, because he knew very well there were still plenty of people to fight in the King's name! There was always the slave trade, and pirates off the coast of Africa as well as in both the East and West Indies.

'How much do you know as yet about what has been agreed, Giles?'

'Not a lot, sir. Only what is in the Gazette. Formal treaty has yet to be signed. There is only a truce at the moment.'

'Yes, and the truce will give everyone the chance to re-arm, re-group and then we will be at each other's throats again!'

'I had rather thought that would be the case, sir.'

'Fortunately, we know that here, for a change, so there will be no throwing good ships and men on the beach. We will be watching and waiting. Who knows, it may even be us who will tear up the treaty first! That would make a change!'

'I am sure that people like Colonel Tandy will be keeping a close eye on things, sir.'

Crompton smiled and held his glass out for Courtenay to refill it. 'Oh yes, I am sure he will be in the thick of it. Now then, most of what our men have given their lives for, been maimed for, is to be returned. The Dutch get the Cape back, the French countless Islands, although we do keep Trinidad, which is good news, and also Ceylon,. which means of course Trincomalee. That is important to us as a base in the Indian Ocean, and for the East Indies. We are also to give Malta back to the Knights.'

Courtenay looked up from filling his glass. 'What? After all we have gone through to get the place? This is insanity, sir! Giving back all the other places is bad enough, but Malta is like a sentinel where it is!'

Crompton held up a hand. 'Rest easy. I have a feeling that the Knights may not get it back, but enough of that for now. There are more pressing matters for us to deal with now that we do not have to worry about the French and Spanish being at our throats. Ever heard of the Barbary Pirates? Of course you have.'

'*Corsairs*. Yes, I have heard of them sir. Cutthroats all. They would sell their own Mother if the price was right.'

'You know that various countries pay 'homage' to three of the Barbary states?' Courtenay nodded. 'Well, they are getting a bit uppity with our Yankee friends. From what I have heard, they have been less than impressed with the amount of the Americans' money they have been giving to them. Started with the Day of Algiers demanding a larger homage, then his friend the Bashaw of Tripoli joined into the act. They had quite an embarrassing time, the Yankees, because one of their ships was forced to sail to Turkey with the Algerian flag at the main, carrying one of the Dey's flunkies. If that had happened to one of our ships, I would have had the Captain court-martialled as soon as I could lay my hands on him. I would have sooner he scuttled the ship that suffer such an indignity!'

'I understand sir. Where do we come into this?'

'We come into it, young man, because the Dey and his friends think that anything which comes anywhere near their states is fair game! Oh, we have protested, and some extent, they all need our help, but the Americans are losing ships to these, these, pirates, and I have the feeling that soon, very soon, so will we! We need to have a presence along the Barbary coats which will make them think twice. The Americans do not have much of a Navy. Oh, they have quite a few ships, but they have never gone in for building ships of the line.'

'They seem to aim for large frigates, sir.'

'Correct. Even a large frigate could be in trouble with some of their ships. Some of them are powered by slaves at oars, so they do not depend upon the vagaries of the wind. They mount a powerful gun in the bows, and, well, I do not need to draw a picture, do I?'

'Indeed not sir. What have you in mind, may I ask?'

'Of course you may. I want you in the Mediterranean with your *Hercules.* I can spare you two smaller ships to work in closer inshore and act as scouts. I want those murdering bastards to realise they are not going to monkey with the King's Navy, nor our merchant ships. I don't care, Giles, how many of them you kill or how many of their ships you sink. If you find them interfering with any of our ships, you are to take whatever action is required. *Whatever action.* Do I make myself clear?'

'Absolutely, sir. Which ships?'

Crompton smiled. 'You need men you can trust. I can't let you have your old *Amazon* because she has been sent off to the West Indies, but I can give you *Aurelia* although Charlton is no longer in command. He was wounded a while ago and is still recovering. Your old friend Spellman has her. Does that suit?'

'It does sir.'

'Then that rascal Fenwick has the brig *Spur.* You can have him for keeping in touch with the Flag Officers at Gibraltar and Malta and running between you and Spellman.'

'Thank you sir. When do you want me on station?'

'Not yet. Let us have a little time to get negotiations under way for this peace treaty. Merchant ships will start moving around on their own in the Mediterranean soon. It is then they will be vulnerable. I can give you another month. Is that suitable?'

'Yes sir.'

'Are you short of men? I know how it is Giles. If there is anything I can do to help?'

'I am some thirty short of complement, that much is true, sir.'

'H'mm. The brig *Dove* is due back in Portsmouth in a few days' time. She is paying off because she is to have a refit. That damned puppy of a Captain will be on half-pay if I have anything to do with it, not that he will care, since his family is rich and well-connected.'

'I will send a note to Mr Cressy immediately, sir. I am sure he will have some men ready to, ah, *greet* the brig's crew when they are paid off!'

'Good. Well, that is business concluded. Join me for lunch at the club, Giles? We haven't enjoyed a meal together for a while.'

'I would be delighted sir, but I am afraid I rather promised to take Jessica to lunch. She is outside in the waiting room at the moment.'

Crompton smiled broadly. 'In that case, Captain, it will give me great pleasure to buy you both lunch. There is a very acceptable private dining house just around the corner.'

Courtenay smiled and stood. The Admiral walked to his desk and rang a bell, then went to the doors even before they were open.

'Now then, where's that beautiful wife of yours Captain?' he barked as he passed through the doors, and made for the waiting room.

FIVE

The days which Giles Courtenay and his wife had together gradually ebbed away. It was nearing Christmas when he received his final orders from Crompton, and it was with a heavy heart that he prepared to go to sea once more. He knew from the regular reports he was receiving that his ship was ready for sea. Cressy had done a good job of 'acquiring' new sails and cordage from the dockyard and he had obtained some thirty-five new hands when the sloop *Dove* had arrived in Portsmouth and paid off.

Courtenay spared a few moments to feel pity for its crew. With there seemingly being a peace, or at least for the time being, a cease-fire, they could look forward to receiving their pay, and a share of any prize money, not that there was much of that, and then disappearing away from where there were any ships, or the dreaded press.

Cressy had put a stop to that. He had taken the press himself and had been waiting at the stairs of the quay when the first boatload of men had appeared. Even he had felt sorry for the men when he had seen the look on their faces as they had seen the familiar blue and white of an officer, with a small party of armed men. He had said in his letter of report that he had actually managed to get ten of the men to volunteer, but the rest had tried to make a break for it and had been detained. Courtenay hated having to do it, but do it he had had to in the past, and he could still remember pressing men from his own home port of Tor Quay, when he was Captain of the *Aphrodite.*

Jessica had taken herself of to dressmaker in Jermyn Street, and she had taken Edward with her and a maid from the house. Courtenay said he would try to catch up with her if he could when he was finished at the Admiralty.

Jessica and the maid stopped outside the shop she was visiting, and kissing Edward on the cheek, and ruffling his hair, she went inside, leaving him with the maid outside. He was staring intently at the carriages passing by, and looking up at the horses, when one came to a slow stop near him. The rider, a Naval officer, stepped down, made sure his horse was secured to a nearby post, and then looked down at the child.

He bent down and spoke to him quietly, the maid oblivious whilst she looked in the shop window, no doubt dreaming of herself in one of the fine dresses. Before she really new what was happening, Edward had been picked up by the man, who was smiling at him and talking quietly, pointing at the carriages and his horse.

When the maid felt Edward's hand leave hers, she turned, to see herself looking into the hard, cold eyes of the Naval officer.

'The little boy here would like to sit on my horse for a while,' the man said. 'I am sure that will be in order, will it not?'

'Well, sir…..' the maid started to respond, but the yes grew even harder.

'Pray do not argue with me, girl. I can make life very hard for you if you do. You should not argue with your betters. Mind your own business and all will be well.'

The maid went to take Edward away, but the man turned away, and with his free hand, pushed the maid so hard she fell.

At that moment, Courtenay was coming along Jermyn Street in his carriage and he saw Betsy fall to the cobbles, narrowly being missed by a heavily laden wagon. He saw two things. First of all, Marmaduke Spencer-White placing Edward on the saddle of his horse, and taking the reins in his free hand, and his wife stepping out of the shop, with her hand going into her bag.

Two steps, and as Spencer-White was about to hoist himself into the saddle, she was next to him with a pistol pointed out his head. Courtenay's carriage stopped and he opened the door, his hand going to his sword, although when he caught his wife's icy cold words, he sheathed it, knowing it was not needed.

'You will unhand my son, *Mr* Spencer-White, before I exert some more pressure ion this trigger and blow your head off your scrawny shoulders!' The sound of her cocking the pistol was loud in his right ear.

He stopped immediately, turning very slowly, a smirk on his face.

''Pon my word, Madam, whatever is the problem? The lad here only wanted to sit on my horse. I saw no harm?'

Courtenay was next to his wife, and reaching up for Edward, who gave a big smile and put his arms around his Father's neck.

'Then why did you push Betsy here into the road?'

'She tripped. I went no harm, Sir Giles, I can assure you. I simply wanted to give your son a little ride on my horse. I am sure when he gets old enough he will want to ride like his parents?'

'I am certain he will, but not with you teaching him! I suggest. Mr Spencer-White, that you leave us now.'

Still smirking, the Lieutenant mounted his horse and rode very slowly away. As he did so, the smirk was replaced with a vicious scowl. He had indeed intended to take the boy for a ride on his horse, whilst Jessica was otherwise engaged, but he had not intended to return him. He had some men waiting he would have hidden him away, and, evilly, his intention would have been to have had the lad's throat slit and then the body dumped into the Thames.

Courtenay watched the man riding slowly away and turned to his wife. There was deep concern on his sunburnt face as he saw Jessica's hand holding the pistol was shaking. He handed Edward to the maid and turned his dark brown eyes on his wife, taking the pistol from her and carefully uncocking it.

'Are you alright, darling?'

Jessica looked at him and smiled bravely. 'Yes, I think so. The cheek of the man! In broad daylight as well. Is there nothing you can do about him, Giles?'

'Nothing. He will say he was merely being friendly and ask why on earth he would want to harm a child, and he would be believed. The best we can hope is that somewhere someone will do for him!'

Jessica turned to the maid, who was crying, and cuddling her charge.

'Are you hurt, Betsey?'

'No your Ladyship, just a mite shaken, that's all. I'm right sorry about this. Per'aps if....'

Courtenay butted in. 'Perhaps nothing. It was not your fault.'

Jessica nodded and smiled and patted Betsey's arm.

'I think we should all return home' said Courtenay firmly, and opened the carriage door for everyone to get in. Jake, the coachman, slid the pistol he had drawn back inside his coat, satisfied all was in order.

Once safely inside the carriage, Courtenay looked at the pistol. He looked at his wife.

'This isn't even loaded, Jess!'

'I know. I meant to load it before we went out, but I forgot. Edward wanted me to do something or other and I just overlooked it!'

Courtenay shook his head in amazement.

A week later, Courtenay received his final orders from Lord Crompton.

'You sail in two days, Giles. You know what is expected of you. Is your wife alright after what happened last week?'

'Yes, but something one day will have to be done about Spencer-White, my Lord. Matthias Harding was bad enough, but even he did not make war on children. Although I have no proof of this, we know that Spencer-White was involved in the attack on James Fenwick and his Mother, and the attempt to kidnap Jessica. He is, however, a coward. When we were attacking a French battery on Malta, he, ah, absented himself whilst the attack took place. It seems to run in the family, because I recall very clearly Prankash doing exactly the same thing on the French coast!'

'Well, he is out of harm's way for the time being, Giles' Crompton smiled at his protégé. 'Three days ago, their Lordships sent Cairns off on a diplomatic mission, and with him went his little lap-dog.'

'Diplomatic mission? Where was that, sir, if I may ask?'

'Of course you may, because it may affect you and your ship. He has been sent to see the Dey of Algiers. The Americans are very keen on good diplomatic relations and have sent one of their top men there, so their Lordships felt we would do likewise, but it was thought that perhaps a man with some force behind him might make the Dey a little more amenable to being friendly. It won't last of course. One of these days, Giles, mark my words, we will have to do something about that nest of vipers, although it will not be an easy task.'

'Has Lord Cairns a squadron with him, sir?'

'No. We didn't wish to appear *too* threatening. Their Lordships have sent him in a frigate. A large frigate, mind you, but a frigate, all the same. She's the *Rochester* 40. Captain Sir Hubert Dalrymple. D'ye know of him?'

'Can't say that I do, sir.'

'Steady man. Experienced frigate Captain. Not scared if sticking his neck out for the right reasons. If it comes to it, you will have quite a handy little force to take on the Dey and his friends.'

'Under Lord Cairns' command, sir?'

'Of course. He may be on a diplomatic mission, but he will still be the senior Naval officer on station. You will of course pass your reports to the Flag Officer, Gibraltar, to where you will no doubt repair from time to time to replace your provisions. Vice-admiral Sir Arthur Connolly.'

'Aye sir.'

Crompton watched the emotions chasing across his face as Courtenay stood up and straightened his uniform. 'I will make sure that your wife will be looked after whilst you are away. Jessica will be fine.'

'I have made sure of that sir. Trafford arranged some help when I was away before, and they are still with the household. I have left orders that Jessica is to be accompanied by at least one or two of them wherever she goes.'

Crompton smiled. 'Good, but, in any event....'

'I am sure that she would relish a visit from you on occasion, sir.'

'Good luck to you Captain.' Crompton held out his hand and shook Courtenay's warmly.

The row out to *Hercules* in the barge was lively to say the least. There was a fair lop, even at Spithead, and the oarsmen had to pull hard against the tide. Trafford had guided the barge neatly alongside and Courtenay was up, reaching for the ropes and swarming up the stairs without a shadow of hesitation.

'Good morning, sir. Welcome back' Cressy stepped forward, touching his hat and smiling tightly. Courtenay looked at his senior and thought there were one or two lines where before there had not been any, or was it that he had just not noticed them before?

'Thank you Mr Cressy.' Trafford appeared through the entry port and went ahead and up onto the quarterdeck to go beneath the poop. 'How is everything? I am most sorry that it will Christmas away from home, but we have our orders, as you know.'

'I understand sir. There is little for me at home in any event, sir. I would rather be where I am needed most.'

Courtenay looked at him with concern for a moment, then realised there were some members of the crew staring curiously.

'Is everything ready for leaving harbour, Mr Cressy?'

'Aye sir, we can sail before the tide turns.'

'Excellent. Come aft with me.'

In the cabin, Kingston had anticipated his Master's return with a pot of fresh coffee, and laid out a tray with two brandy glasses and a decanter. Courtenay nodded his thanks and sat down on the stern bench seat with a mug of coffee in his hand. Cressy sat in a nearby chair and toyed with the brandy glass.

'Is there a problem, Simon? At home?'

Cressy looked up, and his handsome face creased into a small smile.

'Not really, sir. There was an arrangement.....more an understanding. One of my parents' neighbour. Their daughter and myself have been friends a long time, and well, I think we both thought that when I returned home there might be an engagement. However, whilst I was away, she became very friendly with an officer in one of the Foot Guards Regiments. You know how it is, sir. Wealthy family, good background. She was taken with him, even though I heard in the few days I had at home that he is a worthless ne'er do well who drinks and gambles to excess, and well, to cut a long story short, sir, she married him.'

Courtenay looked out of the windows for a moment.

'I am so damnably sorry, Simon. It must have come as a terrible surprise.'

'Yes, sir, but well, that is life I suppose.'

'If you need to talk about it further…..'

'Thank you sir, but I am over it. To business sir. I gather we are bound for the Mediterranean again, this time to fight the Barbary pirates?'

'Not necessarily *fight* them Simon, but let us say *discourage* them in some of their pursuits. Lord Cains is on his way there on a diplomatic mission.'

'The Dey and his friend the Bashaw will chew him up and spit him out in a moment, sir!'

Courtenay smiled. 'We can always hope. He has the *Rochester.* '

'She's a frigate, sir, is she not?'

'Yes. Felt she's a balance between someone like us, and something too small, at which the Dey might have taken offence! I do not see our 'squadron' here?'

'No sir. They are to join us off Wight. They are still at Plymouth, but I have sent word to rendezvous with us there later today.'

'Good. We will sail to Gibraltar, and then we will have a meeting with Captain Spellman and Commander Fenwick and I will explain what is to happen.'

Cressy stood up and replaced his hat. 'I will send word when we are ready to up-anchor, sir.'

'Thank you Mr Cressy.'

Trafford came over and took Courtenay's empty mug, refilling it from the pot.

'Bad luck about Mr Cressy, then sir.'

'Yes. It makes me realise how lucky I am, Alex.'

'Reckon you both are, Sir Giles.'

'Let us hope there is no more trouble.'

'Jake and the lads will look after everyone. In any case, sir, I thought that damned whippersnapper, begging your pardon, sir, was at sea with his Master?'

'Yes, he is, but what is to stop him leaving instructions?'

'They will be alright, sir.'

'I hope so. God help me, Alex, if any harm comes to Jessica or Edward, I'll swing for that bastard!'

The voyage to Gibraltar was uneventful, apart from sighting one or two French ships, and it still seemed odd to every man aboard all three ships that they should not be sent scurrying to their action stations as soon as the hated Tricolour was sighted.

Cressy had smiled slightly when Courtenay was examining one of the ships they came across through his telescope and of course, the French were examining *Hercules* closely as well, probably recognising her cut as being one of their own. Courtenay's fingers had been tapping on the barrel of the glass and he had sighed when lowering the same. He had turned away from the side with a brief 'Damned French!' and gone below the poop. Their 'eyes' the brig *Spur* and the frigate *Aurelia* were out of sight. The French must have wondered what on earth a British 74 was doing, wandering along on its own.

Gibraltar. Still the most important base for the Royal Navy in the part of the world, the gateway to the Mediterranean, and beyond. Once, Britain and France had fought over the Mediterranean bitterly, and there had even one period when the Royal navy was all but excluded from the Sea.

Hercules dropped her hook in the still clear waters of the harbour, which was crowded with shipping, although there were very few warships. Courtenay had half expected to find Lord Cairns tarrying there, delaying his trip to the Dey of Algiers in the hope he would be recalled first, but there was no sign of the *Rochester*. *Aurelia* anchored outside the main harbour, and Commander Fenwick in the brig was patrolling just to the east, more out of sheer habit than anything else. However, the evening after Courtenay's command came to a rest, Fenwick steered his small ship into the anchorage. Courtenay wasted no time in hoisting the signal for his friends to repair on board, and a lively supper was enjoyed by the three of them, with the addition of Cressy.

Tim Spellman had hardly changed at all since Courtenay had last seen him. He was his usual tall gangling self, still wearing his old-fashioned mutton chop whiskers, although Courtenay noticed a tinge of grey in them, and there were some grey hairs in his head as well. He felt sad as he noticed them, because Spellman was a similar age to himself and they were both young to be showing grey. James Fenwick was obviously relishing his first command and could hardly wait to get going again. He and Spellman shook hands warmly, with Cressy eyeing both of them curiously. These were two men who had been his Captain's Seniors in the past, now with their own commands, their own worries and concerns.

Spellman toyed with a glass of port and dug his knife into a piece of cheese before looking at his friend.

'I half expected Cairns still to be here, you know, Giles.'

'So did I, Tim, but he is obviously taking his orders seriously.'

'What do you require of me, sir?' asked James Fenwick, glancing sideways at Cressy, who was examining his glass of port against a cabin lantern. Courtenay knew he was being formal because Cressy was there, and Fenwick did not know the man.

'Ah, I think you may take *Spur* out tomorrow and have a look into the Dey's harbour for me, although not too far in. My orders are that you are to act as a messenger between me and *Rochester*. You might as well see if she is there first of all. We will not be far behind. Tim, you take *Aurelia* further along the coast and keep an eye open for any of our shipping along there. Give any protection they might need.'

Tim Spellman frowned. 'Expecting trouble, Giles?'

Courtenay looked at his friend's twin epaulettes glinting in the light from a lantern. A Post-captain as well now. How far it must seem from the days of the *Seagull* when on the day of that last bloody fight with the pirate *Le Corsair,* Spellman had run the woman pirate through to stop her killing Courtenay.

'Yes. Lord Crompton said that the Dey and the Bashaw and their friends are not averse to taking our ships if they wander too close to their shoreline. I have heard tales of them taking ships which are well away from their shoreline! They have some of these craft which have no need of the wind for their power.'

'Galleys. Rowed by hundreds of slaves.' grunted Fenwick.

'Yes, I believe I have heard of them as well. They mount a cannon in the bows and they can move freely into whatever position is best suited' added Cressy. He coloured a little as the others turned to look at him. 'Dose of grape and double shotted 32-pounders might teach them a lesson in manners!'

'Well said Mr Cressy!' exclaimed Spellman. Fenwick looked at Courtenay and smiled. He nodded to Cressy.

'That's all very well for you, safe and snug in this floating fortress, but spare a thought for us in the rowing boats!'

The others laughed.

'Regretting your command sir?' smiled Cressy.

'No, Mr Cressy, not at all. I will just make sure I keep well out of the way of any of those craft!'

The supper party broke up an hour or so later, and both Spellman and Fenwick shook hands warmly with Simon Cressy. Courtenay walked with them to the entry port whilst Cressy excused himself. He guessed that his Captain would want a few moments with his friends.

'Now, James, take care when you go poking your nose into the Dey's back garden. Just have a look for me and see if *Rochester* is there, that's all. We will rendezvous a way up the coast, where we agreed.'

'And I will sail to the east and keep a watch from that side.' added Spellman.

'I have not had the chance to enquire after Jessica, Giles.' Fenwick said quietly. Courtenay was quietly pleased. His friendship with James Fenwick was as strong as ever.

'She is in rude good health, James, thank you, and she made me promise that I was to pass to you her very best wishes. And, she says it is about time you settled down!'

There was a roar of laughter from Tim Spellman and a wry grin from Fenwick. He was one for the ladies, and Jessica Courtenay knew it.

'H'mm.' was all he said. Then he touched his hat to Courtenay and the side-party formally and with a last smile, disappeared down into his gig.

Spellman shook hands, and followed.

The following morning, *Spur* had gone, and *Aurelia* was shortening her cable. Fenwick had quit the harbour under cover of darkness and had set sail for the east. Spellman made more of a show of going, and Courtenay watched as the frigate tacked smartly and settled on her course, also to the east. He turned as he felt someone beside him.

'Ah, Alex. Hope we didn't keep you up too late?'

Trafford smiled. 'Good to see Mr Spellman again, sir. He hasn't changed at all, has he?'

'Bit greyer, Alex,' said Courtenay thoughtfully, 'but then, we all are!'

Steven Jeffrey appeared.' Good morning, sir'

'Good morning Mr Jeffrey. You have the watch, is that right?'

'Aye sir.'

'Good. I intend that we shall depart soon, but I do not want anyone watching to make it appear that we are the other ships are together.'

Jeffrey's young face creased into a frown. 'I thought we were at peace sir?'

Alex Trafford guffawed and Courtenay smiled.

'So we are, Mr Jeffrey, so we are. At least, with the French and the Spanish, but they are not the only people to have spies in this part of the world. I daresay the Dey and his friends have a very efficient spy system. Lord Cairns is supposed to be on a diplomatic mission, so there would be no need for us to have several ships with him, unless we meant some kind of business, yes?' Jeffrey nodded. 'And so, we go our own ways. In fact, you may ask the master to lay off a course to the west. That is where we will head first of all, wind permitting, but we will slip back through the Straits under cover of darkness.'

'Aye aye sir.'

'You reckonin' on trouble, Sir Giles?' asked Trafford

'I think that wherever there are despots like the Dey and the Bashaw, there will be trouble. They take too many of our ships and hold them to ransom. God help any of them who I find have taken one of our ships. I'll run every last man up to the mainyard as common pirates, God help me! Now, I fancy that by now Kingston may have prepared some breakfast. I will go and enjoy it and some coffee.'

'Aye sir.' Trafford watched his Captain stroll beneath the poop, nodding to some seamen who were rubbing down brasswork nearby.

Later in the day, anyone watching from the shore, and there were plenty of curious people wondering where such a large warship would be going in this time of peace, would have seen *Hercules* moving slowly, gracefully, away from the harbour, and turning on a westerly course. What they would not have seen was that under cover of darkness, the ship reversed its course, and headed back through the Straits and into the Mediterranean.

Dawn found the ship fifty miles inside the sea, on a south-easterly course, with the sun coming up and another fine day in prospect.

Courtenay was on deck as the sun appeared, and he saw the Master, Jacob Wetherby, looking at the sky and sniffing the air. He smiled and crossed the damp planking.

'Something ails you Mr Wetherby?'

'Just a feeling sir. You know this Sea as well as me or anyone else aboard, and there are some here who have spent a fair amount of time in these waters. The weather can change without any warning, and in a matter of no time at all!'

'I agree entirely. Let us hope we find if the Admiral and his ship are still with the Dey before any storm brews!'

Although the clear skies were replaced during the forenoon watch with some greyish clouds, the wind remained steady, and the ship was able to make good time. They had the North African coast in sight all the time to starboard, and Courtenay kept the ship on a course that maintained that view, although at the same time being sufficiently far away that he would not be caught on a lee shore if the weather did change. Greyer clouds appeared during the afternoon watch and some rain fell, and Courtenay noted that even though they had replenished their water supplies, the cooper still had some of his men on deck to catch what rainfall they could. There was a brief downpour, but that was all. The cooper seemed pleased though, judging by the smile on his pale face.

The wind rose during the night, and Jeffrey, who had the hated middle watch, 12 midnight to 4am, decided to take in a reef rather than be caught with too much of a press of sail. Courtenay had heard the watch being piped to the braces, men scampering aloft, when he roused briefly during the night, and although he climbed out of his cot and looked at the weather through the stern windows, he was not called for, and he climbed smiling back into his bed. Kingston was awake in his pantry, and Trafford had heard the pipe and heard the men, noting that his Captain had not been called for. He hoped Steven Jeffrey had got it right!

'That's the Dey's anchorage, sir, that indent in the coastline.' Wetherby was saying as they approached. Courtenay had his glass up as they cleared the coastline which was in the way of a clear view of the harbour.....and its defences.

'We will anchor off the harbour, Mr Wetherby. You will however be ready to make sail again.'

'You expecting trouble sir?' asked Cressy.

'You sound like my cox'n, Simon. Always, always be prepared. Let us just say that I am not taking any chances.' He closed the glass he had been using. 'There is no sign of the *Rochester*. I wonder if that means the Admiral has already left.'

In the meantime, *Hercules* was approaching the area where Courtenay wanted to anchor, and Wetherby caught his eye. A brief nod, and Wetherby was yelling the anchor party to let go, and Cressy was ordering the men on the yardarms to take in the sails. The ship came to a stop, and rode easily in the slight swell coming offshore.

'Boat coming out to us, sir!' called McMasters.

'Thank you Mr McMasters. I do believe we saw that for ourselves!' replied Cressy, but he smiled as he said so, robbing the words of any offence.

It was a grand looking boat, with a blue canopy over the middle part, and what seemed to be a large number of brightly coloured cushions with a large man in equally brightly coloured clothes sitting on them.

'Man the side Mr Cressy.' ordered Courtenay rather shortly. 'Yonder craft does not appear to be a bumboat!'

For a large man, he climbed up the side quite nimbly, and stood for a moment looking around him. Courtenay thought for a moment of going down to the entry port to greet him, but something about the man, whom he now saw sported a large turban stopped him. He smiled as he detected a frown on the man's face but stood firmly rooted to the spot, making the man climb the starboard ladder to the quarterdeck.

The man stopped in front of Courtenay's six foot frame and had to look up at him. He saw firm dark brown eyes and a steely glint in them that made him think twice about what he was going to say, but he remembered the orders he had been given by his Master.

'Whom am I addressing?' he asked in heavily accented English.

'I am Captain Sir Giles Courtenay, and this is His Britannic Majesty's ship *Hercules*. And whom may you be, sir?'

'I am Ali Habib Mansoor, Ambassador to his Most Glorious Majesty the Dey. I must remonstrate with you *Capitaine* for not affording his Majesty with a salute of your guns. I understand that it is the custom with you to salute your own King George?'

'Yes, but unfortunately, I have no idea how man guns salute your Master requires and I did not want to insult him with the wrong number.'

'It is 25'

Cressy was muttering under his breath and Courtenay distinctly heard Lieutenant St Clair utter 'Damned cheek of the man!' The King warranted a 21 gun salute.

Courtenay smiled at the man. I shall remember, but our own gracious King George only has 21.'

'That is his sorrow, *Capitaine.*' replied the fat man with an oily grin. 'Now, my Master commands me enquire as to the honour of this visit.'

'I understand that Vice-admiral Lord Cairns has visited here? He was under a duty to come and see your Master.'

'Indeed, and he is still here.'

'How is that, when his ship is not?'

'Ship?'

'Yes, the one he arrived in. The *Rochester.* Where is it, if he is still here?'

'The ship has gone. Lord Cairns and, and…..'

'Lieutenant Spencer-White, his Flag-Lieutenant?'

The man smiled slightly. 'Ah, yes, that was his name. He went with the ship. The Admiral is still here as my master's…….guest.'

There was an intake of breath from some of the nearby officers and Trafford turned away breathing in hard. For 'guest' read prisoner or hostage!

'Why, M'sieur?'

Mansoor smiled politely. 'Why not?'

Courtenay lost his patience. Diplomacy was not his strongest suit. 'I wish to see Lord Cairns.'

'That is not possible. He is not ….well at the moment.'

'Even more reason why I should see him. I must insist. Whilst Lord Cairns is.ah, a *guest* of the Dey, I am the Senior British Officer in these waters, and I have to speak to him.'

'I will gladly take him a note from you, *Sair* Giles.'

Courtewnay almost laughed out loud. 'I do not think so. I wish to see him, and without delay'

'And what if he does not wish to speak to you?' Mansoor was getting cocky.

'I can assure you, you do not wish to know!'

'You can see our defences, *Capitaine,* are they not, how you say, impressive?'

'Yes, they are, but we have a saying in our country. There is more than one way to skin a cat.'

'I am sorry?'

'Do not worry. Return to your Master. repeat my demand.'

'It would be best to say it was a polite request, *Capitaine.*'

'I don't care what you call it. Just pass it on.'

Mansoor left, very unhappy, and was back within an hour. This time, he had Cairns with him. However, Cairns made no effort to get out of the boat. Courtenay went down to the entry port, and without hesitation, climbed down into the boat. He looked at Cairns. The man was pale, but appeared healthy otherwise.

'Is there something wrong, my Lord?' asked Courtenay.

'Cairns forced a smile. No, Courtenay, nothing wrong. The Dey asked that we do him a little favour, and I was pleased to agree, in the interests of harmony between our countries.' Courteney turned away from Mansoor who was trying to listen to every word, and Cairns had to turn with him.

'Harmony, my Lord, with these, these murdering scum?'

Cairns' face was stiff. 'I have my orders, Captain, and you have yours.'

'You are a prisoner, sir, is that it?'

'More a kind of….guarantee.'

'Where is the *Rochester,* sir?'

'She is away doing the favour for the Dey.'

'And what favour might that be, sir?' a suspicion was forming in Courtenay's mind, one he did not much care for.

'I have been asked to transport some gifts to the Dey's ally in Cyprus.'

'I thought the Americans did something similar, a few months ago?'

'You are correct. These are more gifts.'

'The Americans had to fly the Dey's bargee, sir.'

'Yes. So does *Rochester*. Dalrymple was given no alternative.'

'I cannot believe you allowed this to happen, my Lord.'

'I had no alternative. I am here to further good relations with the Dey. He is taking enough of our merchant ships as it is, for God's sake. If we can stop that, what I had to agree to is little enough Courtenay!'

'But to allow a King's ship to sail under the colours of a Barbary State!'

'My nephew was sent with her to make sure she comes back. There are some gifts to come back to the Dey, and he wanted to make sure he got them. Also, one of the Dey's favourite nephews went. He wanted to make sure he came back as well.'

'What is to stop you climbing aboard my ship here and now sir, and me sailing after your frigate?'

'I gave my word, Captain. The word of a gentleman.'

'Do you really think that the Dey understands what a gentleman is, my Lord?'

Cairns actually smiled. 'Oh yes, Courtenay, the Dey knows what a gentleman is, rest assured. He has no need of being one himself, but he understands what being a gentleman means.'

Mansoor interrupted. 'It is time we return. Goodbye *Capitaine.'*

Courtenay turned and touched his hat to the Admiral before climbing up the stairs. He stood at the top and looked down. There was a brief glance from Cairns and then the boat was moving away.

SIX

It was two weeks since the meeting with Cairns at the Dey's stronghold. Courtenay had had plenty of time to ruminate on what had happened, and he was firmly of the view that in some way the Vice-admiral's hand had been forced. Surely, he reasoned with himself during many an hour pacing his cabin, a King's officer, especially a Vice-admiral, would not allow his ship to be used by a foreign power, especially one such as that of the Dey. Together with his allies along the Barbary coast, they would rape and pillage any merchantman which came within their grasp. A fine ally to the British. In time of war, some strange alliances were forged. But they were not at war. All the same, Courtenay and many others like him realised they *were* at war, but perhaps in a different way.

See a French ship flying the red blue and white of the Tricolour, and you knew who your enemy was, or the red and gold of Spain. Britain was not at war with the Dey, or the Bashaw, at least,. he thought grimly, not officially.

Hercules was on the starboard tack. A fair wind was coming off the North African coast, pushing up on the ship's quarter. It was fine sailing weather and Courtenay was glad of it, but he was concerned as to the whereabouts of the *Rochester*. With good weather, the frigate should have reached its destination and be on its way back.

He had sent *Spur* into Gibraltar with a despatch for the Flag Officer there. He should know that Cairns was effectively a prisoner of the Dey, and he would put whatever diplomatic procedures were possible in motion. Courtenay had little doubt that the Dey would laugh and send the messenger on his way.....if he was lucky.

Aurelia was patrolling ahead of them. Spellman, acting on his own initiative, had gone further north and east than Courtenay had intended, but Timothy Spellman was no idiot. He had carefully worked out what the most likely course would be back to the Algiers, although he had returned to their meeting place flying the large black flag which said it all. *Negative.*

Courtenay was on the quarterdeck, hatless, coatless as usual, when there was a yell from the mainmast look-out.

'Deck there! Sail to the nor' east, sir!'

Cressy was on deck, and the Third, Alan Frobisher, was officer of the watch. The three officers levelled their telescopes in the direction indicated by the look out's yell, and for a moment saw nothing, but on a rise on the slight swell, they saw a small sail.

'Merchantman.' grunted Frobisher.

Cressy lowered the glass for a moment and smiled. 'Like enough, Mr Frobisher'

Courtenay looked over at where McMasters was waiting with his signals party.

'Show the colours Mr McMasters and make our number'

'Aye aye sir!'

For what seemed an eternity, the ships grew closer, and then McMasters was able to confirm the approaching shop was a British merchant ship. Just as Courtenay was about to ask the Midshipman to signal the Merchant ship to heave-to, the look-out yelled again.

'Deck there! Another ship, sir, coming off the shore!'

'What?' asked Cressy, of no-one. 'What the devil?'

The glasses swung round and Courtenay was the first to see the ship. Single-masted, with a brightly-coloured burgee at the truck, it was moving swiftly, despite only having the one main sail.

'Chebeck. Powered by man-power.' was all he needed to say. It was clear what the pirate intended. He was going to get to the merchantman before *Hercules* could intervene. Or so he hoped. 'Get the Royals on her Mr Cressy, if you please, and have the gunner prepare the bow-chasers. I'll be damned if that pirate is going to take one of our ships from under our noses!'

Wearing an impressive array of sail, the liner was almost leaning forward, an impressive bow-wave forming a bone in her teeth, whilst the gun-crews of the bow-chasers hurriedly cast off lashings and ran the guns in to load them. The Gunner, a lean, dark man named Henry Anderson, was fussing around the guns as if they were his own children.

'Mr Mallory,' said Courtenay to a young Midshipman near the binnacle. 'Go forward and give Mr Anderson my compliments. Tell him, he is to fire when ready. There is no need to await my command.'

The youngster touched his hat and walked to the starboard ladder. When he reached the fo'c'sle, and passed on his message, Anderson turned and raised his arm to his Captain by way of acknowledgment.

The Chebeck was closing on the merchantman, whose Captain had set more sail, but the wind was not as kind to him as it was the *Hercules*. There was a puff of smoke from the bows of the pirate and a few seconds later, the sound of a gun. A feather of spray showed where the ball had fallen short, but the next one was closer. The merchant ship had run out her artillery, but they were pop-guns compared even with the gun the Chebeck carried. Another cloud of smoke, another bang, and this time, Courtenay saw through his glass a puff of something from the side of the merchant ship and realised it was wood being pounded into splinters. Now the Chebeck had the range, they would pound the ship and try to get aboard and take her before the British warship could intervene.

Hercules was powering through the water at a speed which would do credit to a frigate, and although Courtenay was willing the Gunner to get on with it, he knew the man was waiting for the range to fall away. He started as there was a sudden bang, and saw smoke funnelling in over the bows. Anderson had opened fire.

The ball fell in what appeared to be direct line with the advancing Chebeck. There was a large plume of water, but Anderson was already at the other gun, which almost immediately fired.

Wetherby, in between watching his sails, had his glass up, and he gasped 'Damme, that was good shooting sir!'

He was right. The second ball landed almost immediately in front of the onrushing ship, which in the meantime, had fired at the merchantman again. The first bow-chaser boomed again, and this time there was no splash. Instead, the Chebeck appeared to slow, and when they all looked again, they could all see that some of the sweeps near the bows had gone. The pirate was momentarily in confusion, and that was the delay they needed. The larboard bow-chaser fired again, and the ball dropped in among the men at the stern of the boat. As Courtenay lowered his glass, he fancied he saw a severed limp flung overboard by the force of the impact.

While the crew of the Chebeck were trying to restore order, *Hercules* was getting within range of her lower-deck 32-pounders, which in fact had not been cleared for action. The British ship of the line swept down upon the unfortunate Chebeck, and Courtenay watched coldly as it started to disappear beneath *Hercules'* bows.

'You goin' to ram, sir?' asked Trafford quietly.

'No, there are the slaves to consider, but I want to get close enough to fire on the ones which count.' He turned to Cressy. 'Swivels and small arms, Simon, pick off the pirates. Mr Wetherby! Three points to larboard, if you please!'

Hercules swept round to larboard, bringing the damaged Chebeck onto their starboard side. As she did so, there was a storm of small-arms fire from her, and several swivels blasted grape at the many men in brightly clothes and turbans. Merrilees had his men at the side and they poured a volley into the pirate as she drifted down the side.

The Bosun had his men throw grapnels, and the Chebeck was quickly shackled. There were still men aboard the ship who were not willing to give in, and who waved ancient muskets and broad-bladed scimitars. One or two of these tried foolishly to climb *Hercules'* side, and were shot out of hand for their trouble.

After a few moments, what was left of the crew threw down their weapons and Merrilees sent a squad down into the ship to take command. Incredibly, one man thought he would start a new fight on his own, and raised a sword to strike down a Marine, but another red-coated figure thrust forward with his musket and impaled the man on his long bayonet before throwing him over the side.

Cressy turned to his Captain and smiled briefly. 'What do we do with the slaves, sir?'

'Have the blacksmith strike off their shackles. Try to make them understand they are free. They can get the ship back to the shore and I am certain from there they will make good their escape. What is left of the crew bring aboard in irons and we will take them back to where they belong!'

'Might be a useful bargaining tool sir?' piped up Frobisher. Cressy turned to him wearing an exasperated expression but Courtenay spoke quietly.

'I am afraid not, Mr Frobisher. The Dey will care not for his men, especially so since they have been caught red-handed in an act of piracy. I am sure that the Dey will have their heads.'

Whilst Cressy was making all the arrangements, the Merchant ship had closed to within hailing distance. Courtenay told the Captain that he would escort him to a point where they would be safe from the pirates' attention. The man had not seen *Aurelia.*

After escorting the merchant ship to a point where she would be safe, *Hercules* turned in her tracks and made her way back to patrol along the coast. Of *Aurelia* there was still no sign, but this changed after they had been beating up the coast for four days. The mainmast look-out, Lees, reported a fast moving sail approaching, and he was soon able to identify the same as their frigate. He also hailed down there was another frigate in company. Courtenay had looked at Trafford, and the cox'n had simple mouthed '*Rochester,* at last?'.

Within fifteen minutes it was clear that the other ship was indeed the missing frigate. Spellman in his *Aurelia* signalled to the effect. By the time they were close enough to talk it was growing dark. But not dark enough to see the burgee of the Dey of Algiers flying from the mainmast instead of the Red Ensign (Cairns was an Admiral of the Red Division) flying from the mizen gaff. Courtenay had grunted and said nothing, but inside, he was seething with anger. His officers sensed it, and kept clear, especially Steven Jeffrey, who knew his moods only too well. He left everything alone during darkness, but at first light, he ordered that the ships hove-to and he had himself rowed over to the *Rochester*.

Dalrymple, the Captain of the frigate, was just the sort of person Courtenay had expected. Aristocratic, arrogant, tight-lipped. He and Cairns were a perfectly matched pair. And of course, there was Marmaduke Spencer-White. He hovered around whilst Dalrymple and Courtenay talked in the former's cabin. He was dying to intervene, but he could not. He did not have the influence or protection of his Uncle here. The Dey's favourite nephew had decided that discretion was called for and had not been on deck when Courtenay had arrived. Dalrymple had coloured deeply when he saw that the first thing Courtenay did was to look at the foreign colours at the mainmast truck. The sneer on his face said it all.

'Now, Captain Dalrymple, perhaps you would so good as to explain why you are flying that filthy rag from your mainmast? My God, sir, is this still a Royal Navy ship, or is it not? How could you possibly agree to fly another Country's colours instead of your own, especially.......of *that* man!'

Courtenay heard the cabin door open and turned to see a slim man enter dressed in fine silk clothing, with a magnificent turban. At the front of the turban was a large diamond.

'Please excuse me.' The man said in good English. 'Who do I have the honour of addressing?'

'I am Sir Giles Courtenay, Captain of His Britannic Majesty's ship of the line *Hercules,* and at the moment, the Senior British Officer here.'

Dalrymple made to say something, but changed his mind,. He had been going to say that in fact *he* was the Senior officer, because he had been a Captain for a small amount of time longer than Courtenay, but Giles commanded a third-rate, whereas Dalrymple did not. That made Courtenay the Senior British Officer.

'Well, Captain Courtenay, the reason my Uncle's flag flies on this ship is because he made a special request to your Admiral that it should be so, and he was gracious enough to agree.'

Courtenay faced him and looked the man straight in the eyes.

'I know the difference between a man being a guest and a prisoner. The Admiral, I am sure, was left in no doubt as to what would happen if he did not agree.' He smiled, but Dalrymple felt a chill pass through him, and so did the young man in the bright coloured robes. Courtenay turned back to Dalrymple. 'You will strike that Flag now, Captain Dalrymple. I have already sent a report to the Flag Officer at Gibraltar, and I am sure he will require a full explanation from you. You will replace the same with our own colours, and then, we will return to the Dey and recover the Vice-admiral.' He sensed the young man smiling.

'You find something amusing?'

'Yes, Captain, I find it amusing that you feel, obviously, that you can intimidate my Uncle.' His tone became hard. 'It will go ill with your Admiral if my Uncle sees anything but his flag flying from this ship when it enters the harbour.'

'We will not be entering the harbour. If you mean that harm will come to my Admiral, then let me say to you one thing, and be assured, I mean every word. If any harm should come to him, the last sight you will have of your precious Uncle will be as you swing from the mainyard, with a rope round your neck. Think on that as we return to Algiers. Captain Dalrymple, you will have this 'gentleman' escorted to his quarters and a guard placed outside. He is not to go anywhere. Can I trust you to do that?'

'Damme sir, of course you may!'

'Then do it!'

Courtenay turned to Spencer-White. 'How did this come about, Mr Spencer-White?'

Marmaduke Spencer-White coloured slightly. 'You will be aware, Sir Giles, that my...the Admiral was sent to negotiate with the Dey. Unfortunately, the Dey took exception to what was being proposed. He said that he wanted some precious cargo being taken to his friend, the ruler of Cyprus, much as he had done with the American ship, and he made it perfectly clear what would happen if the Admiral refused. He agreed, and I was sent to make sure that Captain Dalrymple did not simply throw the Dey's nephew over the side the moment we were out of sight of land.'

'In other words, the Admiral put his own skin in front of his duty?'

Spencer-White remained silent. Courtenay smiled. Dalrymple did not like the smile at all. He decided there and then that Courtenay was not the sort of person to trifle with. He had already heard tales about Spencer-White and the antics of Cairns' previous Flag-Lieutenant, and he knew who had come out on top.

Courtenay replaced his hat and said curtly. 'Well then Mr Spencer-White. It seems it is for me to attempt to retrieve the situation. I shall return to my ship. Captain Dalrymple will obey my orders, is that clear?'

Sprencer-White nodded, his face showing his anger. Dalrymple was in over his head and he knew it.

By the time Courtenay was back on his own quarterdeck he was calm again.

'Mr McMasters. You will signal *Aurelia* that she is to lay off a course for Algiers and scout ahead. You will then signal *Rochester* that she is to take station one cable astern of us.'

'Aye aye sir!'

Cressy hid a grin. That would take some station keeping on Dalrymple's part, since even with a Captain like him, the frigate would be a faster sailer than the liner.

'Something amuse you, Mr Cressy?'

'No sir.'

'Good. I find nothing amusing in our situation.' He turned and strode to the windward side of the quarterdeck where the wind whipped his longish hair as he removed his hat and breathed in deeply.

Trafford passed close by the First-Lieutenant. He liked Cressy. He was a good officer and a fine seaman. 'Don't take any notice of the Captain, sir. He's just bloody angry, beggin' your pardon.'

'Perhaps someone ought to be, Trafford' Cressy smiled briefly and turned to berate some seaman for not coiling a rope properly.

Dalrymple managed to keep station on his senior officer all the way back to Algiers. Courtenay had little doubt that the man had been on deck for the entire time, not wanting any of his officers to let him down. As the small Squadron approached Algiers, Courtenay sent the *Aurelia* back to the East to patrol the coastline, with orders to keep a sharp eye for any of the Dey's fast Chebecks.

Hercules dropped anchor off the harbour, well away from all the local shipping, with *Rochester,* wearing her proper colours, in this case the Red Ensign, just slightly closer in. Where Courtenay had chosen to anchor gave them a perfect view of all the harbour defences, and a small number of the Dey's warships. There was one which was a smallish two-decker, probably carrying 50 guns, similar in size to the *Leander* which had been at the Nile when Courtenay commanded the *Amazon.* The ship had been captured by the French when on passage back to Gibtraltar to report about the Nile, and had been later taken back. This ship was probably of Turkish origin judging by her shape and appearance.

Courtenay ordered Trafford to call away his barge and had himself rowed over to the *Rochester.* Dalrymple had seen him coming and the side party was all spruce and proper as he climbed through the entry port.

'May I ask what you intend, Sir Giles?'

'Of course you may. I intend to obtain the return of your Admiral, what else?'

Dalrymple was a smallish man, and along with his arrogance was a petulance, although held in check. Courtenay was thinking where he had seen that attitude before when he suddenly remembered. Edmund Prankash. They had been Midshipmen together in the 74-gun *Claymore* and then later, Courtenay had served as Prankash's First-Lieutenant in the sloop of war *Seagull*. He had been killed off the French coast by a metal splinter, and Courtenay had taken over command. The Prankash family had never forgiven him. Cairns or Spencer-White as he had been before becoming a peer, was a patriach of that family. What a small world he was thinking. Dalrymple watched a wry grin appear on the other man's face and shifted his feet a little.

'Have Flags bring your 'guest' on deck, and run a halter up to the mainyard.'

'Surely you do not…'

'Captain Dalrymple. You have shown yourself lacking in anything approaching courage or even duty. Just do as I ask!'

The other man melted away. Spencer-White appeared on deck with the Dey's nephew. The man smiled when he saw his home, then frowned as he saw the halter being run up to the mainyard.

He turned to Courtenay. 'Are you intending to execute someone, Captain?'

'Yes. You, if your Uncle does not do as he is requested.' With that he deliberately turned away. Trafford hid a grin and looked over the side. He saw the fancy boat approaching.

'Looks like that that chap Mansoor coming again, Captain.'

Courtenay had seen him. 'Yes.'

Mansoor stood up in his boat as it came to a rest next to *Rochester,* and Courtenay could see him looking up at the mizen gaff where the Red Ensign was flapping in the offshore breeze. Courtenay could see his quizzical expression. When no-one made nay effort to go down to him, he realised he had to go to them, and with a small amount of difficulty, climbed the stairs. He was puffing slightly as he at last arrived on the starboard gangway, where he saw Courtenay and Dalrymple waiting for him, and behind them, his Master's favourite nephew. He also saw the rope hanging from the mainyard.

'We meet again, Sir Giles.'

'So we do. Where is the Admiral?'

'He, ah, he said he would continue to enjoy my Master's most generous hospitality.'

'Really?' said Courtenay sarcastically. It was not lost on Mansoor.

'Sir Giles, I have noticed before that you appear to doubt my master's hospitality to your Admiral, and of course, to your good King George.'

'Enough of this small talk. I have come to take Vice-admiral Lord Cairns back to Gibraltar.'

'And what if he chooses to remain here, Sir Giles?' Mansoor's voice was silky smooth. 'You have but two small ships, and my master, well, look around you.' He was smirking.

'This is the Dey's favourite nephew, yes?'

'That is so. He is the son of his favourite Sister, a most beautiful lady who walks with grace.......'

'Yes, I am sure she does. You see that rope?'

'Yes. Are you going to hang one of your men for some offence? I commiserate with you having to do this within sight of our harbour. I am sure there will be a large audience. What has the poor man done?'

'Rest assured, that if I was hanging one of my men, the last thing I would be do it within sight of your Master. It is your master's nephew I intend to run up to the mainyard, unless the Admiral is back aboard this ship in one half-hour. Do you understand, am I clear?'

Mansoor was aghast. He also looked totally terrified, transformed from arrogant to desperate in two seconds.

'But you cannot, you cannot. It is.......it is inhuman!'

'You dare to talk to me about inhumanity? A few days ago I had to intervene to prevent one of your master's Chebecks taking a merchant ship. A *British* merchant ship, clearly flying British colours. What would you have done, kill everyone and sell the women and children into slavery?'

Mansoor's eyes glinted. Courtenay had struck a chord.

'Your face betrays the answer. One half-hour, otherwise.......' He nodded to the maindeck and Mansoor's eyes widened in alarm as he saw a line of seaman standing by the free end of the rope. He hurried through the entry port and down into the boat.

Dalrymple had taken his courage in his hands and confronted Courtenay.

'You cannot do this, Captain Courtenay! It is barbaric! God, you are an Englishman for God's sake! We do not do things like this!'

Courtenay turned on him, eyes blazing. 'And what would you do, Captain? You would not have recovered the Admiral until the Dey had decided he would release him, and what else would he blackmail out of us before he did? That man needs to be taught a lesson in manners. Oh, and by the way, I am only part English. The rest of me is Scottish. The clan MacPherson?'

Spencer-White was hovering.

'If anything should happen to my Uncle......'

115

'I would not worry too much Mr Spencer-White. I think you will find your Uncle will be safe.'

He turned and walked away, pulling out his pocket watch. Trafford watched him, and found he was alternating watching his Captain and looking at the shore. Twenty-five minutes had passed when Trafford turned and nodded to Courtenay.

'Boat's coming back, sir.'

Courtenay held his hand out for a telescope and a slim, tanned Midshipman whose face was familiar handed him one. He snapped it open and looked through it.

'The Admiral is on board.' He turned to Spencer-White. 'It would appear the Dey values his nephew more than Lord Cairns.' He turned back to the Midshipman, handing the glass to him. 'You are Mr…..?'

'Wyvern, sir. My elder brother had the great honour to serve with you sir.'

'Yes by God. We were Midshipmen together, and he was my First-Lieutenant in the *Amazon*. I am proud to count him as one of my friends. How is he?'

'He is very well, sir. He commands a fine sloop.'

'You will give him my very best wishes when you next write?'

'I would be delighted, sir/'

The boat was alongside the frigate and then Cairns' cocked hat appeared above the decking as he pulled himself through the port. Courtenay touched his hat.

'Welcome back, sir.'

Cairns looked at a loss for words, but grunted a reply. 'Damned glad to be out of that rat-hole, but I fear you have made an enemy of the Dey, Courtenay. Didn't take too kindly to his nephew bein' strung up, I can tell you!'

'And I did not take kindly to a King's Admiral being held hostage, my Lord'

Mansoor was guiding the nephew down into his boat. He looked at Courtenay and there was hate in his eyes, but Courtenay also detected something else. Cairns saw it too. For once he actually smiled.

'You certainly gave the Dey something to think about Sir Giles.' His tone was pleasant, far more pleasant that Courtenay had heard before. 'That chap Mansoor is for it. I think the Dey has something unpleasant reserved for him. Blames him for not hanging onto me and getting his nephew back. Probably the strappado, or perhaps a couple of hundred swipes with the *bastinado*?' He actually chuckled. 'Serve the man right!'

He turned away and spoke to Spencer-White.

'I shall return to my ship and continue with my duties, my Lord. Will you go to Gibraltar?'

'I think that may be for the best, Sir Giles.' He held out his hand 'This is not the first time you have got me out of a tight spot, Sir Giles. I would not blame you if you would not take my hand.'

But Courtenay was not that sort of person, so he shook the Admiral's hand.

Ten minutes later he was back aboard *Hercules* and giving orders to make sail to the east. *Rochester* was already shaking out her sails and raising her hook.

'Was everything satisfactory in the end sir?' Cressy was asking as *Rochester* gathered way and settled on a course for Gibraltar.

Courtenay looked at him for a moment. 'Yes, Simon, thank you. It was.'

'I was watching through a glass sir, and I had the guns manned, just in case. Would you have done it?'

'H'mm.' Courtenay smiled briefly and walked away. Trafford just grinned at the Lieutenant and followed his Captain.

Jeffrey, officer of the watch, turned from making sure all the sails were drawing properly, and joined Cressy.

'Would he have done it, Steven?' Cressy asked quietly. 'Would he really have run that fellow up to the mainyard? You know him better than any of us!'

'Except Alex Trafford!' Jeffrey thought for a moment. 'In truth, Simon, I do not know. I would say that he is capable of it, of that I have no doubt at all. Sometimes, desperate situations call for desperate measures!'

SEVEN

For the next two weeks, *Hercules* and her consorts, divided over the area they had to cover, sailed back and forth that stretch of the North African coastline named The Barbary Coast. Their presence gave heart to the merchantman who came within relatively easy sailing distance of the three states which made up the coastline. The Dey and his cohorts had been somewhat quiet, but neither Courtenay, nor the Royal Navy as a whole were fooled. They knew that both the Dey and the Bashaw had nothing which would match the British 74, and they were clearly worried that *Hercules* might just happen along when one of their Chebecks was attacking a British merchantman.

The Americans had ships in the area as well. Courtenay saw one of their large 44 gun frigates on a number of occasions, patrolling along, trying to make sure their countrymen kept out of harm's way. They also had a brig in company, but Courtenay thought that such a ship would not be equal to even a Chebeck. The latter was highly manoeuvrable and would have the ability to get alongside a brig and then overwhelm it with sheer numbers. *Hercules* was different. A far higher tumblehome, far more guns….and far more men.

Fenwick was presently patrolling to the west of the Coast in his brig *Spur,* and had reported rather oddly that although he had sighted two or three of the Dey's fast moving galleys, when they had seen his ship they had sheered off, even though there was a juicy merchantman in view. Courtenay agreed that it was odd, but perhaps the Dey was being a little circumspect for the time being. The Flag Officer at Gibraltar had been livid about the way Vice-admiral Lord Cairns had been treated, and rightly so. A note had been sent to the Dey warning him of his future conduct if he wished to continue to receive British aid, in other words, money.

Courtenay could never understand the reasoning. The man robbed, pillaged, and stole from any ship his men could lay their hands on, who then proceeded to rape and kill as much as they pleased. Giving this despot money did not make him more amenable to British ships. The Gibraltar Admiral had been fulsome in his praise for what Courtenay had done, even if he was concerned that perhaps their Lordships of Admiralty, snug behind their desks in London might not see it in the same light.

Aurelia had been sent in to Gibraltar to re-provision, and when she returned, she would take over *Hercules'* area and Courtenay would take his ship in to re-stock with provisions. Spellman would then be the senior British officer. Of the *Rochester* there had been no sign, and Courtenay was curious to know what Cairns would do now. He would not go back to Algiers, obviously, and it was unlikely, although not impossible, that anyone else would be sent in his stead.

The day *Aurelia* returned coincided with *Spur* being within signalling distance, so Courtenay took the opportunity of inviting his friends for supper. Courtenay also invited some of his officers, including Steven Jeffrey, whom Spellman had met briefly in Ceylon.

The following day, *Hercules* took her leave, and four days later, her best bower plunged down into the still waters of the busy anchorage.

Courtenay reported to the Flag Officer, a fat Vice-admiral who was also quite short and completely bald. His eyes were also uncomfortably close together, but he had a quick brain.

'Damn good work, Sir Giles, damn good. As I said in my letter, their Lordships may not view it the same way, but they are not here and do not have to deal with this damn pirate taking our ships. My God, we pay him as well! No, young fellah, your actions might just teach him some manners, what?'

Courtenay smiled politely. He very much doubted that *anyone* could teach the Dey any manners. 'Let us hope so, sir. Now, if I may deal with the matter of provisions.......?

The Admiral smiled. He knew Courtenay was really only interested in getting his ship re-provisioned and back to sea.

'Certainly Sir Giles, but only after you have joined me in a glass of Madeira. Got a fresh case in yesterday. Good stuff.'

They stayed in Gibraltar two days to re-stock, and to replenish their waters casks, and another day because the wind was against them. On the fourth day, the men aloft dropped the sails from their yardarms, the hands on deck pulled on the braces, and the liner elegantly moved out into the Mediterranean. An envious Vice-admiral had watched, had seen how smartly the ship spread her sails.

Whilst they had been at anchor, there had been no sign of the other frigate, the *Rochester*. The Vice-admiral had told Courtenay that Cairns had already left for home. Courtenay had also asked about the plans for handing back Malta to the French, as that was part of the agreement reached upon which the truce was based.

'No idea, Captain. Haven't heard a word about it, and why we should give up anything we took from the Frogs is beyond me anyway! The place is damned important. Ought to keep it!'

Courtenay watched as Gibraltar slipped away, in the end hidden in a slight sea-mist. He tucked his hands behind his back and strolled across the quarterdeck, oblivious to the hustle and bustle around him. He was wondering about his wife in London, and what Spencer-White would get up to knowing that he, Courtenay, was thousands of miles away. He had no need to worry. Not only had Sir Geoffrey taken care of that, but so had Trafford. Ned and his lads would keep an eye on the family. Sir Geoffrey had hired a second coach driver, an ex-Marine, and a footman who went everywhere who had served in the Army. If one team was not with her, the others were. Jessica was far from stupid. She knew instantly what the men were who were hired by her father, and she knew of Ned anyway.

So Courtenay and his ship went back to the dreary round of patrol.

Two weeks later, whilst he was still beating up and down the North African coast, there was another 'chance' meeting in London involving Jessica and Spencer-White. Jessica had been out with Edward, this time without her maid, and had arranged to meet a friend, who had two small children of her own. Her friend had elected not to bring her children to the meeting, and was more than a little surprised to see Edward.

'Why should I leave him with the servants, Eliza?' she had asked 'I am not one of these parents who leaves their children with their servants all the time. You know that!'

Her friend had coloured slightly. They were walking through the park, St James's, when a familiar figure was seen walking towards them. Eliza also saw him.

'What a handsome man that is coming towards us, Jessica. A Naval Officer I do believe. He has one of those rather lovely gold braid things on his shoulder. He is looking at us, or, I should say, you. Do you know him?'

'The braid is called an *aguilette*. And yes, Eliza, I do have the misfortune to know him, and so does Giles. He is not a man to be trusted.'

'Oh, how can you say such a thing about some a handsome man?'

'Very easily, dear. Just keep walking.'

Marmaduke Spencer-White stopped in front of them swept of his hat and bowed.

'Why, Lady Courtenay, and young Edward. I hope I find you well?'

Jessica was all for pushing her way past, but Eliza stopped, and smiled.

'Are you not going to introduce me to your friend, Lady Courtenay?'

Jessica wanted to say. 'No.' but manners dictated otherwise.

'Eliza, this is Lieutenant Marmaduke Spencer-White, Flag-Lieutenant to Vice-admiral Lord Cairns. Mr Spencer-White, may I present Lady Frensham. Her husband is Lord Frensham.'

'Your servant, Lady Frensham.'

Jessica said acidly, and much to her friend's surprise, 'I thought you were in the Mediterranean?'

'You are well informed Lady Courtenay. I returned just the other day, with his Lordship. Your Husband, I fear, is still there!'

'And so is the pistol in my bag, Mr Spencer-White.' she said coldly, 'and it is loaded.'

'Of that I have no doubt whatsoever, Lady Courtenay.' He smiled at Lady Frensham's shocked appearance. 'We are old sparring partners, Lady Frensham.

Unfortunately, Lady Courtenay seems to feel for some mysterious reason that I wish harm to herself or to young Edward here. I can assure both of us that I have no such intention, and it causes me great concern to know that you think so ill of me.'

'Well, it was pleasant to meet with you, Mr Spencer-White, but Lady Frensham and myself would like to continue our walk.'

Spencer-White continued to stand in their way, with a smile on his lips, but the smile was changing slightly and two things made him bow again and move out of their way. The first was Jessica's free hand slipping into her bag, and second was the sight of two hard-looking men who had appeared and who were looking straight at him, with their right hands inside their coats.

He walked away.

'He seemed charming enough, my dear,' said Lady Frensham as they continued their walk, 'until the last few moments when the mask slipped. I have seen men like him before. My Husband employs one.' There was the trace of a sneer. 'He calls him his 'remedy man'. '

'He would kill Giles if he had the chance. Or at least, he thinks he would be able to!' Lady Frensham looked at her friend for a moment.

'Do you really have a pistol in your bag?'

'Oh yes. And it is loaded, as I told that terrible man!'

'Can you use it?'

'I wouldn't have one in my bag, loaded, if I couldn't use it. My Father taught me, years ago, and Giles has also helped.'

'And you would use it?'

'I already have!'

Lady Frensham giggled.

'Remind me not to fall out with you, Jessica!'

Jessica looked briefly at the two men who had appeared and made a slight signal with her free hand. They knuckled their foreheads and slipped away.

Meantime, Captain Sir Giles Courtenay was oblivious to all this, standing on the quarterdeck of his ship as she ploughed along on the larboard tack, running to the west along the North African coastline.

They saw some ships almost every day. Local traders, ships of all nations, and a growing number bearing the Stars and Stripes of the United States. A new nation, flexing its trading muscles. They did cross paths with the odd American warship and Courtenay knew he was not alone in realising the oddity of the situation. On board the Yankee warship there was probably more British sailors than there were true Americans. It was a fact there had been many desertions over the years from the Royal Navy to the United States Navy, where the pay was better, although from what Courtenay had heard, discipline was still enforced in the same old way. The Red Baize bag apparently had its place, even with a new Country and a new Navy.

Courtenay mentally shrugged his shoulders as he watched a Yankee brig closing with them, passing them by starboard to starboard. He was surprised. however, when he realised the Yankee was shortening sail, and changing course to run closer to them.

'Mr Wetherby, shorten sail, if you please.'

Wetherby looked at him, then turned to roar his orders, sending the watch aloft to fist in the sails. Courtenay watched the brig as it slowed. They were within hailing distance, and he watched as an officer climbed into the shrouds and raised a speaking trumpet.

'Ahoy there!' the metallic voice called. 'I would like to come aboard sir'

Courtenay's eyebrows lifted and he looked at Trafford, who had appeared from nowhere.

'He wants to what?' said Jeffrey, who was officer of the watch.

'He wants to come aboard, Mr Jeffrey. He must have a reason, as I am sure he is not merely being friendly so kindly hail him and confirm he is welcome. I shall be in the Cabin.'

Ten minutes later, Courtenay was standing near the sternlights when the Cabin door opened and a shortish American officer was shown in. He turned and walked across the canvas floor covering.

'Welcome aboard sir. What can I do for you?' Courtenay watched as the American's eyes moved around the Cabin.

'I am so sorry sir, I am Commander Van Buren of the United States Ship *Maine.*'

'I am Captain Sir Giles Courtenay, and I am sure you have noted already this is His Britannic Majesty's ship *Hercules.* What may I do for you, Commander? Are you short on supplies of some description?'

Van Buren smiled. He had a pleasant face, with a pug nose, and the skin around his eyes was well creased. He was clearly a seaman through and through.

'It is not what you can do for me, Sir Giles, but rather what I can do for you.'

'I am all ears, Commander?''

'Well, Captain, it's like this.'

'Do sit down, Commander. A glass, perhaps?'

'A measure of Rum would be most welcome sir.'

Kingston appeared with a tray, and the first glass disappeared in short order. Kingston refilled it, and Van Buren looked at the contents with appreciation. 'Fine stuff, sir.'

'You were saying?' Courtenay prompted. Trafford was thinking, get the Commander drunk, run out the guns, overpower the Yankee, and search it for deserters, then run them up to the yardarm. Courtenay looked at Trafford, read his thoughts and smilingly shook his head.

'I saw one of your ships the other day. Very smart sloop. We sailed past each other. I waved and one of your officers responded. '

'Excellent.' commented Courtenay. 'I am glad the Royal Navy is courteous.'

Van Buren smiled. 'We share a common enemy, Captain, in those bastards along the Barbary Coast. Hardly a day passes where we come across some poor wretch who is about to be attacked. Sometimes we are too late and by the time we get there, all there is is a ship with a dead crew. We had a tussle with one of the Dey's Chebecks a while ago. Bastard thought that because we are a brig that he was going to swamp us, but my lads know better than that, ' he paused as a knowing smile appeared on Courtenay's face, 'and with excellent gunnery, we beat him off.'

'Good. Well done.' said Courtenay, smiling encouragingly.

Van Buren noted that his glass was full again. He took a sip. 'Thing is, Captain, that earlier today I saw one of the Dey's ships acting what you might call suspiciously. It was hugging the coastline, and not making any effort to actually come out to sea.'

'Perhaps it did not want to get too close to your excellent ship, Commander?'

The other man smiled. ' I am sure it was not that, sir, because he was far larger than us. It was a small two-decker, probably mounting fifty guns if I'm any judge.'

He got the reaction he wanted. Courtenay looked up immediately at Cressy, who started. 'We saw…..' He began.

'Yes, Mr Cressy, we did, did we not?' Courtenay looked back at Van Buren. 'Why do you think he was hugging the coastline, Commander? In which direction was he sailing?' Courtenay already knew the answer.

'He was heading along the coastline to the West, sir, and I think he was hugging the coastline so as not to be seen.'

Van Buren stood up and faced Courtenay squarely. 'I'm not sure what our Navy Board what say, sir, but I cannot allow this to go. I think he is after your sloop, sir. I have heard a number of examples of Chebecks being severely damaged, or even sunk, by a British sloop in the area.'

'Commander, I am most grateful to you, and I wish you a speedy passage to wherever you are bound.'

He shook the man's hand, and Cressy showed him out. A few moments later he returned.

'Simon, set all sail to the Royals. If that bastard is after *Spur,* we need everything we can carry.'

'Too bad we left *Aurelia* to the East the other day, she could have joined us, sir.'

'Yes, but someone has to be around to keep watch for other attacks.'

Cressy left. Trafford walked around the cabin, and paused by his Captain.

'Might be a trap, Sir Giles?'

'What, go after the sloop, and know that we would come running, and suddenly find ourselves under attack from a superior force? I realise that, but we have to rely on the intelligence we have, and the fact of the matter is that the Dey has nothing large enough to face us on equal or better terms. Neither has his friend the Bashaw. We will, nonetheless be circumspect Alex, and leave nothing to chance.'

Peverse as ever, the wind veered slowly and then more persistently so that they were forced to tack one way and then the other, but Courtenay was slightly mollified by the fact that it would be the same for the ship they were chasing.

It took seven days for *Hercules* to reach the point where the Yankee brig Captain had seen the Dey's small two-decker, and then the wind changed to a more favourable direction, and they were able to make some real progress.

Courtenay paced either the quarterdeck, or away from the curious eyes and stares of his men, his Cabin. Trafford watched over him on deck, and both he and Kingston did so when he was in the Cabin. He drank endless mugs of coffee, and prowled around morosely during the middle watch when he should have been asleep, only just resisting the temptation to go around checking all the sails himself to make sure nothing was being lost. Even he realised in his concerned state that this would be suggesting he had no faith in the officer of the watch, or indeed the Master's Mate of the watch. So he held back, but not without difficulty.

Eventually, four days after leaving the point where the Yankee Captain had seen the 'enemy' ship, and as he was about to go below to shave and have some breakfast, Courtenay heard a hail from the masthead look-out just after the man had climbed up there to begin his watch. It was only just light, and the officer of the watch, Alan Frobisher, had only just ordered the lookouts aloft.

'Deck there! Gunfire to the nor-west!'

Courtenay heard it at the same time, a low rumble in the distance. He turned in his tracks and hurried back to the wheel, looking quickly at the compass card. Frobisher turned towards him, his mouth opening.

'Thank you Mr Frobisher, but I heard the look-out. There is nothing wrong with King's eyes, but if Lees was up there, we would know already who was fighting who!'

'Shall I take a glass up there, sir?' Frobisher looked a little anxious.

'If you please Mr Frobisher. Quick as you like. Tell me what you see, but take your time. Tell me what you see, not what you *want* to see, you understand?'

'Aye sir!'

Frobisher hurried to the shrouds and was soon running up the ratlines at a pace which would put an experienced topman to shame. He climbed out and around the barricade at the lookout's position and settled himself in the crosstrees. In the meantime, Lees had appeared on deck, and was standing at the foot of the mainmast, looking first of all up at his fellow lookout and then at the quarterdeck. Courtenay saw him, and motioned for him to stay where he was.

'Deck there!' Frobisher was calling down. 'Tis the *Spur,* sir! She's fighting a larger ship. Looks like that small two-decker we saw!'

Cressy and Wetherby were now on deck and both of them were looking at Courtenay for orders. They were not kept waiting for long.

'Mr Wetherby, alter course two degrees to starboard, then check all the sails carefully, make sure not a glassful is lost. Mr Cressy, get Mr Frobisher down, and then clear for action.' He looked around for the Midshipman of the watch. 'Ah, Mr Cook. Do not hide yourself sir. I need all my officers about me this day. Present my compliments to the Gunner and tell him I would like the bow-chasers cleared away, and for him to oversee them being fired.'

'Aye aye sir!' The twelve-year old Harvey Cook, son of a Post-Captain, grandson of a newly deceased Admiral, walked calmly to the companion. He had always been taught an officer did not run. He went down to the gundeck below, where the men who served the guns were already casting off lashings and then down and down into the bowels of the ship where the Gunner presided over the Magazine. The Gunner, a wizened man with a face which could tell a hundred stories, looked at him quizzically.

'Lost your way, young gentleman?'

'No. The Captain sends his compliments and would you clear away the bow-chasers and take command of them.' Cook nodded to himself as he finished, confident he had remembered all the order given to him.

'Do ee knows what for, young sir?'

'I'm…..I'm not certain, but the *Spur* is in trouble with a larger ship.'

'I got you, young sir. If I knows the Cap'n, he wants me to try and scare t'other ship off with them. Right-oh. We'd best go then.'

When Cook returned to the quarterdeck, he reported to Courtenay that he had passed the order, and found Cressy and Wetherby with their glasses to their eyes, watching what was going on.

'Very well, Mr Cook. Thank you. Remain here. I may require you for further messages.'

The ship was going to quarters. The guns were being run in, checked, and loaded. Men were scurrying around apparently aimlessly but they knew where they were going and what they were doing. In less than ten minutes, the ship was ready for action. Courtenay closed his watch and smiled at Cressy.

'I'm going aloft to see what is happening, Simon.'

A few moments later, Courtenay was smiling at the surprised lookout called King as he settled himself and opened his glass.

'Mornin' sir!' said King. He had never known the last captain to climb all the way to the masthead.

'Morning King. Now, let's have a look shall we?'

He looked carefully. Their sloop was indeed being attacked by the two-decker they had last seen in the Dey's harbour at Algiers. They were not yard-arm to yard-arm and he could see that Fenwick was doing his best to keep the bigger ship at bay with constant changes of course. The sloop was the more agile of the two, and even as Courtenay watched, the sloop luffed, came about and poured a slow broadside into the bows of the enemy ship. Courtenay knew however that Fenwick would not be able to keep that up. Sooner or later, the bigger ship would get alongside and then the sloop's company would be overwhelmed by the number of men the bigger ship would be carrying. Even as he watched, the Dey's ship fired a ragged broadside at the sloop and it was bracketed by water splashes. Nothing came down but the sloop seemed to straighten her course and not take any further avoiding action, and as he lowered the glass he knew that James Fenwick had lost his steering.

Two minutes later he was on the deck via a backstay.

'*Spur* has lost her steering.' he said to Cressy. 'She was doing well to keep out of the way, but it must have been a lucky shot. The enemy ship will go alongside and overwhelm her by sheer numbers. 'He looked down the length of his command and saw the Gunner looking at him.

'Mr Cook. Go forrard and tell the Gunner than he may open fire at the enemy ship when he feels appropriate. He is to keep firing.'

'Aye aye sir!'

'Are we going to get there in time, sir?' asked Trafford.

'Please God, Alex, we will. Perhaps the Gunner can put the fear of God into them with the bow-chasers.'

There was a boom from the bows as the first bow-chaser fired and a plume of spray as the ball crashed down at a point which appeared to be almost level with the stern of the two-decker, which was now facing them. Courtenay could also see from the quarterdeck that the ship was firing into the sloop as it sidled towards her, ready to go alongside. *Hercules* was bursting through the blue sea at an impressive rate as the other bow-chaser fired. This time the ball slammed down just behind the enemy's stern.

'Good shooting' muttered Wetherby with admiration.

They were closing the distance, but there was a sudden sigh as the sloop's foremost suddenly fell and went over the side. A bow-chaser blasted the air again and this time, the ball smashed the sternlights of its target. There was cheering from up forrard, which Jeremiah Smith, the Bosun, instantly stopped.

The enemy ship was starboard side on to the damaged sloop.

'Mr Wetherby, we will engage along *Spur's* disengaged side. Steer for her accordingly. Mr Cressy, upper larboard battery only. As we come alongside *Spur,* we will give that ship half a broadside and see how he likes that! I'll teach him to fire into a King's ship!'

As the gradually drew closer to the embattled ships, Courtenay's blood ran cold as he heard the noise coming from the Dey's men. He forced himself to place his hands behind his back and pace up and down the quarterdeck, even when Trafford appeared with his sword and he slipped the crossbelt on, settling his sword at his hip. He partly pulled the sword out of its scabbard and then thrust it home with a distinct click which caused the Master's Mate nearby to turn around in alarm.

'Tell the Gunner to cease firing the bow chasers.'

'Aye aye sir.' said Cressy quietly. A silence settled over the ship. All they could hear now was then noise of the fighting.

On the sloop, the men were fighting for their lives. They were outnumbered, but the large ship had taken a while to get alongside, and Fenwick had seen help coming. Despite the hits on the stern of the ship, the Barbary pirates did not seem to notice the larger ship coming in their direction, but James Fenwick had other things to think about than the help which was arriving. He had to stop his ship being swamped before help actually arrived.

His ship's company had armed themselves, and a number of the deadly swivels, mounted on the side of the ship,. discouraged the first wave of boarders as they got ready to cross over from their ship to the *Spur*. However, with the two ships gradually being swept together, he knew that the time had come to engage in deadly hand to hand combat. He drew his sword and ran to the larboard side.

On his own deck, Courtenay was now staring at the two ships and willing his own command to get there more quickly. He could see the bowsprit beginning to overlap the sterns of the ships ahead and could imagine the figurehead, the craved figure of the Greek Warrior, with shield and short sword raised, as the bows approached the ships ahead.

Fenwick felt the shadow of the larger ship cross his small quarterdeck as the swarm of Pirates dropped onto his deck and started cutting down his men. He hardly felt the pistol ball which slammed into his left arm, and waved his sword wildly to his men.

'*Huzza,* lads, here's the *Hercules* to our help. To me, *Spurs!*'

With a roar, his men leapt to the attack and a number of the pirates who had dropped onto the deck were killed where they had landed, and thrown over the side. One lost his footing, faced with the wave of cheering men, and fell between the hulls. There was a short scream as they came together and crushed the life out of him.

Courtenay was at the rail, hatless, longish hair streaming in the wind, hardly the image of a Captain of a King's ship of the line, as his ship surged past the sloop's starboard quarter. He had his sword raised. His men waited expectantly, looking for the sword to come down, ready to fire at the enemy,

On *Spur,* Fenwick screamed to his men.

'*Spurs, down!*'

The men dropped like stones, and the men from the Dey's ship suddenly realised something was wrong. For many of them it was the last thing they ever thought. As it surged alongside, *Hercules* opened fire with her upper battery of 18 pounders. Double shotted, with a charge of grape, the murderous fire scythed across the deck of the sloop, and cut down the pirates who stood on it, before slamming into the side of the ship.

Already, the small two-decker was sidling away from the sloop. The sails were being set and the ship was moving clear. The Captain was obviously quite happy to abandon his men to get away.

Courtenay saw all this as his guns battered the other ship. He saw the pirates cut down, and saw Fenwick's men rise after the onslaught and attack what was left of the boarders. No quarter was given. He saw Fenwick, his left arm tucked inside his sword belt, run a pirate through and then turn to wave at *Hercules* as she ploughed past.

The Algiers two-decker was turning away, trying to run, but she was no match for the British liner, and before her Captain had got the sails set properly, *Hercules* was alongside. This time, she felt the full force of her artillery.

'*Broadside!*' yelled Courtenay, and felt the deck buck as the entire larboard battery, 24–pounders on the lower deck and 18-pounders on the upper deck, fired in unison. The Algiers ship leant to larboard as the weight of metal crashed into her. The guns were reloaded and ready for another broadside when the burgee at her masthead came fluttering down.

'Cease firing!' Cressy ordered and the men stood back from their guns which had been reloaded and run out again.

Courtenay looked over at the other ship and wondered exactly what he was going to do with it. He was tempted to put a prize crew on board, sail her to Algiers and sink her outside the harbour. Or, he could taker her back to Gibraltar, and leave the Flag Officer there to deal with the diplomatic side of things. He had done his job.

Then, an odd thing happened. Suddenly, the guns on the other ship, which had been run in, were being run out, and as Cressy turned to Courtenay with an enquiring expression on his face, those guns opened fire. At the same time, the enemy Captain was trying to set some more sail, as if he was hoping to escape.

A number of balls slammed into *Hercules'* side, but most of them whimpered overhead. The men at the upper deck guns looked at their Captain and saw the rage on his face.

'If that is the way he wants to play it, Mr Cressy, so be it!'

Cressy turned to the gundeck, and lifted his arm. It swept down, and once again, there was the double ripple of flashes along the side of the ship as the guns belched fire and smoke. The latter funnelled inboard, but no-one noticed. There was haphazard return of fire from the other ship, then another broadside from *Hercules*. This time, there was no return fire, but Courtenay was not going to take any chances. A third broadside rang out, with the ships growing close together. When the smoke cleared, he could see that the Algiers ship was in a terrible state. Her foremast had gone by the board, and she was suffering from a starboard list. A white flag was waving.

The guns were reloaded, but no effort was made to run them out again. The two ships sailed along slowly, with almost complete silence. Courtenay looked at the other ship, waiting for some sign, and then once more, the guns were run out and she opened fire with what guns were left.

Balls slammed into the British ship again, but this time, when *Hercules'* upper gunners replied, they had loaded their guns with a charge of canister. Apart from the deadly cannon balls, the musket balls packed into their canisters swept across the decks. When the smoke cleared, there was no firing from the enemy ship, and in fact on her decks, there was hardly a man standing. The Captain stood by the wheel, desperately trying to stem the flow of blood from his shoulder, which had no arm. The deck was red with blood from his men, and the wheel itself was a splintered wreck. He slipped to his knees and hardly realised that the British ship was now well alongside and that grapnels were flying from her. His last recollection was that swarms of British sailors were swinging onto his ship and that a man in white shirt and breeches with long hair and holding a naked sword in his hand was striding towards him with what he dimly recognised as murder in his eyes. He looked up at this man, feeling blackness creeping over him. The man in the white shirt and breeches was saying something to him, but he could not make out the words.

Courtenay looked down at the man who was lying on his side, and saw the blood from his shoulder cease as he died.

He turned to Trafford. 'What the devil did he think he was doing? He surrendered twice, for God's sake!'

He looked around. There was dead and dying everywhere. He saw Smith, the Bosun, looking at his for orders.

'Mr Smith, take off the wounded and then open the sea-cocks. She can go down here, to an unmarked grave!'

The Bosun turned away and started barking his orders.

EIGHT

It was December, 1801. The New Year was three weeks away. A new beginning? The Treaty of Amiens had not been completely ratified, but, to all intents and purposes, Britain was at peace with most of the World, although as often had happened during peace-time, the Navy had this time not laid off large numbers of men, nor laid up countless warships. The Government knew that what Bonaparte was really up to was simply re-stocking. This time, they would be ready. They might even re-start the war rather than wait for the little Corsican to call the shots.

Captain Sir Giles Courtenay was back in London. His stay on the Barbary coast had been mercifully short, but Crompton had a reason to bring him back. *Aurelia* had been left to patrol the long coast of North Africa until more ships arrived, and for a short period, the gangling Tim Spellman has been the Senior Naval Officer on that station. *Spur* had accompanied *Hercules* back home, but Fenwick, who was going to take a little time to recover from his injuries, knew that she would be back at sea soon enough. However, it would not be with him. The Admiralty had replaced him, owing to his wounds, with a new captain. Commander Marmaduke Spencer-White. Quite how he had got his command was a mystery to everyone. Even Lord Cairns, his Uncle, would not confirm his patronage had made his former Flag-Lieutenant climb to the dizzy heights of command. It was not unusual for an Admiral, especially as senior one such as Cairns, to use his patronage in such a way, and no-one would have criticised him if he had, but he had not. Somewhere, Spencer-White had found a new friend.

Courtenay was seated in Crompton's club, a blazing log fire yards away, and the remains of an excellent meal between them. Courtenay studied the fine cut-glass Brandy glass in front of him, and sipped some of the contents. He smiled.

'I suppose the Club will be re-stocking its cellars with fine French cognac during the peace my Lord?'

Stafford Crompton smiled. 'Whatever makes you think the Club started to run out? Ask no questions and ye shall be told no lies, my boy, but I have reason to believe that the Club's supplies came from, ah, let us say an unauthorised source?'

'You mean they buy from the smugglers?'

Crompton looked aghast. 'Did I say that Giles?' He picked up the matching cut-glass decanter and poured another measure. He moved his leg, and then looked at Courtenay.

'Is Jessica well?'

'Aye, she is very well.'

'No more, er additions to the family just yet?'

Courtenay smiled. 'Not yet!' He stopped smiling. 'Why, my I ask, sir?'

Crompton seemed to hesitate. 'Got a little job for you.'

'I've only just got back from the Mediterranean!'

Crompton was unabashed. 'I know that Giles, but I have a favour to ask of you. Should be nothing more than a cruise in the sun. Of course, if you would rather go on half-pay.......'

Courtenay gave up. 'What is it you want me to do now? And that's blackmail!'

Crompton smiled. 'Yes, I rather suppose it is.'

'Jess will kill me. Or rather, she'll kill you……sir.'

'Everything will be fine. The last thing your lovely wife wants is for you to be moping on the beach on half-pay. She knows you to be a fighting sailor, as do I, not someone who wants to sit on his backside and get fat!'

'That's all very well, but it would be nice to be able to spend some time with her….is that why asked if there are any more children on the way?'

'Yes. If Jessica was with child again, I'd not send you away in peacetime.'

'Well, she is not. What is you want this time?'

Lord Crompton smiled inwardly. Giles Courtenay was the perfect Captain to put his plans into action, but he meant what he had said. Had he found that Jessica Courtenay was with child, he would not have sent Giles off in peacetime. War was something different.

'On the 14th, that is, tomorrow, the French are sending a large force of ships and soldiers to Saint Domingo. I believe you know where that is?'

'Yes, sir, I do believe I do! I was there with *Pegasus*. Isn't that the Island run by that extremely clever negro – Toussaint?'

'Yes, it is. The intelligence which their Lordships have gained tells them that the French want to have their Island back. Toussaint rather took control for himself and his Islanders. That did not go down at all well with the French people there, nor with Bonaparte. He is using the peace to send an expedition there to get the Island back.'

'So what is this to do with us, sir?'

'His Majesty's Government feels that it would like to know what is going on in part of its backyard. After all, neither Antigua or Jamaica are that far away. So , their Lordships thought that we would send someone over there. Just to see what is going on, of course. Not to interfere.'

'Not to intrefere.'

'Of course not. Their Lordships have decided, in their infinite wisdom, to send just a token observer, so as not to upset the French, you understand..'

'A token observer.'

'You are sounding remarkably like one of those parrots they have in the tropics. Don't you want to know who they have sent, or should I say sending, since he has not as yet sailed?'

'I am sure, my Lord, that you are going to tell me anyway!'

'Commander Marmaduke Spencer-White, and as you already know they have given him *Spur.*'

'But that is James's ship!'

'Was. He is ill, remember, and their Lordships have used the excuse to put Spencer-White in command. Quite what they think they are doing, I have no idea.'

'Well, I heard about the promotion, and if he can get a command, next thing we know, the Bosun's mate will get a ship of his own!'

'He is due to sail on the 20th. I know that will be six days after the French, but he should be able to keep up with them, and we don't want him getting too close, after all.'

'Very well, so we have the French sailing to Saint Domingo on some private frog mission and their Lordships sending Spencer-White off probably to get lost in the middle of the Atlantic. Where does *Hercules* come in to this?'

Crompton leant forward on the table. 'I don't trust that dandy nitwit to find his way to the Scilly Isles and back without getting lost! Even if he does manage to find the French and keep up with them, I doubt he will do what he has been told to. So you are going as well. That is between you and myself. You will, of course, have your written Orders from me, since we cannot have you wandering around the Oceans without orders, but you will keep an eye on things generally in that neck of the woods. Your orders will tell you that you are on an inspection cruise, between Antigua and Jamaica, at my request, but you will, at all times, keep a close eye on what the Frogs are up to.'

'And what will young Spencer-White have to say about all this?'

'He will say nothing. I doubt he will even know you are there! If you do see him, you have your orders. Will you do this for me, Giles?'

'Of course I will sir. My ship, and myself, are at your service.'

'Thank you my boy, but I think I will leave you to tell your wife yourself, if you do not mind!'

'What! You are off again? When?' Jessica Courtenay was not best pleased. In fact, she was downright angry.

'Not yet. Lord Crompton has agreed that I may remain at home until Christmas, but I have to sail after that.'

'Dearest Giles, you have only been home for a few days.' She was beginning to get upset, but she remembered what she had promised herself before she married him, and pulled herself together.

'I know, but I was only away a short amount of time, and there are a lot of people less lucky. And besides….'

'I know, you don't want to be thrown on the shore.'

'Beach.'

'What?'

'Beach. It's 'thrown on the beach' not the shore.'

'You wouldn't be happy on half-pay.'

'It is not that. You know very well that I have been very lucky with prize-money, and mercifully, I do not have to worry about how to support you if I was on the beach. When there is peace, ships are not in great demand, and neither are their Captains.'

'I understand Giles. If you remain with your ship, perhaps that will hasten further promotion? Perhaps you will be given a job in Admiralty?' She watched him a moment, the man she had come to know so well.

'I think that would be a long way off, Jess, and besides……'

'You are a fighting man, and not a quill-pusher. Yes, I know.'

He put his arms around her. 'Where is Edward?'

'Out with his nanny.'

'Are the lads around?'

'Oh yes, they won't let me or Edward out of their sight!'

'Well, they aren't here now.'

'No, and you have some pacifying to do to get me over the thought of losing you again so quickly.'

'What do you have in mind?'

'Come here and I will show you!'

Two days after Christmas, on a wild grey day at Portsmouth, Jessica was standing on the quayside with her father Sir Geoffrey, her son Edward, and the coachman and footman, as they all watched Courtenay being pulled out to his ship. *Hercules* had originally returned to Plymouth, but a message send to Cressy had left him to bring the two-decker to Portsmouth. Courtenay had not been worried about leaving that to his Senior. He rated a command, but apart from those favoured few, there were none available.

It was a hard pull for the barge crew. It was very windy, and Spithead and the anchorage were very rough. Courtenay turned to wave goodbye, but on the next occasion he turned, the quayside was lost in mist and spray. He wrapped his boatcloak about him, clutched his sword and kept his eyes on his approaching ship.

Trafford, standing above him with his hand on the tiller, glanced sideways at him and sympathised. Right now, he would rather be in the warm, with a large tot in front of him, chatting with the new housemaid at Sir Geoffrey's house in London. He looked at the stroke oarsman, but his eyes were firmly on the job. None of them knew where they were going. Apart from Trafford of course. He also knew something that not even his Captain did.

Back on the quayside, Sir Geoffrey helped his daughter into the coach, and then picked up his grandson, cuddling him for a moment before putting him inside as well. Then he climbed in, slammed the door shut, and wrapped a thick rug around his knees.

'By God, it's cold!' He looked at his daughter. 'You haven't told Giles, have you?'

'Told him what, Father?'

'That you are with child again.'

'How did you know?'

'Oh, Jessica, do come along! I always knew when your dear Mother was expecting you and your Brother. I see all the signs…..and I bumped into Doctor Jarvis the other day. Why didn't you tell him?'

'Had he known, or rather, had Stafford Crompton known, he would not have been sent. I do not want him rotting on the beach, Father. I was going to tell him when he came back home, but everything was happening so quickly that I felt I had to wait for the opportune moment. Then I found out he was off again.'

'Not much of a life for you, Jessica.'

'Yes, Father, it is. I love Giles, and when he is home, I will do my utmost to make him happy, and to have a family to come to.'

Sir Geoffrey smiled, then settled back in his seat as the coach started to pick up speed on a smoother stretch of road.

Simon Cressy had met him as usual at the entry port, and Courtenay shook his hand warmly.

'Any problems, Mr Cressy?'

'None whatsoever, sir. All present and correct. No desertions, and no hands for punishment. We are ready to proceed immediately.'

'Very well, get the hands aloft and let us take advantage of the tide! When we are clear of the land, I will bring you up to date with the latest scandal in London!'

'You mean, sir, with Spencer-White being given the *Spur*?'

'I should have known you would find out about that! There is more, believe me. Later, Simon, when we are clear of land.'

With a fair wind, *Hercules* was soon clear of the Solent, and heading down-Channel. Courtenay stood on his quarterdeck, wrapped in his boatcloak against the cold, and looked at the spray bursting over the beakhead. He tried not to think of his wife. He had a feeling, more a nagging worry in a way that she was expecting their second child, yet she had said nothing, and his concern was why she had said nothing. She had not wanted him to give up this mission, and spend time on the beach, until the next time Britain was called to arms.

He felt, more than heard, Trafford step next to him. His cox'n looked at the face he had come to know so well, and saw the worry. He also knew what the worry was about.

'Miss Jessica will be fine, Sir Giles, never fear. At least that whippersnapper Spencer-White is at sea as well!' When they were alone, it was always 'Miss Jessica', never 'Her Ladyship'. Neither Courtenay or his wife would permit anything else.

Courtenay turned. 'Aye, that is at least something Alex. I wonder what he is up to? D'ye think he is lost yet?'

They chuckled, and the officer of the watch, St. Clair, turned briefly to see his Captain laughing with his cox'n. He shivered inside his cloak, but straightened his back. If I ever have a command, he was thinking, I will never be caught laughing with a common seaman! The look on his face spoke volumes and when he turned back to give his attention to the compass he saw the Senior Master's mate, Fred Poole, look away, but not before he saw the sneer on the man's face. He was about to issue a reprimand, which would have done him no favours at all, when his Captain's voice reached him.

'I think you will find the weather mainbrace needs some attention, Mr St.Clair!'

He turned again, searching out the Bosun's mate, his face crimson. One of the helmsmen glanced at Poole and grinned and was rewarded with an even larger grin in return. Poole put his pipe in his mouth and cursed as spray bounced over the side and soaked it.

'Is there any coffee, Alex?' Courtenay was asking.

'Aye, Kingston had a new pot going when I was down below.'

'Right, in which case I think I will repair to the cabin and enjoy a mug before this wind gets any stronger.'

The wind, he had noted, which St Clair had not, was getting stronger, but he had not had all sail set, and the courses were partly reefed, so he was not too concerned for the time being. Cressy would be on watch at the next turn of the glass, and if the wind grew in strength still further, he would know what to do without bothering his Captain.

The wind did grow for a while, but did not get sufficiently strong for sails to be reduced. Leaning over on the starboard tack, *Hercules* was able to make some good time in the journey south and west.

They were able to pick up the Trades after clawing their way south and west for a few days, and gradually, as they reached further south, the weather grew warmer. The sun shone, and some of the crew were able to try their luck at catching fish. Kingston was always one of the more successful ones, and Courtenay wondered, as he always had over the years the servant had been with him, what little delicacies from the cabin Kingston attached to his line as bait.

Courtenay was on deck, hatless and coatless, enjoying the sunshine and watching the watch change when he heard a cry from the masthead. It was Lees, in his usual position, and the sighting report was firm.

'*Deck there!* Two ships to the sou'sou west, sir! One of them is the *Spur!*'

Jeffrey was the officer of the watch, just on deck. He looked at Courtenay. '*Spur*, sir? What is she doing out here?'

'She is where she should not be, Mr Jeffrey, that is a fact.' He lowered his voice. 'She should have been at her destination by now, in the West Indies. I wonder why she is not?'

Jeffrey smiled. 'I hear tell that Commander Spencer-White is in command?' Courtenay nodded. 'He probably got lost!'

Jacob Wetherby heard the exchange and turned his head away to smother a grin.

'Now now, Steven,' said Courtenay quietly, 'he is supposed to be your superior. However, I am sure you are perfectly correct!'

'*Deck there!* The other ship is a Yankee sir! Looks like *Spur* 'as grappled her!'

'What the devil?' said Courtenay angrily. 'Grappled a Yankee? Whatever for?'

He turned. Cressy had appeared on deck, his eyes asking questions.

'Ah, Simon. *Spur* is to the sou'sou west, and, according to Lees, has grappled a Yankee!'

'Then we had best get there as fast as we can, sir!' He turned, his eyes skimming over the set of the sails, although it was obvious that there was nothing wrong with any of them. The ship was going as fast as she could.

Courtenay climbed into the ratlines and lifted his glass. Trafford, watching his Captain for any trace of emotion saw his lips twitch slightly and an eyebrow was raised. Trafford knew he had recognised the other ship.

As he stepped down, he saw Trafford's look and smiled and nodded.

'She's the Yankee from the Mediterranean. The one who warned us that *Spur* was going to be attacked.'

Cressy turned. 'The devil you say, sir!'

Courtenay smiled briefly, and lifted the glass again.

As *Hercules* swept down on the two ships, neither of them made any effort to part, or indeed, set sail. When the two-decker was close enough, Courtenay ordered that she hove-to and although he was tempted to go over to the sloop and find out what was happening, he simply hoisted the signal for her Captain to repair on board, and sat back and waited. He was still waiting thirty minutes later.

By then he was on the quarterdeck, boiling with anger and pacing this way and that. The men on the quarterdeck with him kept out of his way.

'Mr Jeffrey,' he said at length, kindly take the launch and some men, together with some Marines, go to *Spur,* and enquire as to why my order has been disobeyed!'

Jeffrey was turning away to execute the order when Courtenay put out a hand and touched his arm. 'Belay that Steven, I will come with you.'

Trafford already had Courtenay's sword, which he handed to him, and as he clipped it to his crossbelt, he hefted his own cutlass and thrust a pistol through his belt.

Courtenay looked at him calmly. 'Do you expect trouble, Alex?'

Trafford shrugged. 'Who knows, sir? But why hasn't Commander Spencer-White come across?'

'Why indeed? Come then, and let us find the answer!'

Five minutes later, Courtenay was swarming up the stairs of the entry port on the lithe sloop, anger creasing his handsome face. Behind him was Trafford, cutlass through his belt, and Mr Midshipman Cook for messages.

Courtenay climbed through the entry port and there was the usual ceremony of welcoming a Captain aboard a ship, then he turned and glowered at a tall Lieutenant who was standing looking very apprehensive.

'Well, Mr Jarman, are you going to tell me what is going on?'

'Er, yes sir. The Captain is in his cabin with the Yan......American Captain sir.'

Courtenay looked across the sloop to where the American ship was riding alongside. There were some armed seaman there, muskets pointing at the American sailors. They could have been his own men. He smiled wryly. They were probably mostly from the Royal Navy to begin with.

'Take your weapons away from those men!' he ordered. 'They are not your enemy, for God's sake!' The men did not move, but then Courtenay glared at them and they saw Trafford wrap his hand around the hilt of his cutlass. They slowly lowered their muskets.

Courtenay strode to the wheel and after noticing that the sailing master and his mate, and the other men clustered around waiting to see what was happening avoided his eyes, he grunted and swung down the companion. *Spur* carried no Marines, but there was an armed seaman outside the Cabin.

Courtenay looked at his briefly. 'You are not needed. Get back to whatever your duties are.'

The man looked at him, not knowing who he was.

'Do as you are damn well told!' Courtenay snarled. The man fled. Trafford looked at his Captain in a new light. He had never seen him so angry before.

Courtenay slammed the door open and marched in. Spencer-White was sitting at his desk, with his usual supercilious smile, with the American Captain in a chair on the other side. There was yet another armed seaman near the door.

'Get out!' Courtenay said shortly to him.

Spencer-White rose from his chair, his face red with anger.

'What the deuce do you mean by this!'

'I would remind you, *Commander*, that I am the senior officer here! What the devil is going on? I ordered you aboard my ship over thirty minutes ago. I have had to come and find you! By the way, were you aware that you are miles off course?'

'There was a storm.......how did....'

The American Captain had stood up, and a slow smile spread across his tanned features as he recognised Courtenay.

'My dear Captain,' Courtenay began, striding across the decking with his hand outstretched. 'I never had the chance to thank you for your kindness when we ran into each other in the Mediterranean. As you can see, I was able to save the ship, thanks to you!'

'Yes, Sir Giles, and I thought it was still perhaps Captained by the same man when I saw her this morning, which is why I passed close by to exchange greetings. Instead...'

'Yes, I have to apologise. Perhaps you would explain to me, Commander, why you are detaining the good Captain?'

'He's a damned Yankee, Sir Giles, and I would not mind wagering that all his crew are deserters from our Fleet!'

'Even if they are, they all hold American protections, do they not, Captain?' He half-turned towards the smiling American, who was enjoying himself. He nodded. 'There you are. What are you trying to do, Spencer-White, start a war?'

Spencer-White had gone a deathly pale, and not very attractive colour. He slumped into his chair.

'Come, Captain, I shall see you onto deck and over the side into your ship.'

Courtenay took the man's arm and steered him out of the Cabin. They shook hands before the American climbed over the side onto his own familiar deck.

'Cast off the lashings there!' Trafford roared. This time there was no hesitation. The lashings were cut, and in no time at all the Yankee was sidling away, and her men were aloft, spreading sail.

Spencer-White was on deck, shaking with rage.

'How dare you sir! My uncle shall hear of this and when he does.....'

'And he shall, Commander, never fear. I shall make quite sure he finds out about what has happened today, and I am sure that their Lordships in Whitehall will be very pleased to hear that you nearly started a War! Hell's teeth, Spencer-White, we have only just stopped fighting one! Count yourself very lucky that we happened along. Now, you have a job to do, and so do I. I suggest you make sail and go where you should be going!'

With that, Courtenay left the sloop and returned to his own command, some of his anger assuaged.

Giles Courtenay paused for a white as the familiar tall mahogany doors were opened for him, and as he was announced, strode through into the high-ceilinged office he remembered so well from his days in Antigua

When he had first entered this room, Sir Stafford Crompton, as he then was, had been the Vice-admiral in charge of the Antigua station. He had set the younger Courtenay, then with his 22-gun sloop *Seagull* to work finding the French, privateers, and pirates, and one in particular. The mysterious and vicious man called *Le Corsair*. Only he had turned out not to be a man at all, but a strikingly beautiful young lady. Mercy LeFevre, step-daughter of a wealthy Antigua businessman, who had been her willing lieutenant. He had hung. The last Courtenay had seen of him was his body rotting on a gibbet for all to see. A message. When it came to piracy, not even the wealthy were exempt from due process of law. As to Mercy LeFevre, she had died on the point of Tim Spellman's sword after she had shot Courtenay and tried to kill him.

'Ah, Sir Giles, welcome to Antigua! Although I think you probably know the place better than I!'

Courtenay took the proferred hand and sat down at the Admiral's invitation. Vice-admiral Lord Tarnworth had only been in the position of Flag Officer Antigua for three months. He was tall, well-built, and when he smiled, the lines around his eyes crinkled. He had a friendly face, but Courtenay had been warned by Crompton that there was a good brain behind that face, and he did not suffer fools gladly.

'Thank you sir. I have not been here for a while.'

'Yes, that damned business with the slaves on St Kitts. You did a good job there, Captain. Got a baronetcy out of it, and well-deserved if I may say so. Join me in a glass of claret? Good stuff. Brought it with me from home.'

'Thank you sir.' Courtenay looked around the room as the Admiral, who obviously eschewed servants, poured two generous glasses. He handed one to Courtenay and they silently toasted each other.

'Well, Captain, it is always good to see a face from home, but what exactly is it I can do for you? Judging by the look of your ship and the appearance it made when arriving, I am certain it does not need the services if my dockyard?'

Courtenay smiled. 'No sir. It does not. However, Lord Crompton thought that since my ship will be, er, operating in your backyard so as to speak, it would be good manners for me not only to report to you but also to hand a despatch to you direct. It is from Admiral Lord Crompton, sir.'

'How is the old rascal, Sir Giles? I used to be a Lieutenant under him many years ago.'

Courtenay smiled even more broadly. 'He is very well, sir, and he commanded me to pass to you his very best wishes and, ' Courtenay paused wondering if Crompton had really intended him to say what came next, 'he said he hopes you are making a fortune in prize-money.'

Tarnworth roared with laughter. 'The old rogue!' He looked at Courtenay, who was smiling, but only slightly. He took up the despatch which Courtenay had placed on the polished desk and slit it open. Inside the envelope was a smaller one. He put that to one side and opened the orders.

'I am to afford you all and any assistance you may require, within reason.' He stopped reading and looked up. 'What exactly is it you are doing here, Sir Giles?'

'The French have sent a large expeditionary force to Saint Domingo, my Lord. The Admiralty believes it is to re-take the Island from the person who has, apparently, been running it for them.

'Toussaint. Yes, I know. I have some good agents in the Islands. But what is your job, Captain? Even if you were to try and stop them, first of all we cannot as we are not at War with them......yet, and secondly, with all due respect, what can one 74 do against a fleet?'

'Nothing sir, and that is a fact, but I am instructed to, er, keep an eye on things, or as my Father would put it, hold a watching brief.'

Tarnworth smiled. 'Father a lawyer eh? Must have been shock to him when you chose this rather unhealthy occupation?'

'He was very supportive sir.'

'What about that sloop that passed through here a few days ago, the *Spur*? My intelligence packs are not up to date. I expected to see a Commander Fenwick in command and instead found it to be a member of that........a member of the Spencer-White family.'

'Ah yes, sir. Commander Fenwick was wounded in action in the Mediterranean with some of the Dey of Algier's men. We were serving together at the time. He was not fit enough to resume command in time.'

'So that whippersnapper Marmaduke Spencer-White got some patronage and the ship, is that it?'

'Just so sir.'

'He should have been here weeks ago.'

'I know sir. Perhaps he got blown off course?'

'Lost his way more like! Another glass, Captain?'

'Thank you sir, but no. I must return to my ship. I would like to top up our water casks sir, if I may, and take on board some fruit and vegetables?'

'Of course. Send your Purser ashore and get what you require. If you need any help whilst you are in my area, please let me know.'

'Thank you sir.'

Twenty minutes later, Courtenay was back aboard the *Hercules* and thankfully shedding his heavy dress coat, the stock which had been threatening to strangle him in the heat, and his hat. He opened his shirt and stood near the stern windows. Kingston placed a cool glass of wine on his desk. There was the thump of the sentry's musket butt on the decking outside the cabin, and the roar of '*First-Lieutenant, sir!*' and the door opened and Simon Cressy, as dapper as ever, walked in.

He threw his hat on a chair and took a glass from Kingston. 'How did it go with Lord Tarnworth, sir?'

'Fine Simon. No problems. We will get whatever help we need, and God knows what that might, since I am still not altogether certain what it is we are doing here in any event! Get the Purser ashore. You know what we need, fruit and vegetables. As much as he can lay his hands on, and see if he can get some poultry. I am sure the lads would like chicken for a change. The water lighters will come alongside in the first dog-watch. Then, we can be on our way.'

'Any sign of *Spur,* sir?'

'Yes, she was here a few days ago. Although Tarnworth did not say anything, I have a feeling that young Marmaduke said something that upset him!'

'He wouldn't do a thing like that, sir, would he?' When Courtenay looked at him he saw a sarcastic smile on his face.

'I am sure he would not!' They laughed quietly. Trafford came into the Cabin and fussed around for a few moments.

'Kingston will have your lunch ready in a few moments, Sir Giles.'

Courtenay turned and smiled. Then a thought crossed his mind, and he looked at Cressy. 'Has the mailboat been here yet, Simon?'

'Yes sir. There were the usual letters for you and I think one or two personal ones.'

Trafford pulled them out from under the official ones.

'They came separate sir. Must have been a mail packet sir. Couldn't have got here any other way!'

Cressy smiled and made his excuses. He had a lot to do. Ship's First-Lieutenants always did.

Kingston laid a place at the table for Courtenay's lunch whilst his Captain sat down on the bench seat and opened the personal letters. One was from his family, and the other was from Jessica.

'Dammit! ' he exclaimed. 'I knew it.'

'What's the matter, Sir Giles?' asked Trafford, although he knew the answer.

Courtenay looked at him. 'Jessica is expecting our second child.'

'Aye sir, congratulations. Well done!'

'Did you know?'

'Not actually sir, but I did hear one or two things, you know, the way they get about below stairs.'

'You didn't think to say anything?'

'Not my place sir, in any case, if Miss Jessica had wanted you to know before we left, don't you think she would have told you?'

'I suppose she knew that if I knew of it, I would have told Lord Crompton he should find another Captain?'

'That's about it, Cap'n.'

'I would have done.'

'I know sir, and so did Miss Jessica. May I ask if she is all right, Sir Giles?'

'Of course you may. She is, and she sends her warm wishes.'

'She is very kind.'

'Yes, Alex, she is. I hope to god she stays safe.'

'She will be fine, Cap'n. The lads will see her right, never fear!'

NINE

It was two bells of the forenoon watch. His Britannic Majesty's ship *Hercules* was on the starboard tack, a fair wind coming in off the starboard quarter, and making good time towards Santo Domingo. The Admiral had provided Courtenay with what information he had, and it was, in fact, a fair amount. His spies had noted the French Fleet, and although Tarnworth had thought about sending someone to shadow it, he accepted he did not have the resources. They might not be fighting the French or the Spanish anymore, but there were still the privateers and the pirates. Now that at least the first two were off the agenda, and he could turn his ships to the other menace.

They had passed into the Caribbean by St Kitts and the sister island of Nevis, and were passing to the south of Peurto Rico. The water was a deep blue, broken by the white of the foam pushed aside by *Hercules'* passing. Courtenay knew from the ship's books that she had never served in these waters before, and that meant that a fair number of her men, but not all, had never seen the Islands either. Courtenay had himself checked when the Purser had returned to the ship, and found the man had not followed instructions.

'I gave firm instructions that you were to obtain as many fresh vegetables and as much fresh fruit as you could!' He blazed at the man, 'and look what you return with! My God, Parker, what do you expect the men to eat in this climate? I have been here before, and you have not. Plenty of fresh food and good drinking water is what they, and you, will need before long. Now, get back ashore and do not return until you have followed my instructions!'

The result had been quite spectacular. The man had returned with carts of vegetables and fruits of all kinds. Courtenay had nodded, and left it at that.

Some of the men were suffering from sunburn, but they would all be hardened to it soon.

Cressy looked at him as Courtenay walked to the binnacle and checked their course. 'Do you think that Commander Spencer-White is on station yet, sir?'

'In other words, Simon, do I think he is lost again? Let me put it this way. By now he should be on station, been observing what the French are doing, and then thinking about we are doing out here as well.'

Cressy allowed himself a short laugh. 'If you say so, sir.'

Courtenay turned a questioning eye on him, but said nothing. He thrust his hands behind him and walked to the windward side of the quarterdeck. He was in fact quite worried. He had little faith in Spencer-White being able to find himself in the right place at any given time. He had the chart of Saint- Domingo in his mind, and he was thinking about where he would be landing troops if it were him carrying out the exercise.

Clearly, Santo Domingo and Port-au-Prince were the two main places to land and take control, and then there was a fort in Mancenille Bay. He wondered how exactly the troops would be divided, but it was only an exercise in tactics, because he was not there to intervene, or cause any trouble. He was just there to watch.

Hercules continued her passage. The ship's company were able to add fish to their diet of fresh fruit and vegetables and it made a good change to their usual salt beef or salt pork. Courtenay was thankful that Cressy had been alive to the dockyard victualler's usual trick of giving out condemned meat, or casks already several years old. The meat was hardly fresh, but it was not too bad. They had plenty of chickens, in coops, and when his men were called upon to fight, Courtenay knew that they would do so on full bellies and that they would be healthy. And fight, he knew they would.

For that reason, he drove them with all the old force which would have been applied if they were at war. The younger hands could not understand why, in a time of peace, their Captain was driving them so hard, but the older men understood. As one of them put it, 'Listen sonny, we may not be at war with the frogs, or the dons, but this is the Royal Navy. We're always at war with *someone!* The Cap'n is simply making sure we are prepared, that's all, and if that takes some sweat, well, that's too bad!'

On the morning their sights told them they were approaching Saint-Domingo, Courtenay ordered a shortening of sail, so that their approach would be a slow and gentle one. When the masthead look-out reported he could see ships ahead, off Santo-Domingo, Courtenay ordered a slight change of course to head a little further along the Island.

The look-out reported that a French frigate was heading in their direction, which brought a smile to Courtenay's face.

'No doubt he is going to ask what the devil we are doing here!' he observed to St Clair, who was officer of the watch. They all watched as the frigate grew closer, and the Tricolour grew larger.

'Run up the colours Mr McMasters,' ordered Courtenay shortly. The White ensign broke out from the mizen gaff and they saw the moustache of foam at the bows of the approaching ship grow smaller. Her captain was clearly unsure of himself, but since the gunports on the British ship remained closed, he closed to within hailing distance. He tried using a speaking trumpet, but Courtenay pretended he could not hear the man.

'Heave-to if you please Mr Wetherby. Let us see what he does.'

Hercules came to a stop and so did the French ship. After a short delay, Courtenay could see a boat being lowered into the water. His lips twitched a little as he nearly ordered sail to be set again, but he refrained and waited until the French Captain came up the side in a hurry.

'Excuse please, who do I have the honour of addressing?' He said in an arrogant tone. He was short, fat, and looked totally ridiculous with the usual red, white and blue sash around a generous waistline.

'I am Captain Sir Giles Courtenay, and this is His Britannic Majesty's ship *Hercules*. And you are sir?'

At the name *Hercules* the French Captain's jaw dropped a little. Courtenay helped him to lower it even more.

'Yes, *M'sieu,* she used to be the *Hercule*. I am afraid that the Royal Navy took it from your lot.'

'Excuse please, your lot?'

'Your Navy. Who did you say you were? *Comment s'appelle vous?'*

'Je m'appelle Citizen Captaine Jean-Luc Vincent. Mon Vasseau et Le Citoyen Paris.'

'Thank you Captain. Now, what can I do to help you on this fine morning?'

The Frenchman paused and took out a huge handkerchief to wipe his perspiring face. Courtenay half expected it to be red white and blue. It wasn't. It was a dirty white. He saw Cressy turn away holding his nose.

'I 'ave been sent by my *Amiral* to enquire as to what you are doing in this location. This is a French island, and this is nothing to do with the Royal Navy.'

Courtenay smiled. 'I know that, Captain. Believe you me, I am not here to intervene, but we were just, er happening by as you might put it, and we thought we would stay and watch the fun. What are you doing? It would appear you are mounting an invasion of your own Island?'

Vincent was getting angry. 'Whatever it is we are doing is nothing to do with you and I must insist you leave the area.'

Courtenay narrowed his eyes and Vincent took a step back.

'Are you going to force me, Captain?'

'There are many ships here for that purpose.'

'You go back and tell your Admiral that I am perfectly happy here. I shall be pleased to watch your invasion and report back to London how efficient the French are at launching such an operation. We must all be on our guard, obviously.'

Vincent did not know how to take it. It sounded as if Courtenay was being sarcastic, but he was not sure.

'Please leave the area, Captain' was all he said, and with that, he stomped off to find his boat.

'Oh dear, he appears to be a little sensitive to our presence!' Courtenay said to the quarterdeck at large, and there was a roar of laughter from the men working there, as he knew there would be. Cressy smiled and even St Clair, grim-faced as he was most of the time, managed a smile.

The laughter reached the men in the boat below, and there was a sea of grinning faces from the British seamen as their French counterparts pushed away from the ship to row back to their own.

Courtenay turned to Cressy. 'He didn't say anything about seeing another one of our ships, Simon. So what the devil has happened to *Spur?*'

'Shall we spread sail and move further along the coast, sir?'

'Yes, I think we will, but only slowly, and let the French see some of us watching them carefully through our glasses, eh?'

Hercules moved slowly through the clear water with hardly enough way to give her steerage, but that was enough for Courtenay's purpose. He took his time studying what the French were doing. He could see that they had, in fact, already made their attack on Santo Domingo and were storming some batteries and a fort. There were a great number of explosions and the sound of musketry carried clearly in the still air. It was quite a novelty to stand and watch other people fighting.

Eventually, as they reached the other end of the Island, and Courtenay was thinking about coming about and heading back for another look, the masthead look-out sighted the missing sloop.

When it was close enough, Courtenay signalled for it to heave-to, and for Spencer-White to repair on board. This time he did not have to wait.

'Commander, correct me if I am wrong, but I thought your orders were to observe what the Frogs are up to?'

'Yes sir.'

'Well, where have you been?'

Spencer-White was his usual arrogant and petulant self. 'There was a storm, sir. Add to that the sheer incompetence of my Sailing Master and the inability of the crew to understand simple commands, and I am afraid we were blown off course. That is why we have approached from this end of the Island, sir.'

'Storm, Commander, what storm?'

'There was one two days ago, sir.'

'Really? That's odd, because we did not come across any storm.'

'You were indeed fortunate in that case sir. It was quite bad. It was only by good seamanship that I was able to avoid losing a spar or two.'

'I thought you said your Sailing Master was incompetent?'

'So he is sir.'

'So it was you who saved the day, was it?'

'I do not understand what you are trying to say sir. May I ask what you are about in this place sir? I hardly see the requirement for both our ships to be here at the same time.'

'My orders are for me to interpret Commander, not for you to question.'

Spencer-White saw the look on Courtenay's face and decided not to press the point.

'Return to your ship, Commander and take up your duties. You will find the French Fleet anchored off Santo Domingo, and there are some Transports with their escort a little further along the coast in this direction. They seem to be ashore in great numbers, and I would imagine that if disease does not carry them off, the French soldiers will prevail....in time.'

Spencer-White left.

Trafford looked at Courtenay in a disapproving way.

'You didn't tell him about the French frigate, sir. How could you?'

Courtenay smiled. 'Oh yes, I forgot that. Oh well, too late now, but Spencer-White will find out all about that in due time!'

After a few days of sailing up and down, Courtenay was growing restless. It was unusual to be in the situation whereby they were unlikely to get called to action at a moment's notice, and he was surprised to find he was growing bored, as were some of his men. One morning when Cressy came into the Cabin and was greeted by Kingston with a mug of coffee, Courtenay had a chart open on his desk and was looking intently at it.

'Ah, good morning Simon. Got some coffee? Good. Come and have a look at the chart. The French have made their landings, as we know, but they do not seem to be getting very far. The other day, when we were a little further up the coast, they were still battering away at those forts, and Santo Domingo had not fallen. Obviously, Toussaint is proving a tough nut to crack. There is a small bay, just there.' He put his finger on the chart. 'Not large, but big enough for us.'

Cressy looked up sharply. 'If you intend what I think you are, sir, that is a little dangerous, surely. This is, after all, a French Island.'

'Come, come Mr Cressy, all I intend is to anchor in this bay to repair some damage we occasioned in that squall yesterday, and to have a little walk inland to find some water. I am sure our new friends would not object?'

Cressy said nothing. He was looking at the chart again. There had not been a squall the previous day! And, they were not short of water….yet.

'Where is that sloop again sir?'

'Probably frightened away by the ferocious Capitaine Vincent.' Courtenay rolled his eyes and Cressy smiled. There had been no sign of the sloop for some days.

'So, today, we will anchor in that bay, and you will send down some spars, Simon, so as to create the impression we have some storm damage. When we are certain we are not being disturbed, I will take a party ashore. We will even take some casks ashore with us, although they will be left secreted in the undergrowth. I am sure the cooper can find us some casks which will not be missed if they are left behind.'

'He was only complaining about some the other day, sir.'

'Good, then we will take them.'

'What are you going to do, sir?'

'I am going to have a look and see exactly why the French are having such a job. Who knows, it may stand us in good stead in the future when we are back at war with them again.'

'Do you think we will be, sir?'

'Don't you?'

'Yes. Seems inevitable, as long as Boney is in power.'

'Well, then. We will be gathering intelligence. Anyway, I could do with stretching my legs.'

'I ought to go, sir.'

'No, You will take command of the ship. If some nosey Frenchman turns up and you have to up-anchor and leave, you can come back once he has gone. I will take Mr Jeffery as my second in command and Midshipman Fulford. Ten of the lads ought to be enough.'

'Aye aye sir. I will tell Mr Smith to detail ten men.'

'No Simon, we are at peace, remember? Ask for volunteers.'

Cressy nodded, and having looked once more at the chart, left.

The launch pulled strongly for the white sandy beach. Beyond the sand was the colourful backdrop of lush green vegetation, palm trees, and brightly coloured plants and flowers.

Courtenay sat in the stern of the boat with Trafford next to him, hand on the tiller. As well as the oarsmen, there were ten volunteers and Midshipman Fulford, a big grin all over his young face. Courtenay admired his enthusiasm, and saw one of the men checking the pistol which the Midshipman had thrust through his belt. He was sixteen, and the second senior Midshipman. He also had a fine sword on a crossbelt, which was not standard uniform for a Midshipman. The sword was a gift from a rich Uncle, in anticipation of his receiving his commission in the years to come. Clearly, he thought the usual dirk was of no use when it came to defending himself, and Courtenay approved. In fact, it brought back memories of another Midshipman aboard his sloop *Seagull* . He had eschewed the usual dirk when it came to fighting as well.

Courtenay had left firm instructions with his First-Lieutenant. No colours were to be shown, and if there came a snooping French ship, Cressy, who spoke excellent French, would give out the story of illness aboard ship. In fact, if necessary, Cressy had the huge Yellow flag ready to run up to the gaff. That would deter anyone. At night,. there were to be no lights. Courtenay did not plan to be away too long, but there had to be contingency plans.

The stem of the boat ran through the crystal clear water and Courtenay could see the sandy bottom reaching up towards them. The boat grounded, and immediately, three men were over the side and sprinting up the sand to act as cover.

Merrilees had been aghast at the idea of his Marines not taking part, but all Courtenay wanted was to have a look at what was happening. He did not want a large party. Ten men, himself, Fulford and Trafford, could flit along, keeping hidden, and staying away from anyone they might hear coming. What Courtenay did not know was that Cressy and Merrilees had agreed between them that a squad of Marines would be kept ready at all times, the cutter in the water ready, just in case there was any hint of trouble.

Courtenay dropped over the side and splashed the last few feet up to the beach. He was wearing white shirt and a pair of white trousers, rather than breeches, so that if anyone did see them, he would not look like an officer. Fulford was dressed in a similar way.

'Very well. Austin, take the point. We will move out to the right. According to the map, there is a road which goes to Fort-Dauphin. I want to have a look at what is going on.'

The man called Austin smiled broadly as he realised his Captain actually knew his name, then doubled away through the undergrowth. When Courtenay and the rest of the party followed, they found Austin at the edge of what could hardly be called a road. It was more like a wide track.

'This it, sir?'

'Must be. Off you go then.'

Austin moved off down the road, keeping to one side. Courtenay led the rest along the other side, further back. At any sign of anyone coming along, they would step off the road, and be swallowed up in the undergrowth.

They continued in such a way for an hour, had a break and a small drink of water, then moved on again, and soon they could hear the familiar popping of musketry and the louder crashes of artillery pieces.

As they grew closer, Courtenay took them off the road, pushed through the light jungle and they found a hill in front of them. They moved slowly up the hill to the crest, where there was some cover, and blessed shade, and crept up to the crest.

At the top, they could see across to where Fort-Dauphin lay. It was being heavily invested by French troops and even as they watched, they could see that the French were getting the upper hand. They had breached one of the walls and men were pouring through. Ladders were against another wall, and through the air, they could clearly now hear not only the sounds of musketry and artillery, but the other sounds of battle. Men screaming as they were shot, blasted by grape, sliced by sword or run through by bayonets.

Courtenay tensed as he noticed some blue uniforms beneath the hill on the front slope and a file of French soldiers came into view. Some of the men drew their muskets closer, and one started to cock his, but Fulford reached out a hand and stopped him, appreciating the position they were in, and simply placed a finger to his lips.

The men went around the hill, and disappeared in the direction from which Courtenay's party had come. Courtenay rubbed his chin for a moment after they had gone. He looked at Trafford and Fulford.

'How many did you count?'

'About twenty, sir.' said Fulford

'Aye, the lad's right.' agreed Trafford.

'I wonder where on earth they were going? The fight is over there, and I would have thought the French commander would want every single man.'

'Perhaps they have some mission, sir?' offered Fulford.

'Well, we have to return that way, so let us be inquisitive, shall we?'

'Shall I take point again, sir?' asked Austin.

'Thank you, but be very careful. Do not cock your musket, just in case. Keep close to the undergrowth.'

They went back to the road and moved cautiously along. After half an hour or so, they found Austin waiting.

'They moved off the road sir, and went down this track.' He gestured to a track on the right, which ran down a slight incline between typical tropical bushes and shrubs.

'Well, let's see where it goes.' Courtenay gestured and Austin padded silently along the track, the others about twenty feet behind him. They moved along silently, disturbed only when a bird rose into the air making a noise, then Austin stopped, and made a motion with his hand that they should move into the undergrowth, which they did. Courtenay moved up to Austin, with Trafford at his shoulder. Courtenay noticed he had drawn his cutlass.

'What is it Austin?'

'There's a sentry just ahead, sir, and I could just see, beyond him, a small village. Nothing great by the look of it, several huts.'

'Why leave a sentry?' asked Trafford.

'Because they are going to do something they don't really want anyone to know about, that's why, Alex.' He turned to Austin. 'What do you think, Austin?'

'I could have a closer look, sir. That sentry won't hear me. I could also slit his throat for you?'

'We are not supposed to be at war at the moment, so have a look and then report back.'

Austin nodded and was gone. Courtenay had a drink of water, then the man was back, his face angry.

'What is wrong, man?' demanded Courtenay.

'There's a village ahead, sir, as I said. That sentry is to stop anyone going in and stopping his friends, because they are rounding up the men, and herding the women into their huts. I think these lads have decided that Fort-Dauphin is too dangerous a place, sir, and they want some fun instead. I think they are going to rape the women, then probably kill them. Dead men tell no tales sir, and neither do dead women.'

'And they will probably take the men off somewhere and kill them as well.'

'Like enough sir. You ain't goin' to let that happen, are you sir? I mean…'

'We are not at war with France. We are not even supposed to be here. Look at us all. We look more like some desperate buccaneers than members of the King's Navy!'

'Even so, sir……' added Trafford.

'Sir….?' started Fulford, but he was cut short by a shrill scream.

'Austin, can you remove that French sentry without anyone knowing?'

The man smiled. 'No problem, sir. Are we going to do something then, sir?'

'Yes, we are. Silence that sentry first. Mr Fulford, get ready to bring the men up when I give the word.'

Courtenay moved as far up as he dared, and then heard a slight sound, followed by a low grunt. Austin came back, bloodied knife in hand, just as there was another scream. They crept up to the edge of the undergrowth which surrounded the village and saw a group of French soldiers, hats off, muskets stacked, loosening their clothing. Clearly, the fun was about to start. One was passing round a bottle. As they looked over to the far side, they were in time to see about eight French soldiers herding the man away, down another track. Courtenay was thinking quickly. He needed to dispose of these men in the village quickly and silently. Then they had to go after the others. He did not have enough men to do both at the same time. He thought of his Marines, but knew he had been right to only bring a small party.

He watched coldly as one of the soldiers chased a young girl, no more than about twelve, and caught her. He pulled her towards one of the huts which was closest to where Courtenay and his men lay hidden.

He stood up and walked behind the hut, so that he was hidden. Trafford was behind him in a trice. He looked through a window, just an opening in the side of the hut, as the soldier dragged the girl, terrified, into the hut. Trafford stepped up to the window, knife in hand. The soldier saw him, but had no time to cry out before Trafford's knife sliced into his throat. Courtenay and Trafford were through the window in a flash, Courtenay smiling at the girl and holding a finger to his lips, for which he received a shaky smile. He looked at Trafford, raising an eyebrow. They both had the same thought.

'Call out to one of the others in French, Cap'n?' said Trafford.

Courtenay smiled, and called out as if he was having a problem. One of the other soldiers laughed, and strolled over to the hut. As he entered, Courtenay was waiting with drawn sword. The man turned in surprise, reaching for his bayonet, but never had the chance. Courtenay's blade sliced into his chest and the man was dead before he hit the bare floor of the hut.

They hurriedly stripped the tunics off the dead men, and pulled them on. Then, heads down, they walked outside and over to the remaining two soldiers. Screams and moaning coming from some of the huts identified where the rest of their comrades were. The two were the worse for wear for drink, and did not take too much notice until one of them suddenly realised that one of their comrades was carrying a sword. He made a grab for his musket, but like his dead friend in the hut, he was too late. Courtenay's sword thrust through his throat and blood spread down the front of the man's filthy uniform. Trafford jumped the other man, and his knife flashed briefly before plunging into the man's chest. The man tried to scream, but with Trafford's hand clamped over his mouth, nothing came out. The blade came out, Trafford hesitated, picking his spot, and the blade plunged down again, snuffing out the man's life.

They looked round, and Courtenay waved for his men to advance. Fulford, his sword drawn and ready for use, led the men into the centre of the village.

Courtenay indicated the huts with his hand. 'The French are in those huts. I reckon there are about eight left. Ready? Let's go. No-one gets away.'

Courtenay headed for the hut the furthest away, Trafford following, while Fulford and the rest of the men split up. Inside the hut, Courtenay just had time to see a French soldier divesting himself of his trousers, a frightened girl doing her best to cover herself up and keep away from him before the man realised someone else had come into the hut and turned round. He reached for his musket, but Courtenay's sword slashed into his ribs, and as he fell away, came down on his neck. Blood was soaking into the floor as the girl collapsed, crying quietly. Trafford spoke to her quietly, and some of the fear went from her face.

'Had no reason to believe we were any different to the others, sir.'

'Remember Manula Island, Alex?'

'Aye sir. That I do.'

Courtenay smiled at the girl and spoke to her in French. She nodded and smiled bravely.

Courtenay and Trafford went outside and although there were some short screams and the sound of crying from the huts, there were no musket or pistol shots. Then it all went quiet apart from the crying of the women. The men came out of the huts, dragging the bodies of the French soldiers after them. They were pulled to the edge of the village and laid in a line.

On the older women approached Courtenay, who was wiping his sword blade in the dirt.

'M'sieu?'

'Yes, Madam?'

A look of surprise crossed her face. 'You are English?'

'British.'

'What are you doing here, M'sieu? We were told that Britain and France were at peace?'

'So we are, Madam, but we are here, er, unofficially.'

'And I thank God you were, M'sieu, but the French pigs took away our men!'

'I know. I have sent one of my men to follow them, and that is where we are now going, if you will excuse me.'

'But why are you doing this, M'sieu?'

'We are not fighting the French. Madam. Those men were not soldiers, they are mad dogs. In our country, you shoot mad dogs.' Courtenay gave a short bow, and then motioned to his men.

'Follow me, and not a sound!'

Courtenay had sent Austin off to follow the French soldiers with their captive villagers. They ran along a hard-packed pathway, and then slowed as they came to a bend. Austin stepped out of the undergrowth in front of them.

'Just along here sir, to the left is a track that goes off this path. It goes down to a small gully, with a large pool next to it. Perfect, sir.'

'You mean…'

'Aye sir. You tie the poor buggers' hands and feet, shoot or bayonet them, weight them with some rock, and throw them into the pool. They would be gone for ever, and no-one would ever know where they were.'

'Right, let's move out. How many were there, Austin?'

'Twenty prisoners and eight guards, sir. I'll lead.'

Fulford was next to Courtenay. His face was haggard. He looked as if he had aged several years. 'What are we going to do to those bastards, sir?' He was gripping his sword hilt tightly, and the blade was covered in drying, sticky red-black blood.

'We are going to see what the situation is first of all, Mr Fulford, and then I will decide.'

He turned, and with Trafford right behind him, moved along the path and then turned off to the left down the track. It would downwards gently, and they were taking it very slowly, so that it took several minutes to get near the bottom. Austin held up his hand and the men came to a halt. Courtenay looked all around. They had in fact picked a very good spot. They were down below the level of the Island all around them, with walls of trees and shrubs on both sides. He could see the water glinting in the dying sunlight, because the sun was beginning now to disappear, and he could see the scene clearly in front of them.

There were, as Austin had said, twenty villagers, some of whom were already tied hand and foot and the rest were being similarly tied. They were being watched carefully by the soldiers who had their muskets ready to shoot, with their bayonets attached. The village men were lined up along the edge of the pool and there could not have been one of them who did not know what was about to happen. There were two or three elderly men, and two boys, hardly more than ten or twelve. One of the soldiers was piling loose rocks nearby. Fulford pressed up alongside Courtenay, and his face grew hard as he looked at the picture in front of him. He was about to say something when Trafford touched his arm, holding a finger to his lips.

Courtenay was weighing up his chances. He had wanted to charge the soldiers, since his men outnumbered them, but the French would not worry about using their muskets, and he suspected that some of them at least would be cut down before they got to grips. The French would only have time for one shot each, but that could be enough. He was thinking about the men using their muskets. He had two men with him who were very good shots, as was, he knew, Fulford. The trouble with that plan was that he might well hit some of the villagers with their shots.

'Very well. Mr Fulford, you, I am told, are a good shot with a musket. Is that true?'

'Not bad sir.'

'Right. Maxwell, Johnson, come here. Austin, hand Mr Fulford your musket. You three will remain here. When I give my signal, which will be to blow my whistle, you will fire at the French soldiers. The rest of us will be on each side of them, and will rush them as they are returning your fire. That is, of course, if they can figure out where you have fired from! If you have time, you may take a second shot each, but then, come in and join us.'

He turned back to the seaman. 'Austin, I'm rating you a very temporary Petty Officer. Take four men, and go slightly to our left, as quietly as you can. I will take the remainder round to the right. I will allow you enough time to get into position. On my whistle, you will charge in. Clear?'

'Aye sir. Thankee sir!'

Courtenay smiled. 'Don't get any ideas, it is only a temporary promotion!'

He took three men and very quietly, very slowly, they edged away. Courtenay and Trafford took the rest of the men further round to the right. It was hard, working their way through shrubs and bushes without making any noise, but they did it, and collapsed sweating on the edge of the undergrowth. One of the men reached for his water bottle, but Courtenay stopped him. 'Later.'

He looked towards the scene in front of him. The villagers were now all bound hand and foot, and the soldiers were conferring, probably to decide the best way to carry out the execution. Eventually, they started to spilt up and that was when the men with Courtenay saw him put the whistle to his lips and blow.

There was an answering crackle of musket fire from where they had left the others, and with most of the Frenchmen in a group, the balls were going to find a target somewhere. Three men were down, two kicking, one silent, but Courtenay was already out of cover and racing towards the soldiers. He saw the other men under Austin charging out of their cover. There was another volley from the hidden men and one more Frenchman went down. One or two of the soldiers tried to fire back, but the shots went wide as they fired in panic.

Then Courtenay and his men were amongst them, not that there was a lot of fight left in them, outnumbered as they were. Courtenay took the first one he faced by slashing across the stomach, dragging the keen blade slowly so that it cut through the man's dirty uniform, and blood spilled down across his equally dirty trousers. With his insides falling out onto the ground, he screamed in agony and fright, but not for long. One of the seamen with Courtenay drove the bayonet on his musket into his back and silenced his screams. The next soldier tried to run Courtenay through with his bayonet, but he slashed it aside, and having turned the point, the soldier was at a disadvantage. Courtenay run him through the stomach and left the man dropping to the ground, dead.

It was soon over. All the French soldiers were dead. Courtenay had thought he had seen one trying to surrender, but after seeing what his men had, they were in no mood to let any of them live. He had been cut down even as he screamed for mercy.

'What do we do with them, sir?' asked Trafford, just as Fulford ran up to them.

'First things first. Cut those men free.'

His men walked over to the villagers, who started to cower away. However, as soon as two of them had been released, they realised they were safe and soon, they were all jabbering to each other. One of them, clearly the elder, turned to Courtenay, seizing his hand and shaking it over and over again.

He was speaking in French, and was surprised when Courtenay was able to reply in the same tongue.

'We cannot thank you enough, sir, but our women and children.....'

'Are safe. We have just come from there. They are all safe and well. However, there are a number of dead Frenchmen there. I fear they will have to be moved and it is now almost dark.'

The man smiled. 'We will do to these men what they were going to do to us, sir, and then we will return to the village. We will bring the rest of the dead here, and put them in the pool as well. No-one will ever find them. They will have disappeared.' He looked at him, taking in the first time the lack of uniform.

'Excuse me, sir, but you are British?'

'Yes.'

'Where have you come from?'

'My ship is a little along the coast.'

'It will be too dangerous for you to get back to the ship tonight. There are French patrols everywhere. I fear that by now Saint-Dauphin has fallen. You will stay with us. We will make sure you are safe. Trust us, sir. After what you have done, we owe you our lives.'

Courtenay nodded, and after the villagers had weighted the French bodies, they were kicked into the pool. The elder said it was a very deep pool, with an underground channel. Then, they set off back to the village. By now it was a dark tropical night.

Back at the village, arrangements were made for the French bodies to be moved to the pool, and whilst the men were away, Courtenay and his men were made welcome and the women began preparing a meal.

Courtenay posted a sentry at the entrance to the village, but when the men returned, he was recalled and the villagers posted their own sentries to make sure they were not disturbed.

Although they were well cared for by the villagers, Courtenay spent a fitful night. He was more awake than asleep, and Trafford woke well before dawn to see his Captain prowling around the village, unable to rest. He was glad when, in the half-light before dawn, he gathered his men together and returned to the bay where they had first landed.

Waiting on the beach he found a squad of Marines, well hidden in the undergrowth, but not so well hidden that Austin and Trafford did not see them. Merrilees, no less, was in command and Courtenay saw him breathe a sigh of relief when the small file of men tramped onto the sandy beach.

'What is this, Captain Merrilees, a welcoming committee?' asked Courtenay sternly.

'Mr Cressy was worried that if you were found, you might be fighting a rear-guard action. He judged it a good idea to be prudent, and asked me to send some of my men to cover any withdrawal.'

'I see. Very kind of you Captain. As you can see, we are unscathed, although we did run into some French soldiers.'

'If you could call them soldiers' muttered Trafford under his breath. Fulford was hiding a smile and Merrilees looked from one to the other, raising an eyebrow in a questioning manner.

'I think it might be as well to return to the ship, Captain Merrilees?' said Courtenay finally. 'I could certainly do with a good shave!'

TEN

'That is my report, sir.' Courtenay placed the report on Vice-admiral Tarnworth's desk, and stood back, hat under his left arm.

Tarnworth looked at the sealed parchment for a moment, seated in his comfortable chair, his fingers steepled. He had nothing on his desk, apart from a decanter and two glasses.

'I have received a complaint, Sir Giles.' he started slowly. He had clearly been giving himself time to think. 'About you and your ship.'

'A complaint, sir?' What sort of complaint if I may ask?'

Tarnworth was clearly more than a little irritated. 'Dammit Sir Giles, we are at peace with the Frogs by way of a change! I know you had your orders, but they were not to start another war!'

'I am afraid that I do not follow you, sir.'

'It is perfectly simple. I have had a complaint from the General in charge of the French troops on the Island of Saint Domingo. First of all, the complaint is that you sailed too close to their ships, when they were in the process of their operations on the Island, and second, that you were seen on the Island, and that the General has reason to believe you may have been instrumental in him losing some of his men.'

'Losing men, sir?'

'Don't start sounding like a bloody parrot, Captain!'

'They are the complaints, sir?'

'Yes.'

'I did not sail close to their ships, sir. I kept a prudent distance from them. I did, however, receive a rather arrogant French officer on my ship who most bitterly complained that I should not be where I was. Since I was well away from their operations, sir, I judged I was not interfering.'

'What did you say to him?'

'I told him we had come to observe on how an amphibious operation ought to be carried out, sir. When he left, we sailed on.'

'What about his missing men?'

'I do not understand that part of the complaint sir. Why does he consider my men were on the Island?'

'You were seen, or rather, some men looking like privateersmen were seen.'

'Why would that be us, sir?'

'A two-decker, wearing no colours, was seen anchored in a small bay. When a boat approached, the ship ran up the Yellow Jack. I know you had orders to observe what the Frogs were getting up to. It was not difficult to put two and two together.'

'I see, sir. But what about their men, sir. Why is that down to us, sir?'

'There was a patrol of French soldiers in the area where you undoubtedly were. They have gone missing. Just disappeared. Vanished off the face of the earth.'

'I do not understand why that had to be us, sir?'

'I agree, but your appearance there is a coincidence, is it not?'

'I suppose sir. What have you told the General, sir?'

'I sent a note back denying any involvement.'

'Who took it sir?'

'Commander Spencer-White.'

'He was supposed to be patrolling off Saint-Domingo, sir. What was he doing here?'

'Said he ran out of water. I think he was bored!' Tarnworth paused. 'Did you not see him off the Island before you left?'

'No sir. I have not seen any sign of the sloop for about three weeks.'

'I hope he has not got himself lost.' He gestured for Courtenay to sit down and poured two glasses of wine. 'See here, Sir Giles. Nothing you say will go out of this room.'

Courtenay raised his glass and took a sip. 'They were going to rape, then kill all the women and young girls in a village. They had led off the men, and they were going to kill them as well.'

'Did you kill all of them?'

'Every single last one. The villagers helped us to hide the bodies.'

'I hope they have been hidden well.'

'They will never be found where they are, sir.'

'How do you know they were going to kill all the men?'

'They were taken to a quiet spot, sir, with their hands tied. Then their feet were tied, and the French were piling up rocks. They were next to a deep pool.'

'May I assume that the French are now where they intended their victims to be?'

'You may sir.'

'Best place for them if you ask me, Sir Giles. Your health, sir.'

An hour later, Courtenay was back aboard *Hercules,* sorting through the letters which had arrived for him. There were three from Jessica, and in each one she said how well she was, that she was being well cared for, and that she was greatly looking forward to the birth of their second child.

All this did for Giles Courtenay was to make him feel even more guilty that in this time of peace, he was thousands of miles away from where he really needed to be.

Trafford did his best to cheer him up, but even his efforts were flagging.

'Look sir, and I beg your pardon if you think I am speaking out of turn, but it Miss Jessica's idea that you be here. She could have said afore you left that she was having another child, but she didn't. She knew that she has to share you with the rest of us. She will be all right, sir. She has plenty of people looking after her.'

Courtenay turned his dark eyes on his cox'n and for one bad moment Traffotrd thought he had stepped over the line. Then he relaxed a little as the eyes softened and a small smile appeared for just a moment.

'She's one in a million, Sir Giles' he said quietly.

'Aye, she is. Thank you Alex. See if you can persuade Kingston to make some fresh coffee, will you?'

Two days later, *Hercules* was back at sea again, ploughing through the deep blue waters of the Caribbean, retracing her steps to Santo Domingo. Courtenay wanted to take a look at how many French ships were still there. He had heard that the man who used to run the Island, Toussaint, had in fact been arrested by the French, and that he had been taken aboard one of their ships, which seemed a cruel fate for him. According to the intelligence report he had seen, the man had put up a spirited defence against the French, but he had been supposed to be running the Island for them, and he had instead been running it for his people. That was not the way the French wanted their possessions to be run at all. In the end, his men had been overcome by the superior French forces, but Courtenay wondered how many of them had perished by fever, and how many of them would perish in the months to come.

And so, Courtenay and his ship sailed back to Santo Domingo, and to meet again with Commander Spencer-White and his sloop. That, at least, was the plan.

One of Tarnforth's courier schooners had been given instructions for Spencer-White as to positions where he should rendezvous with *Hercules*. Courtenay was not silly. He had given a number of alternatives, so that Spencer-White would not be able to plead weather conditions, and therefore deliberately avoid meeting with them.

When *Hercules* arrived at the south-eastern tip of the Island, Courtenay had not really expected *Spur* to be there, and he was not disappointed. She was not. However, as they sailed further along the coast, there was still no sign of her, and she was most certainly not where she was supposed to be.

Courtenay and his officers noted that the number of French ships was diminishing. Their job done, the Island taken, most of the French fleet would be on its way home, or elsewhere. Courtenay harboured the thought that perhaps some of them would find harbours away from France so that when the countries returned to hostilities, they would not be subjected to an immediate blockade.

By the end of the first dog watch on the fourth day after they had raised Santo Domingo, Courtenay was becoming concerned.

He was staring out to where the Island was dim on the horizon, as usual hatless and coatless, his shirt open to catch the breeze. Jeffery had the watch, and after looking at his Captain for a few moments to judge his mood, crossed the broad quarterdeck to stand next to him.

'Good evening sir.'

Courtenay turned. 'Good evening Steven. Is everything in order?'

'Aye sir. Sails pulling fully, everything is fine sir, at least, it is with the ship.'

Courtenay raised an eyebrow.

'I have a feeling sir that all is not well with you. Forgive me if I go too far, but is *Spur's* absence causing you a lot of concern?'

Courtenay smiled briefly. 'Let us take a turn around the deck, Steven.' They turned and walked up and down the quarterdeck, watched curiously by the Master, who had come on deck a few moments ago, ready for the change of watch.

'Yes, I am very concerned about our sloop. I gave Commander Spencer-White enough options for meeting us, as you know.'

Jeffery paused, testing the water. 'Do you think that he has gone off on his own somewhere, sir, looking for prize-money somehow in the shape of privateers?'

'I doubt even he would do that, Steven. He has written orders from me, much as he may dislike the fact, and I have the duplicates in my strongbox. No, I am concerned that something has happened to the ship.'

'Probably not more than he has lost himself sir' said Steven Jeffery seriously.

Courtenay laughed. 'Now, now, Mr Jeffery, you should not criticise your superiors in front of your Captain!' Then he stopped laughing. 'I think she has been taken.'

'By whom, sir? Surely no pirate or privateer would get the better of a King's ship?'

'No, I think the French have taken her.'

'Why, sir, if I may ask?'

'Who knows? Perhaps Commander Spencer-White got too nosey and they decided they would teach him a lesson in manners.'

'He could do with that.' said Jeffrey drily.

'We will see. Your watch is at an end Mr Jeffrey, and I hear tell that you have some kind of stew tonight. Enjoy it. Any of that cheese the wardroom picked up in Jamaica left?'

'I think there is some, sir, and there is still a plentiful supply of port to accompany the same.'

'Excellent. I wish you an enjoyable supper.' With that Courtenay nodded to his Fourth Lieutenant and walk away beneath the poop.

Two days later, Courtenay, now very worried, ordered a change of course, and they headed back to Antigua. They were about two days away when Lees, the mainmast look-out, spied a fast moving brig heading for them. It was one of Admiral Tarnford's messenger brigs and its Commander lost no time in passing over a message on a grass line before hurrying off again.

Courtenay was opening the canvas envelope as Cressy came into the cabin. He sat down as Courtenay motioned to a chair and waited until Courtenay had finished reading.

'Trouble sir?'

'This is a message from the Admiral. He requires us to return to English Harbour at once. He has received a message from the French General commanding at Santo Domingo. They have *Spur.*'

'How did the French let you know that they had *Spur,* may I ask, sir?'

'Of course you may ask, Captain Courtenay.' Vice-admiral Tarnforth was striding up and down his office whilst Courtenay stood, hat under left arm, watching him. The pacing up and down reminded him of how Admiral Crompton had limped up and down in the same way when he was thinking. 'They sent me a note, simple as that. They said they had every reason to believe some of my men were responsible for some missing soldiers and they had taken the sloop into 'protection; as they put it, until an explanation was given and the men responsible for the outrage were handed to them.'

'I see. How exactly did they know that something had happened to some of their soldiers, sir, did they say?'

'Apparently, someone saw some men who were obviously sailors, but who were not French, and had all the appearances of being British. They were in the area where some of their soldiers were last seen, and well, I suppose the French can add two and two and arrive at four.'

'But we were not dressed like British sailors at all, sir. I was not in uniform, and neither was Midshipman Fulford, nor even my own cox'n. No sir, no-one could have linked us with the Navy at all, even if we were seen, and I am fairly certain we were not. We could have been anyone, including privateers.'

'But your ship was seen. remember?'

'Yes sir. We discussed this last time I was here. Someone did try to investigate, but Lieutenant Cressy ran up the Yellow Jack pretty quick, and no-one came near. Also, my ship is a French prize, sir, so the cut of her would have been recognisable.'

'Yes, I know the background of your ship, Captain. Well, if you are certain you were not seen, and you were not dressed in anyway which would associate you with the Navy, what on earth is this man blathering on about? Could someone else have been there?' He stopped and looked at Courtenay. 'Do you think it was Spencer-White?'

'No sir. There was no sign of anyone else where we were, and I think if he had been ashore, in the same area, I would have seen him.'

'Well, any ideas, man?'

'No sir, not at the moment, but I think I know a way to find out, if I may be permitted to sail as soon as possible?'

'Sir Giles, you are not under my command, remember? I can at least truthfully say that none of my men were responsible for whatever happened to the French soldiers. What do you intend?'

'I shall make contact with the villagers I met, sir. They were the only people who knew who we were.' Courtenay held up a hand. 'Never fear, sir, I shall be very discreet. I shall go ashore with my cox'n and no-one else.'

'Just make damn sure that the Frogs don't catch either of you.'

'Aye, sir.'

'Now then Simon, I intend that we will close the shore tomorrow night, and I will take Trafford and meet with Jean-Christophe at his village. You will take *Hercules* and stand off-shore for the day. . I will go ashore at night, obviously, and Trafford and myself will find a place to hide until daylight. We will make contact with the village, and then return that evening. I will take a lantern, and we will show a light at the appointed time. You will have a boat standing just off the beach, and when the signal, two flashes, is shown, the boat will come in and collect us. I will arrange with Jean-Christophe as to when he will let me know if he has found out anything about the whereabouts of the *Spur*. Have you any questions?'

'Are you satisfied you can trust this villager, sir. For all we know, he is the person who told the French about your presence there before!'

Courtenay smiled. 'I can trust him. His wife and daughter were about to be raped by those animals, and then, no doubt, killed, so that no-one would ever be able to talk about what had happened that day. I am, however, most curious to know exactly how the French General found out about us, because I am absolutely certain we were not seen.'

'Why is that, sir?'

'Stop and think, Simon. If we were seen by French soldiers, do you not think they would have attacked us, taken us prisoner, and used us to embarrass our Government, and the King? No, I am certain we were not seen.'

'Then it must have been one of the villagers, sir, unless one of the French soldiers was not dead?'

'No, they were all dead, and even if one was pretending, he ended up at the bottom of the pool with a heavy stone tied to his body, so he would have drowned.'

'Curious, then sir.'

'Yes. Very well, I will come on deck and speak to Mr Wetherby.'

They went on deck and found the Sailing Master at his usual station, near the big double wheel, supervising the helmsmen. He was looking upwards at the clouds, which were thickening, although they did not threaten rain or a storm, for which Courtenay was grateful, since if there had been a storm, he may not have been able to close the land, and even if he could have, he would not have been able to leave the ship to Cressy. As good a seaman as he was, it would not have been fair to leave him with the responsibility.

Wetherby turned and touched his hat.

'Cloud is building, sir. That will suit us tonight. Doubt there will be any moon. Should be as black as pitch.'

'Can you still take the ship to that cove?' asked Cressy.

Wetherby gave him as much of a withering glance as he dared, whilst Courtenay hid a smile. 'You may rest assured, Mr Cressy, that I will be able to guide the ship to the right place.'

Cressy nodded, and then turned to examine the perfectly drawing sails with quite a lot of interest.

'I have given Mr Cressy his instructions, Mr Wetherby. You will hove-to off shore, and I will go in with Trafford. You will then leave the area, and return tomorrow night, by which time, hopefully, I will be back at the cove to be collected.'

'Aye sir.' Wetherby was unhappy.

'You appear not to be happy about something, Mr Wetherby. You ought to know my ways by now. If there is something troubling you, please say what it is.'

'Taking a risk, begging your pardon sir. Could you not send Mr Fulford? He was with you last time, and he knows where to go.'

'Oh, I am certain Mr Wetherby that young Mr Fulford would be delighted to go, but there are things I have to find out, including how exactly the French knew were there last time, when no-one saw us. It would be wrong to entrust such a mission on such young shoulders.'

'If you says so, sir.'

'I do, Mr Wetherby. I shall be perfectly safe, never fear' Courtenay just wished that he felt the confidence that his words were meant to bring to his Sailing Master. Someone had told the French that some of their soldiers had been killed by British sailors. It had to be someone in the village.

The ship slowly approached the cove. It was pitch-black, and anything which might make a sound had been bound, or greased. Without there being any shouting of orders, the topmen ran aloft to shorten, then take in sail, and the ship ghosted to a near stop. The gig was lowered, and Courtenay, Trafford, and the oarsmen were into it, and pushing off from the ship's side in just a few moments. Gordon, one of the Bosun's mates, was also there to make sure the boat found its way back to the ship,.

The boat headed into the shallows, and grounded on the fine sand. Trafford and Courtenay were out of the boat into the shallow water immediately, and with drawn weapons in their hands, walked slowly up the beach to the treeline. All was quiet. Gordon was with them, bared cutlass in one huge hand.

'All quiet Gordon. Return to the ship.'

'Aye sir.' He paused and Courtenay knew he was summoning up courage to say something.' Take care o' yourself, sir. And you, Alex. See you tomorrow night.'

He ran down the sandy beach and helped to push the boat clear. There was a final look back, but there was no sign of either his Captain or Alex Trafford. He shrugged his shoulders, and climbed into the boat.

In the meantime, Courtenay and Trafford worked their way into the treeline, and found themselves a space between some palm trees where they could rest until daylight came. Courtenay wanted to be up and on the move as soon as it was dawn. They were both dressed as if they were refugees from a privateer, or, more likely, some pirate ship. Courtenay carried a bare cutlass, pushed through his belt, rather than his usual sword, and was dressed in ragged shirt and trousers. He had a pistol as well, and a bright red bandanna tied around his neck, which he had borrowed from the Bosun, Jeddediah Smith. Trafford was similarly attired, although without the red bandanna.

They took turns to sleep and keep watch, but as soon as dawn started to appear, they worked their way through the trees and shrubs and found the road again along which they had travelled before. They walked along slowly, pausing at the bends, and once, they were forced to drop off the road into the jungle as they heard hoofbeats. They had only just secreted themselves when a patrol of French Dragoons trotted past, some ten in all. Just before they reached the point where they would turn off the road, the sound of marching feet and voices made them find somewhere to hide again, and this time they watched as some French infantrymen trudged past, looking neither right or left.

Eventually, when Courtenay considered it was about noon, they reached the outskirts of the village. Trafford realised that Courtenay was not likely just to go walking in, and was not surprised when his Captain moved off the track, and they skirted the village to a point where they could watch what was happening, without being seen.

After an hour or so, they were satisfied that there were no French in the village. The villagers were eating their midday meal, which made them feel hungry, although they had brought plenty of water with them. Trafford produced some hunks of bread from a bag he had been carrying on one shoulder and some cheese, and they had to make do with that.

The village settled down for the afternoon siesta. Outside the huts, the sun beat down remorselessly, and although Courtenay and Trafford were in the shade, there was no cooling breeze for them. When all was quiet, Courtenay led Trafford out of the trees and to the edge of the village. They had their cutlasses in their hands in case there was a French soldier or two hiding, but there was not. Courtenay remembered where Jean-Christophe's hut was, and went straight there. He looked through an open window, and saw the village elder lying on a bed next to his wife. His daughter would be in the room next door. He looked through the window, and saw that there was room to get through, so he climbed in, with Trafford following him. They then moved to either side of the bed, and gently, but firmly, clamped their hands over the mouths of Jean-Christophe and his wife. They awoke immediately, fear springing into their eyes, but seeing only smiling faces instead.

Courtenay and Trafford took their hands away, but Courtenay placed one finger to his lips.

Jean-Christophe leapt off the bed, and took Courtenay's hands in his own.

'My friend!' he exclaimed quietly, 'I did not think that I would see you again. Is something wrong?' His wife came up to Courtenay and gave him a small hug, and did the same to Trafford.

'Whatever it is that you need, Captain, if it is in our power to give it, we will.'

There was a noise at the door which led to the rest of the hut, and Jean-Christophe's daughter appeared, rubbing her eyes. They opened wide at seeing the two British sailors, and Courtenay had to once again raise a finger to his lips. She nodded, and sat down next to her father.

'You remember when we were here last?' started Courtenay.

'But of course, how could I forget!'

'Well, according to the French, someone saw us. They have taken a ship of ours, and are holding the same, with the crew, prisoner, until the men who killed their soldiers are handed over to them.'

'Did someone see you, my friend?'

'Not as far as we are aware. And if someone did see us, why did they not do something about whilst we were here?'

'That is true. What is it that you wish of us?'

'We know that our ship is not being held at Saint-Domingo, or at Port au Prince. If it was, our patrols would have seen it. Therefore, the French must be holding it somewhere else. Is there any way in which you can find out where it is for us? It is a smallish ship, like what the French call a Corvette.'

'Ah yes, I think I know. Did you hear what happened to our beloved leader?'

'Toussaint?'

'Yes, that is him. He has been taken to France. We will never see him again. Those cowardly French, they will find someway to kill him and make it appear he has died naturally. They dare not murder him!'

'I am sorry for your loss, my friend.'

'I have friends in some of the other villages. Friends who will keep their mouths shut. But you say that the French General said you were seen?'

'Yes.'

'I do not believe it. There is something……leave it to me, Captain. Very well, it will look wrong if we start to move around during the early afternoon, so make yourselves comfortable and enjoy our humble hospitality, and when it becomes cooler, I will start to make enquiries for you. Are you remaining here?'

'No. I wish to be back at the cove where we will be meeting our ship later tonight. We can arrange when I should return.'

'Very well. I shall guide you back to the cove. Let us arrange to meet again in three nights. I should then have information for you.'

Courtenay and Trafford spent the rest of the afternoon and early evening in the hut, resting in the cool shade with a gentle breeze fanning through the open windows. Marie, Jean-Christophe's wife, and their daughter Jade made them some food, and very soon, it was dark again and Jean-Christophe was there to lead them through the darkness to the cove. When they were away from the village, he let them know what he had been doing.

'I have visited some of my friends in two other villages, and they will speak to their own friends, but there is a rumour that a small ship has been anchored in a bay to the west of the Island for several days. It carries no flag, and local people have been told to stay away.'

'That could be the ship, but of course, equally, it may not be.'

'What is the name of this ship, captain?'

'The *Spur*.'

'And where would it be possible to see the name of the ship?'

'Across the stern. The ship's name will be painted beneath the stern windows.'

'Very well. My friends and myself will see what can be done.'

'This must not be mentioned to anyone else in the village.'

'Do you not trust us, Captain?'

'Of course I do, but this is for their safety, Jean-Christophe.' That was of course only partly the truth. Courtenay most regrettably did feel that someone from the village had spoken out of turn to the French.

'We had to avoid two patrols when we were going to your village yesterday.' Trafford pointed out.

'Yes, they do have many regular patrols these days. I think they are doing this to make sure that none of us Islanders dare to rise up against them.'

They reached the cove without mishap, and Trafford found the lantern he had hidden. He lit it, and then opened the shutter twice, slowly. Nothing happened for a few moments, and for a couple of minutes, Courtenay was worried something might have happened to his ship. Then, he saw the dim outline of the gig approaching, and as it beached, Lieutenant Jeffrey, sword drawn and pistol in his left hand, ran up the beach.

'Good evening, sir. Is everything in order?'

'What are you doing here, Mr Jeffrey?' asked Courtenay, smiling.

'I volunteered for the duty sir. I have some men with me, just in case.'

'Well, let's be getting back to the ship. There have been several French patrols around, and it would not be a good idea to tarry unnecessarily.'

Courtenay turned to Jean-Christophe, and clasped his hand. 'I will return in three nights, Jean-Christophe. I hope you will have some news for me then.'

'I shall do my best for you, Captain.'

Jeffrey climbed into the cutter, and Trafford was already there, seated next to the tiller. Two seamen stood up to their knees in the surf, and as their Captain approached, started to push the boat into deeper water. Courtenay waded out, and climbed over the gunwhale. In a few moments, with several strong strokes from the oarsmen, the boat was lost to sight in the inky blackness.

The next three days dragged unmercilessly for Giles Courtenay, and for the men of his ship. When he and the rest of the boat's crew were back aboard, Cressy had ordered that they make sail and they had moved away from the Island. They patrolled up and down, well out of sight of the land. The weather was exactly the same each day. Clear, impossibly beautiful blue skies with a witheringly hot sun, and deep, shark blue seas. The crew amused themselves trying to catch flying fish, and even once managed to snare a small shark. Dolphins would regularly swim alongside the ship, leaping out of the water to plunge back gracefully. Their performances never failed to draw an audience from the men of the *Hercules* and although there were a number who fancied the taste of Dolphin meat, Smith, the Bosun, put a stop to any such notion.

At last, it was time to turn the ship's head and point the bowsprit back to Santo Domingo. They closed the land slowly, look-outs searching the seas all around them as the light started to fade for any sign of French ships in the area, but there were none. Courtenay had sent telescopes up to the look-outs to assist them, and had doubled their number. Lees, typically, eschewed a telescope. His eyes were keen enough without, and no-one, from Giles Courtenay down to the youngest and newest ship's boy, was prepared to argue with him.

With no sign of any French ships, *Hercules* crept in under topsails only, her huge courses clewed up loosely ready to let drop at the first hint of trouble, but none arrived. All was quiet.

The cutter beached, and Courtenay was out in a moment, wading the last few feet up the shelving beach. Trafford was behind him, cutlass bared, and Steven Jeffrey, pistol in his right hand, followed. The men in the boat looked around the darkness nervously, holding their weapons and listening carefully for the slightest wrong sound.

Everyone's heads snapped up as there was a slight whistle, but Courtenay smiled in the gloom. 'Easy, men, that is the signal. All's well. Remain here with the boat Mr Jeffrey.'

Courtenay and Trafford moved towards the tree-line and then two men stepped out of it. One was Jean-Christophe. The other was a stranger.

Courtenay and Jean-Christophe clasped hands warmly.

'Captain, this is Baptiste. He is headman of a village further round the coast.'

'You have found our ship?'

'Yes we have, but that is not all we have found.'

Courtenay looked at his face in the darkness, and could see sadness there.

'What is it?'

'I have found out how the French knew you had been here. It was the daughter of one of my villagers. It seems that during her visits to the Town nearby, she formed quite an attachment with a young French soldier who was very kind to her one day. He was hardly any older than she. One day, she let slip she had some men, not in uniform, and who spoke neither French nor Spanish. She speaks both, but did not recognise the language, although she guessed it was English. She did not say they had been to the village. She was mot that stupid, for she knew that would bring trouble on all of us. From the young soldier, it reached upwards to the General in command of the Island.'

'How can you be sure she will not say anything about your disappearances in the last few days?'

'She will not, after what her Father has had to say to her, but in any case, she will probably not see her friend again. Her Mother went to the market today, and when asked where she was, she explained that her daughter was unwell. One of the young soldier's friends said that he was also unwell. He has the fever. He is unlikely to recover.'

'Where is the ship, Jean-Christophe?'

'Have you a chart, Captain?'

'I have, but it is hardly safe to look at it here?'

'We will be safe. The last patrol was two hours ago, and there is unlikely to be another one, at this time of night. In any case, I have men near the road. If there is any sign of a French patrol, we will be warned.

A lantern was lit, and Courtenay opened the chart, spreading it on the sand. The man with Jean-Christophe pointed to a bay, round to the west of the Island.

'Your ship is there Captain,' he said slowly. Courtenay rubbed his chin.

'Good sized bay, Baptiste. Easy approach by the look of it, although I shall consult with my Sailing Master.' He paused, looking at the chart. Trafford was looking over his shoulder one side, and Jeffrey the other.

'Looks almost too easy, sir.' commented Lieutenant Jeffrey.

'Yes,' it does.' agreed Courtenay. He looked at Baptiste. 'Why do I have the feeling that it has been put there deliberately? Why did they not anchor it in Sant-Domingo? There is a large enough anchorage, and it would have been safe from attack there' Baptiste shrugged his shoulders and then smiled.

'The French think she is safe enough there as well, Captain.'

Courtenay looked at him. 'Why?' Then a slow smile spread across his face, and Jeffrey snapped his fingers.

'It's a trap. sir'

'I do believe it is Steven. Tell me Baptiste. Are there are any other ships there?'

'No, sir. But the French have sited six cannon at the head of the bay, and two more on each side.'

Courtenay smiled. 'How big?'

'I do not know, sir, but they are large. About nine or ten men to each one.'

'How did you find out about these?'

'Our village is nearby, sir, and they think we are only ignorant savages!'

Courtenay reached out and touched the man's arm. 'You are far, far from that, Baptiste, and I am most grateful.'

'Is this all you need from us, Captain?' asked Jean-Christophe.

'Yes, and I am in your debt.'

'No, Captain, we were in yours. I wish you luck, and I hope you recover your ship.' With a final handshake, the two men melted into the treeline.

Twenty minutes later, Courtenay and the others were back inboard of *Hercules*.

ELEVEN

Courtenay gripped a ratline as *Hercules* lifted her bowsprit to allow a swell to pass beneath. It was overcast, an almost welcome diversion from the usual procession of blue skies and blinding sunshine. There was a stiff breeze, and there had been a swift shower which had passed overhead and disappeared almost as soon as it had arrived, but not before, forewarned by the Master, the cooper had arranged casks and canvas funnels on deck to gather the precious cargo. There had not been much, but it all helped. The decks were steaming with the water drying in the heat.

Cressy approached and touched his hat.

'We are almost there sir.'

'Good. Time for some discretion, I think.' He turned and sought out the Sailing Master. 'Mr Wetherby, lay off a course which will take us away out to sea. Winds permitting, I intend that we shall claw round in a circle and approach the land again under cover of darkness.'

'Aye sir. Reckon if the weather stays more or less the same we ought to be all right.'

They had been approaching the bay which had been identified by Jean-Christophe and his friend as to where *Spur* was being held. Courtenay knew very well that the French had planned a trap, and he was certain that if he ventured too close, look-outs would soon see their topsails and then they would be alerted. They would move out to sea and come back during the night, but first of all, there was something which had to be done.

'Mr Mallory. My compliments to Captain Merrilees, and I would be most grateful if he would join me in the chartroom.'

'Aye aye, sir!' The Midshipman of the watch walked swiftly to the companion.

Courtenay motioned Cressy and Wetherby to join him and they went into the chartroom. The Marines Captain was there within a few moments. His face was red, and he was buttoning the top of his immaculate tunic.

'I hope I did not disturb you, Captain?' asked Courtenay lightly.

'No sir. What can I do for you?'

'How many ex-poachers or gamekeepers have you among your men?'

The question took the Marine off-guard, but his keen mind soon slipped into gear.

'Six, sir. One is Sergeant Jackson. He was a poacher. One of my best shots. Then there is Corporal Wilson........what do you have in mind sir? Do I gather it is something which requires stealth?'

'Yes, Captain, it is. Look at the chart. You see this Bay?' The Marine nodded. 'Well, I have it on very good authority that there are three batteries guarding the anchorage.' He pointed to the locations Jean-Christophe had told him about.

Merrilees looked at the chart and then rubbed his chin. 'Well sited if that is where they are, sir. Covers the whole anchorage. What size guns, sir?'

'No idea, but I think we can rest assured they are not six pounders!'

'May I ask what the importance of this bay is, sir? After all, the Island is French, and we are at peace with the frogs....for the time being.' He looked up and saw Simon Cressy smiling.

Courtenay looked him in the eye. 'That is where, I am told, the frogs are holding *Spur.*'

'The devil you say sir!' He rubbed his smoothly shaved chin. 'What do you in mind sir? I assume you are going to cut her out?'

'You assume correctly, Captain, but I am obviously concerned about those batteries. I would like you to send your lads ashore, and check the location and size of the batteries. Can they do that without being caught, or seen?'

'I will want to know the reason if they cannot, sir! I would like to see the day when any frog is better than a......sorry, sir. Yes, my lads can do that. When, sir?'

'Tonight. We are clawing back out to sea at the moment. When we are out of sight we will reverse our course, winds permitting, and turn under cover of darkness.'

'I would suggest sir, with respect, that perhaps two lads to each battery. They can take a note of what size the guns are, how many, and what men are serving them.'

'No red coats, Captain. Better dress your men as if they were privateers. Sorry about that, but you understand the reason?'

'Of course sir. Do not worry. May I ask what you intend about the *Spur?*'

'All in good time, Captain, but you may rest assured that we are not going to leave her there. I would rather burn her down to the waterline than leave her with the damned frogs!' Merrilees was quite taken aback by the venom in his Captain's voice.

'I will go and instruct my men, sir, if you will excuse me?'

Courtenay nodded and the tall Marine left.

'Well, Simon, what do you think?'

'We will have to silence the batteries sir. I am sure your, er, local intelligence is accurate, but it will do no harm to be certain. If those guns are there, I would wager they are at least 24 pounders, and they can smother the whole anchorage. The problem is sir, that we do not want to start another war! We both know, sir, that this is only a lull at the moment. We will soon be back at each others' throats, but I am sure that our Government would far rather it be when they are ready. I apologise if you consider I have spoken out of turn, sir, but I am sensible of your position here.'

Courtenay smiled grimly. 'So am I, Simon, but I fear that their Lordships would not take too kindly to us sailing away and leaving one of the King's ships in the hands of the people we are supposed to be at peace with. It might be taken as a sign of guilt!'

Wetherby looked from one to the other, suddenly grateful for the fact he would never be put in the position which his young Captain was. He slipped out of the chartroom and noted that the light was going. Then he strode to the double wheel and the conversation in the chartroom was forgotten as he saw that the Officer of the watch, Ralston, the most junior Lieutenant aboard, was not looking after the sails properly.

Hercules was at rest, hardly moving in the very slight off-shore swell. In Merrilees' words, it was as dark as the Earl of Hell's waistcoat. Clouds in the dark night sky meant no moon at all, and that suited them perfectly. They were at anchor just away from the bay where the *Spur* was supposed to be held captive.

The selected Marines, dressed more like scavengers than the men they really were, climbed down into their boats. They each had a pistol and a cutlass thrust through their belts, and they had even darkened their faces with some soot from the galley fire.

Courtenay realised that the men going to the head of the bay had the longest pull, and they were going first. Sergeant Jackson was in the gig, which would move fastest out of all their boats, and was going to look at the battery at the head of the bay. On the way out, he would have a look to make sure that the sloop was indeed there. On the way in, he wanted to keep to the backdrop of the land, against which he would invisible on this dark night. The other men would follow in the cutters. Soon, they had all left the safety of the ship, and now was the time Courtenay hated most of all. He felt he ought to be with them, sharing the dangers, but he knew that they were best suited to the task entrusted to them, and would be able to move about, even in the dark, in total silence. He knew he would not have been able to.

All around the deck, men looked anxiously in the direction of the shore, expecting all kinds of things, from a sudden challenge to gunfire. But nothing happened.

Courtenay snapped open his watch and peered at the face in the light from the binnacle. Trafford was next to him, and Cressy was pacing the deck nearby.

'Be dawn in half an hour, sir.' said Trafford

'I know Alex.'

There was a hushed shout from up forrard. 'Two boats approaching, sir!'

The cutters were back. Then another shout told him the gig was approaching and he breathed a heavy sigh of relief.

'Mr Wetherby. Get the ship under way if you please. I wish to be well away from the area before light finds us!'

A rather dishevelled Sergeant Jackson came onto the quarterdeck a little nervously, and drew himself up before his Captain. He was in a curious condition for a Marine. His clothes were dirty and torn and his face was still black from where they had all used soot from the galley chimney to darken their faces.

'Reportin' back sir.'

'And what did you find, Sergeant?' Courtenay noticed that Captain Merrilees had been at the entry port and had followed his Sergeant up the starboard ladder. His face was burning with curiosity.

'The guns are there, right enough, sir, just like you said they would be. 24 pounders. There are six at the top of the bay, sir, in a good position to sweep the area. There were about sixty soldiers with 'em. I reckon they were artillerymen, sir, by their uniforms.'

'You were not seen?'

The Marine grinned. 'No way, sir. Them frogs never knew we were there! Didn't even have a sentry!'

'Good. What about the others?'

'The other two batteries have three guns each, sir, with about thirty men, so Corporal Wilson tells me. He's a good man, sir, if he says that, you can rely on it.'

'I'm sure I can, Sergeant. Thank you very much. Well done.' Courtenay held out his hand and shook the tough Sergeant's. 'Mr St Clair. My compliments to the Purser. He is to break out a double tot of rum to these Marines.'

Jackson's face creased into a big smile. 'Thank you sir.' Then he stopped smiling. 'There was one other thing sir that Corporal Wilson mentioned to me. Those batteries on the headlands. They've got heated shot.'

'What?' said Cressy in alarm.

Jackson turned to him. 'Crude furnaces, sir, but...'

'Yes Sergeant,' Courtenay finished for him. 'Crude, but effective, nonetheless. Thank you Jackson.'

The Marine turned and left, but not before Merrilees had slapped him on the back.

Courtenay felt the deck start to tilt slightly as his ship headed away from the shore and found sea-room, and thoughtfully walked beneath the poop.

'Very well, gentlemen, this is what we will do.' Giles Courtenay was standing at the table the cabin, with a chart of the bay open in front of him, the positions of the batteries clearly marked. Gathered around the table were all the officers, including the Midshipmen, aside from those on watch. The Warrant officers were also there, in line with Courtenay always keeping these seasoned professionals alive to what he was planning. Wetherby stood, legs astride, stroking his chin, and looking very thoughtful. Doubtless he was worried about what his Captain intended when they were supposed to be at peace with the French.

Courtenay looked around him, at the expectant faces.

'The main battery, as you know, is at the head of the bay, to the rear of where *Spur* is anchored. Sergeant Jackson confirmed that she is indeed there, and she is anchored fore and aft. There are some sixty artillerymen serving those guns. On each of the headlands, if we can call them that, there are another three guns. They have heated shot available. There are about thirty men on each side. We are going to silence the batteries, hopefully without firing a shot. Then, we will cut out *Spur* and take her home.'

There was a murmur around the table. Courtenay waited for one of his officers to say something about was this wise when they were supposed to be at peace with the French, but even Ralston, the most junior officer and not long out of the gunroom, knew the peace would not last, that it was merely something Bonaparte wanted to draw breath before he began again.

'Thirty Marines, under Captain Merrilees, and thirty seamen, under Mr Cressy, will silence the main battery. I want no bloodshed. No man must be hurt, unless absolutely necessary, understand? A sore head is one thing, but I do not want any Frenchman hurt. Bound and gag them so that they cannot intervene. The left hand battery will be taken care of by Captain Merrilees' second in command, Lieutenant Pemberton, supported by Mr Frobisher with twenty seamen. Mr Cressy will have Midshipman Fulford as his second in command, and Mr Mallory will accompany Mr Frobisher.' He paused for a moment then looked at the senior Midshipman, McMasters. 'How long is it until you may sit your examination for Lieutenant, Mr McMasters?'

'Six months, sir.' The voice was confident enough.

'Then it will look fine on your record that you will command the attack on the right hand battery, will it not? Fear not, you will have the Bosun with you as support.'

There was a ripple of laughter around the table, and the Midshipman felt his cheeks burning, but he felt pride at the job he had been given. 'I'll not let you down, sir.'

'Now listen. These instructions apply to all of you. No-one is to wear uniform, not even the Marines. The ship will be out of sight, off-shore. The Master tells me that we will have a dark night. That is what we want. No-one is to take with them anything, anything, which would identify them. Do you all understand? Check all your men, every single man, to make sure this order is obeyed. The worse the men look, the better. Hopefully, if there are no sentries, you will be able to bind and gag all the soldiers without any opposition. If, God forbid, there is trouble, and any of our men are hurt, or worse, killed, they are not to be left behind. I want to make that perfectly clear.' He looked all around, and all those taking part nodded their heads. There were some disappointed looks, and St Clair, in particular, did not seem very happy. Courtenay smiled.

'No need to look too disappointed, those of you not involved, because that is only part of the operation. Having given the shore parties the chance to get to their objectives, I intend to take one hundred of our jack tars and cut out our sloop. Mr Jeffrey will support me, with Mr Macherson, and one of the Masters' Mates. Mr Poole, I think, if that suits, Mr Poole?'

He looked at the smiling face of the Master's Mate, who simply nodded.

'Mr Cressy. When you have silenced the battery, and spiked the guns, and made sure that all the artillerymen are securely bound and gagged, you may return to the boats and move out to support us.'

'Aye sir. Leave something for us?'

'I am sure Mr Cressy, that the frogs will be expecting us, but they will think they have the support of three batteries, with heated shot. They may even allow us to cut the cables and gain control, in the knowledge that the heated shot will put paid to any chance of *Spur* making it out of the bay. They will, I trust, have an unpleasant surprise!'

He nodded to the gathering, which started to disperse. When they had all gone, Courtenay turned to Trafford, who had been feigning a great deal of interest in Courtenay's sword.

'What is it, Alex?'

'Just a mite worried that you could well start a new war, all by yourself, sir! We all know that Boney is only biding his time, and he will declare war against us again, but I don't reckon you will get much thanks from The Admiralty if you starts it again here!'

'Which is why I want to make certain our men look more like privateers than British sailors and Marines, and why no personal belongings are to be taken.'

'Them frogs are not likely to hand over the sloop, sir. There's bound to be a fight there.'

Trafford was clearly concerned, and his worry for his Captain touched Courtenay.

'As far as I am concerned, Alex, and I am certain that the Admiralty will agree with me, France has illegally taken one of our ships. They have no proof that we had anything to do with those missing French soldiers, they are only supposing that in some way, some British sailors were around and they have added two and two and made five. On the other hand, they have admitted they have taken one of our ships. It is hardly going to be a wrongful act to take it back again, is it?'

Trafford sighed. 'I just hope that their Lordships see it the same way, back in Whitehall, sir. Hate to see you on the beach.'

'You mean, you do not want to be on the beach with me!'

Trafford laughed. 'Perhaps I do, sir, but then, you being a gentleman and a Baronet and all, it would come a lot harder to you.'

'I am touched by your concern, but I very much doubt that word of whatever we do tonight will reach Paris for some time, and who knows, by the time it does, *if it does,* we could well be at war again anyway. I very much doubt that Boney would approve of what his General has done, you know. The last thing he wants to do at the moment is to provoke a conflict for which he is not ready. I am sure he would not be very happy if the Government declared war on him because one of his Generals had taken it upon himself to take one of our ships. No, Alex, I have a feeling that no word of this will ever reach Paris.'

'Do you think the crew will be aboard, sir?'

'I have no idea. I would not be at all surprised though if Commander Spencer-White has ingratiated himself with the captors and is probably living comfortably somewhere.'

'So we would have to leave him behind then?' A smile was appearing on his face.

'I really do not think it would be a good idea to start looking for him if he is not aboard with the rest of his men, do you?'

'Be a shame sir!'

'Wouldn't it? Fetch a bottle Alex, and we will share a tot.'

Under a dark sky, the cutter moved slowly towards the beach. The oars, and anything else which might make a noise, were muffled, and the oarsmen were only too well aware of the need for quiet. They were even careful about how they worked their looms, so that hardly a feather of spray could be seen. It was full of men, and there was another boat slightly abeam. The prow ran into the soft sand, and the oarsmen quickly lifted their oars. Everyone sat still for a few moments, then Cressy nodded to Merrilees, and the Marines officer lowered himself over the gunwhale and waded the last few feet up the beach, sword in hand. His men followed and then the seamen. The other boat was disgorging its men and in a trice, they were out of sight of the beach as the undergrowth swallowed them.

Merrilees had sent Sergeant Jackson on ahead with two men, and one of them suddenly appeared amongst the rest, not having made a sound.

'Sarn't Jackson says no noise, sir. We've got about an 'undred yards to go, and then we'll be at the battery, so dead quiet, sir, beggin' your pardon'

Merrilees nodded, and followed the man as he turned and headed back along the track. Cressy looked around him. Dead still, quiet as the grave. He could see his men looking nervously around. He forced a smile, raised a finger to his lips, then raised his sword and waved it for them to follow him.

Back on the right-hand headland, Midshipman McMasters had landed safely in the darkness, and Smith had supervised all the men getting out of the boats quietly. They had a squad of Marines with a Corporal in charge. Two of the Marines doubled up the beach, muskets at the ready, but came back and reported that all was quiet.

Smith looked at McMasters, waiting for orders, wondering if the youngster was up to it. McMasters was something of an unknown quantity. He was good at his job, and his seamanship was coming along, but he kept himself very much to himself, and was never seen, like some of the other 'young gentlemen' racing around in the rigging when they were off-watch. He was studious, and he was quiet well informed about the stars, astrology Smith had heard it called.

McMasters saw the look and correctly interpreted it.

'Very well, Mr Smith. You know what to do. Marines first of all, and tell them to keep very quiet, otherwise we will have some very angry frogs around our ears and that will not please the Captain!' He smiled as he said the words, but Smith recognised the bite of a man in charge and relaxed a little. McMasters looked every inch a pirate. He had two pistols thrust through a broad leather belt, and a fine sword at his side on a cross belt. He had a red scarf tied loosely round his neck, and his shirt was open almost to the waist.

The Marines moved out, and as the last one left the beach, McMasters drew his sword and motioned to his men to follow him.

They came across the battery sooner than they thought they would. One of the Marines came back to McMasters and reported that the guns were just fifty yards ahead.

'Sentries?'

The Marine smiled. 'One sir. Thing is, he's asleep, the lazy bastard!'

'Very well, let's go.' McMasters moved up to the head of the file, with Smith right behind him. They all held their breath as they very slowly approached where the sentry was seated on a rock, musket propped up beside him. His head was lolling, and he was obviously asleep. McMasters took out one of his pistols, and reversed it. Although he had never done this before, he felt he had to show his men that there was nothing he would ask them to do he was not willing to do himself, which he admitted to himself was just what the Captain would do.

As he prepared to hit the unfortunate sentry over the head, he wondered what his father, an Admiral, was doing. The thought almost made him laugh, because he was probably drunk by now, having lambasted his wife for something or other. He lifted the pistol, and brought the butt down hard on the man's head. He collapsed off the rock and McMasters dropped the pistol and caught him. Smith was there in an instant.

'Well done, sir!' he hissed.

'See to the rest, then'

The Marines and his men moved in to the camp and found everyone asleep. At a nod from Smith, they pounced on the rest of the artillerymen, and they were soon trussed up like the proverbial Christmas turkey and gagged so that not a sound could escape their lips. Not a word was spoken the whole time.

Smith beckoned McMasters over. He pointed to the guns and a crude furnace next to them. The furnace was destroyed quickly, and Smith set to work with some of his men spiking the guns. McMasters stood and looked out over the headland, careful to make sure there was no silhouette showing against the dark sky which might be seen. He was wondering what was happening elsewhere.

Cressy was wondering what was happening with McMasters, but only briefly because his men had also accomplished their mission, and without a sound being made. Sixty French artillerymen were securely gagged and tied, and he had directed his men in spiking the six 24-pounders which made up the battery.

He moved out of earshot of the French, who were looking terrified, as well they might. The men who had so easily captured them looked like something out of their worst nightmares. Dirty, scruffy, carelessly dressed, and giving the French evil glances whenever they came close, the French got the impression, which is what Cressy wanted them to have, that they had been captured by a bunch of cut-throat pirates.

Merrilees followed him. 'Do you think the others got their jobs done, Jason?'

'I think they must have done, Simon, otherwise I think we have heard fireworks by now! When is the Captain attacking the sloop?'

Cressy strained his eyes looking out over the dark water. 'He should be in position by now. When we are finished here, we will return to the boats.'

'Right, I will go and hurry them along then. We might be in time for some fun after all!'

Out in the Bay, the boats were silently approaching the sloop *Spur*. The only sound was the gentle lapping of water as the men at the oars worked them as silently as they could. Jeffrey's boat had been in the lead, because he was attacking the stern of the ship which was the furthest away. The gig, with some of Merrilees' best marksmen aboard was going to stand off and offer support to the boats attacking. Jeffrey had the Master's Mate, Poole with him, whilst Courtenay with his barge had a very nervous looking Midshipman Macherson with him. Trafford sat at the tiller, eyeing the Midshipman, and he knew there were bets in the boat as to how long it would take him to crack. He simply did not seem to be the sort of person who would be fit for stand up and fight hand to hand combat. He had taken a cutlass, on the advice of a few quiet words from a Bosun's Mate, and there was a pistol butt showing dully under his jacket.

The barge silently closed in on the bows of the sloop. The oars were lifted and it very quietly coasted in. There was a cry from above them.

'*Qui va la?*'

That was to be expected. They knew very well there would be an attempt to cut out the ship, otherwise there would be no need for the batteries. Courtenay rose to his feet, cupped his hands and called back, in to what the men in the boat appeared perfect French, 'Rest easy my friend, it is only us, from the battery over there. We have run out of wine!'

The boat bumped gently against the side of the sloop and instantly, Courtenay was jumping for the first handhold and his men were swarming up after him. The sentry who had challenged him had stepped back at the reply in his own language, not realising he had been fooled, even though he should have been on the watch for such a subterfuge. It was now too late. As the men climbed over the side, the sentry realised his mistake and unslung his musket, but he was far too slow.

Courtenay waved his sword, 'At 'em my lads!' and lunged at the sentry. The man was helpless, trying to get at his musket and the blade sliced through his chest and into his heart before he realised his fatal mistake. He dropped to the deck as more men appeared from the deck where they had been waiting. Even as they did so, Courtenay's men were dropping over the side in ever increasing numbers, and he heard Steven Jeffrey's voice from aft as he rallied his men.

MacPherson pulled his cutlass and bravely went into the attack as a number of French seamen started towards them. He got two paces. A musket ball took him in the chest and he dropped without a sound. Courtenay paused and looked down at him, then he was pushing forwards with his men. Trafford sliced his cutlass round and caught a French seaman on the side of the neck, opening a huge gash and making blood fountain across the deck. The man gave a shrill scream but before Trafford could finish the job, a seamen was there with a boarding axe. Courtenay looked away, momentarily sickened as the man's head bounced away into the scuppers. One of his men turned away, and vomited over the body, then fell over it as a musket ball caught him in the side of the head. A ball fanned past Courtenay's head as he lunged at an officer and then the area around them cleared for a moment and they were able to cross swords, lunging and parrying, darting and twisting as they sought out any possible weaknesses. Sparks flashed as the steel came together, and Courtenay was pushing the other man back towards a hatchway. The man almost tripped over a ringbolt but saved himself, but even as he thrust up his sword to parry the overhead slash he thought was coming, he knew he had made a mistake. Courtenay paused, and then thrust underneath the upraised sword. There was a short scream as his blade went into the man's ribs then upwards and then silence as he died. Courtenay had to pull hard to extricate his sword blade, and as he did so, he pulled a pistol out of his belt with his free hand and aimed it at a figure darting towards Trafford, who had his back to him. He took quick aim and fired. The ball slammed into the man's head and toppled him against the side. He slumped down, still alive, but pumping blood onto the decking.

There were more cheers and Cressy's men appeared over the side, wading into the attack, not that they were really needed. The fight was going out of the French, and soon they were throwing down their weapons.

'Look's like the ship is ours, Cap'n!' said Trafford, theatrically sounding like a pirate.

'Aye, let's have a look and see what's below.' He turned to seek out Cressy. Jeffrey was coming along the deck, blood dripping from his sword, and pushing a pistol back into his belt.

'Best gather up these frogs, Mr Jeffrey, and batten 'em below until I decide what to do with them!' He winked at Steven Jeffrey who merely raised a hand.

Courtenay, Trafford, Cressy and several others raced down the companion, pistols at the ready, looking for more French, but there were none. What they did find, down in one of the holds, was the crew of the sloop, but no officers. The senior man was a Master's Mate.

Courtenay went into the Captain's cabin and found everything had been turned over. Desk, table, chairs, everything had been wrecked. The Master's Mate was brought in, rubbing his wrists where he had been manacled. His face lit up with relief when he saw Courtenay.

'Beggin' your pardon sir, but it's Sir Giles, ain't it?'

'Yes. You are....?'

'Miles sir. Master's Mate. Right good to see you, sir. Thought you were bloody pirates!'

'That, Mr Miles, is the idea! Where are your officers?'

'Took ashore days ago, sir. No idea where they might be. Sorry, sir.'

'There's no need to be. How were you taken?'

'We were patrolling up and down, sir, mindin' our own business like when the look out reports this frigate approaching. First-Lieutenant didn't like the look of the way it was headin' for us, but the Captain said they wouldn't dare do anything against us. Well, sir, as soon as they got near, out run all their guns, and we were given the option of surrendering or bein' blown out of the water. Captain decided to surrender.'

'He bloody would!' muttered Trafford.

'Perhaps it is just as well that Commander Spencer-White is not here.' said Courtenay. Cressy hid a grin. He was probably being royally entertained by the French at this very moment.

Merrilees appeared at that moment with a French officer. He looked like the Captain.

'Caught this fellow trying to hide, Cap'n. Something of a coward, by the look of him. Shall I run the bastard up to the mainyard, with the rest of his men?'

Courtenay, who looked every inch a pirate, raised an eyebrow. 'We'll see. When we get this girl out to sea, we might have a bit of fun with our 'guests'. Haven't had anyone to keelhaul for ages. Might be fun for the lads!'

The Frenchman's eyes were bulging with terror. Courtenay took hold of him by the collar of his uniform jacket and pulled him close to his face. Before he left the *Hercules* he had swilled rum around his mouth so that when he opened it, the Frenchman thought he was dealing with a drink-crazed pirate.

'We'll have fun with this one first. Get this scow under way, and then we'll see how this chap likes the thought of being shark bait!'

He shoved the man away, and Merrilees grabbed him and held him hard. He grinned at him evilly and the poor man tried to shrink away. Merrilees threw him at one of his men, who grinned and dragged him away.

Courtenay went back on deck to see that the sails were being dropped and sheeted home and Jeffrey was standing next to the wheel, issuing a steady stream of orders. The anchors were being raised, and as the bower came dripping clear, he ordered the wheel over, and the sloop gathered wind into the sails and started to move out of the bay.

Courtenay had the French crew on deck, and he saw them looking nervously at the shoreline. He of course knew what they were expecting to see. All they got was silence. He stepped up to the French Captain.

'Looking for your friends of the Artillery, *M'sieu?*' I am afraid they are all asleep. Some of them will have sore heads in the morning, but *c'est la vie*. At least they will be alive.' He turned and left, and what the Frenchmen did not see was a little hand motion he made as he did so. Suddenly, the French found themselves alone on the deck. They needed no second chance. As one, they ran for the side and jumped into the still dark water. Last seen, they were swimming for the nearest shore as if the devil was after them. The men fell about laughing.

As *Spur* moved slowly, under topsails, out of the bay, the boats from the headlands could be seen joining them, and they simply hooked on and allowed themselves to be towed out to where *Hercules* was waiting.

'A very successful evening's work, gentlemen.' Courtenay was saying, 'but how many men did we lose, Mr Jeffrey?'

'Four dead sir, and half a dozen wounded. Mr MacPherson is one of the former.'

'Yes, he fell next to me. We will take him aboard the ship and later, when we are out of sight of this place, we will bury him and the other brave lads.' he turned to Cressy. 'You are in temporary command, Simon. Make use of the *Spur's* crew. If you need any more, we will call for volunteers. I will give you your orders, which are that you will return to Antigua with all despatch. I have a feeling that our presence here will not have gone unnoticed and I want this ship well away from here by daylight.'

'Aye sir. Thank you.'

'I will recommend you be given her permanently, Simon, but I fear others may have different ideas!'

TWELVE

Daylight the following day arrived with *Hercules* alone on the ocean. *Spur* had already disappeared from view, Lieutenant Cressy in command, with Midshipman Fulford to assist and a Master's Mate. With the sloop's own crew, that would be enough to get them to Antigua, and to pass on Courtenay's report to the Admiral. He wondered what Tarnworth would make of it all. Courtenay had got *Spur* back, and hopefully had done so without making it obvious who had done it. However, the French would know.

St Clair had stepped up temporarily to be First-Lieutenant, but Courtenay knew he did not have the skill as a seaman which Cressy had, and knew he would have to keep a better eye on what he did. Wetherby was not that happy, either. Fortunately, the weather was fine, and there was a fair breeze.

Courtenay wondered where his old *Amazon* was. The last he had heard was that Van der Saar had been ordered to take her to the Caribbean, but Tarnworth had made no mention of the frigate. A smile creased his face. David Van der Saar was probably away looking for pirates off the Main. He would give them a bloody surprise with the armament his ship carried. What he would give to have her in company now.

'Deck there!' A shout from the mainmast look-out, the eagle-eyed Lees.

St Clair leant back and yelled back. 'What is it?'

'Sail to the west, sir! Looks like a frigate, sir!'

'Maintain course Mr St Clair.' ordered Courtenay quietly. 'I have a feeling that might be the French guardship we ran into before. We aren't that far away from where we last met up with her.'

'Aye aye sir.'

Hercules continued to plough through the deep blue water, but all eyes were on the approaching ship, which indeed was identified as the French ship they had met up with off Sant-Domingo.

Eventually, the French ship was close enough to enable her Captain to speak with Courtenay and he made it clear he wanted to come aboard. Courtenay smiled and agreed.

It was the same pumped up Captain who came aboard. He wasted no time with preliminaries.

'*Capitaine* Courtenay, is it not? We met a few weeks ago?'

'Yes indeed, *M'sieu.* I thought I recognised your fine ship.' That brought forth a few grins from men on the quarterdeck. The frigate was in a disgraceful state. Clearly, the Captain had no pride in the appearance of his ship.

'Once again, *Capitaine,* I have to warn you about interfering in French Government business.'

Courtenay smiled. 'Howso, Captain? We are in what I believe to be International Waters. How are we interfering with you? I understand your mission here is complete, is that not the case?'

'Well, yes…..'

'Then, my dear Captain, we are hardly interfering with anything at all. We have the perfect right to patrol this area. There are so many pirates and privateers around, well, you know how it is, I'm certain.'

'Well, yes, but…….'

'I am sure you will wish to be on your way, Captain, as I wish to be about our lawful occasions. Come, I shall see you over the side.'

The Frenchman stood his ground. 'May I ask where you have been, Sir Giles?'

'No, you may not. I only answer to his Britannic Majesty, Captain, not to…..not to Napoleon Bonaparte!'

'You will know we, ah, *detained* one of your ships, Captain, until my superiors had an explanation about a number of our brave soldiers disappearing?'

'Yes, Captain, I know that you took one of our ships by force of arms, at a time when we are supposed to be at peace!'

The Frenchman was unabashed. 'We were entitled, *Capitaine*. '

'That is something the Lawyers will argue over, Captain, if they get a chance.'

'The ship is no longer detained, Sir Giles. It was taken from our brave sailors and soldiers by a gang of cutthroats who murdered each man without quarter!'

'Each man, *m'sieu?* Are you certain?'

'Yes. One man escaped to tell the tale.'

'I thought you said each man had been murdered?'

'Each man, save one brave soul!'

'All murdered?'

'That is what I said. You and I know who took the ship, Sir Giles, and who murdered all our brave men!'

'Do I really, Captain? What are you suggesting?'

'You know very well, Sir Giles, it is no coincidence you are here again, quite close to where the ship was being guarded!'

Courtenay's eyes narrowed. 'What are you suggesting? That we took our ship back, and murdered all your men?'

The Frenchman looked at Courtenay's face and started to have misgivings, but he continued nonetheless. 'Yes, Sir Giles, I believe it was. It is too much of a coincidence you are here again, and the ship has gone!'

'Well, where is it then? Do you see it, Captain? Do my men and myself look like a bunch of cutthroats? How dare you come aboard one of his Britannic Majesty's ships and accuse its Captain and men of murder! By God, Captain, I've a mind to call you out, here and now! I trust you can defend yourself with that sword of yours?'

The Frenchman fell back. 'Well, Sir Giles, I didn't mean to insult you....perhaps I was mistaken....'

'You were all of that, Captain, and your mistake will be even bigger when it reaches the ears of Bonaparte! My God, accusing a Baronet of being a murderer? Whatever next?'

The Frenchman was getting redder and redder.

'I suggest you leave my ship, Captain, before I throw you over the side!'

Courtenay turned his back on the man and strode away. The French Captain had little choice. He almost ran down the ladder to the entry port and was gone in an instant, with derisive cheers from the British sailors ringing in his ears. For once, the Bosun made no effort to stop them.

The ship's head was almost due south-east. *Hercules* was on a course which would take her and her men to the south of the island of Peurto Rico, thence to the twin islands of St Christophers and Nevis, and onto Antigua. There was a fair wind, blue sky and a hot sun shining on the men as they went about their work.

Courtenay was by the larboard nettings, the wind ruffling his hair as usual. The watch changed and he knew without looking of course that the temporary Third Lieutenant had the new watch. He listened vaguely to the usual words spoken when the watch changed, course, wind direction etc and waited for Steven Jeffrey to join him, as he often did unless he had already determined his Captain was in no mood for idle chat.

He turned as Jeffrey approached.

'Good morning sir.'

'Good morning Mr Jeffrey. Is everything to your satisfaction?'

'Yes sir.' He hesitated.

Courtenay smiled. 'What is it Steven? Something is troubling you?'

'I was just wondering what might have happened to Commander Spencer-White sir. Will this cause you more trouble with his family?'

'I doubt that even *that* family could find fault with me there, Steven. We were nowhere near *Spur* at the time, and clearly, he was fooled into allowing the frog to get close enough in circumstances where he should have been a mite more suspicious'

'They might try to say it was your fault because of what we did, sir, have you thought of that?'

'You mean what I did, Mr Jeffrey.'

Jeffrey shifted uncomfortably.

'The French have no proof whatsoever that it was us. They cannot lay the blame on us, and in any case even if they did, Vice-admiral Tarnworth has evidence about the fact French soldiers were going to murder innocent civilians. The French may *think* it was us, but they do not know for certain.'

'Where do you think he is, sir?'

'You know Mr Jeffrey, I have no idea and I care even less!'

With that he turned to look out over the sea, leaving a rather perplexed Steven Jeffrey to return to his watch. Trafford passed by and said very quietly,

'Don't pay any attention to what Sir Giles says, Mr Jeffrey. He cares about where the bastard is alright, but I suspect it is because he would like to run him through!'

Jeffrey grinned, but the smile turned to a scowl as he turned to the helmsmen and saw them watching out of the corners of their eyes. 'Keep your eyes on what you are doing! We'll be steering in a damned circle if you don't watch what you are about!'

Trafford stepped up next to his Captain. 'Where do you think Mr Cressy will be by now, sir?'

'Oh, he ought to be getting up to Nevis by now. Why do you ask?'

'Nothing really sir. Just won't be entirely happy until we know they're nearly back to Antigua. He may have the rest of the crew of *Spur,* but he's hardly got any officers.'

'And he shouldn't need any. He should be perfectly safe from anyone. No privateer is going to attack even a ship like *Spur.*'

'I wasn't thinking of anyone like them, sir.'

Courtenay looked at him sharply. 'You mean you think the French might go after *Spur?*'

'They know we've got her back, Sir Giles. They won't have been fooled for too long by whatever they might have been told by their men about privateers making off with the ship.'

'You may be right. They would know what course she would take to get back to Antigua, but surely even the French would not try to re-take her? If word got out it would be war straight away!'

'If anyone lived to tell the tale, sir.'

Courtenay rubbed the scar on his cheek. 'Well, we will have to hope that Mr Cressy is driving the sloop hard to get back to the Admiral before that happens.'

They slipped past Peurto Rico and headed for Nevis and St Christophers, or, as the locals called the island, St Kitts. There was no sign of any French ships, not indeed anyone else. They might have had the Caribbean Sea to themselves, but they didn't.

The mainmast look-out suddenly yelled down he could see something on the sea ahead of them. A look from Courtenay to Lieutenant Frobisher was enough. He grabbed a telescope and went to the starboard ratlines. A few moments later he was settling himself at the cross trees and opening the glass. Courtenay, leaning back and staring up at him saw his suddenly stiffen, then he turned to yell his message down.

'Deck there! Wreckage in the water, dead ahead!'

Courtenay waved him down. St Clair appeared, straightening his coat, and Smith stood looking up at the quarterdeck, anticipating the next orders.

'Mr St Clair, standby to heave-to when we are closer to that wreckage.' St Clair nodded. Courtenay looked down at Smith. 'Mr Smith, I fear we will need a boat. Call away a launch's crew.'

'Aye sir.'

As *Hercules* was heaving to, the mainmast look-out yelled down that he had sighted a sail astern of them. A few moments later he altered that to two sail. Frobisher had come down, and Courtenay went aloft himself whilst Wetherby and St Clair brought his ship to a standstill. He looked down and saw the launch being swayed out over the side, and a crew running down into it. Then he looked through his glass at the two sail Lees had reported.

'Frenchies.' He said.

'Aye sir, that's what I thought.' replied Lees.

With a nod to the look-out, Courtenay swung out onto a backstay and swarmed down it to the quarterdeck.

St Clair looked at him blankly, but from the look on Wetherby's face he knew what his Captain was going to say.

'French. I'd say they are liners. We'll know better when they get closer. What is that boat's crew doing for God's sake?'

The launch had reached the wreckage and one of the crew was poking about with a boathook. He turned a piece of wood over, pulled it towards him and pulled it out of the water. Ten minutes later, Courtenay was standing looking at the piece of wood, dripping water on the decking.

It was clearly part of the transom of a ship because it had part of a ship's name in gold paint. The name was *Spur*.

There was a commotion down on the larboard gangway, and then Smith's loud voice as he shouted up to the quarterdeck.

'There's some more over to larboard sir, and I think there's a body there!'

The launch was in the process of being hoisted inboard again, but as he yelled the words, the men on the falls allowed it to drop back to the water again.

'Get the launch there, Mr Smith, as fast as you care!'

It took another agonising twenty minutes, in which time the French ships had grown a little closer, before the launch returned. There was a man with the crew, quite badly injured, but alive. He was taken to the sick-bay and Courtenay went down to the orlop to see him.

Turnville was there, examining the man's left arm.

'H'mm. Got to come off, I'm afraid sir. Ball has shattered the bone. I'm surprised he survived as long as he did.'

The man's eyes opened and he looked up to see Courtenay's dark eyes holding his firmly.

'Captain Courtenay, sir. I'm Parker, Bosun's Mate.'

'I heard Commander Fenwick speak of you.'

The man tried to smile, but then he winced as the pain came again.

'What happened Parker?'

'Took by surprise sir. Damn' French frigate came along. Mr Cressy weren't takin' any chances, sir, he sent us all to quarters and stood by ready to run out the guns, not that we could have fought the frog off anyway, sir. Must have been a 38 at least. We all saw the frogs running out their guns at the same time, and orders our guns out, and then the frogs open fire on us. He did his best sir, but we didn't stand a chance. Mr

Fulford, he was a good lad sir, he went down in the first broadside. Ball cut him in half, near as dammit. Mr Cressy was cursing all the time, but trying to get us clear so we could use our agility sir, but he was cut down by a splinter when a ball hit a gun on the quarterdeck.'

'Did he die, Perker?'

'Aye sir. He only lasted a few moments. With both him and Mr Fulford gone, there was no-one really to direct the fire sir, even though we did what we could, then the steering was hit, and the wheel was shot away. I got shot in the arm, but the next thing I knew I was in the water. The ship had blown up. Must have been....'

'Yes, Parker, I can imagine. Spark in the magazine, anything. You rest easy. The Surgeon will look after you.' He turned away, hating to see the fear coming into the man's eyes as he realised what was coming next.

Back on the quarterdeck, St Clair went to say something but fell back when he saw the anger on Courtenay's face. He had never witnessed that look before, although Jeffrey had. By now all the officers were on deck. Courtenay faced them grimly.

'The French sank *Spur*. Mr Cressy and Mr Fulford were both killed, and apart from that man Parker, the rest have perished as well.'

'By God, sir, that is an act of war!' postured St Clair.

'Yes, Mr St Clair, it is, but who is going to prove it pray? Parker is right now having an arm removed. He may not survive Mr Turnville's ministrations, you know that, but even if he does, he is the only witness, and the French will discredit him.'

He turned and sought out the youngest Midshipman, Harvey Cook. 'Mr Cook, take a glass, get aloft with you, and keep an eye on the progress of those two Frenchies behind us.'

'Aye aye sir.'

'I think, Mr Wetherby, we might get the ship underway again.'

'Aye sir.' Wetherby turned away to issue his orders and *Hercules* started to gather way.

'No doubt, gentlemen, those two frogs coming up astern are meant to ensure we do not return to port safely either, so that there is nothing at all we can report. We will have to make sure that does not happen. I intend we shall return to Antigua and that the world shall soon see what sort of people the French are!'

The glass had been turned twice and the French were slowly catching *Hercules*. That was not because she was a slower sailer than the French ships, but rather that Cook had reported they had all sail set to the royals, whereas Courtenay had left his sail plan at the courses and topsails. In other words, he was deliberately allowing the French ships to catch them.

To some of the men working on the maindeck, when word was passed the French were gaining, they could not see much sense in that, and were surprised their Captain had not spread more sail.

'We could show them frogs a fair pair o' heels, Mr Smith!' commented one of the Bosun's mates whilst he was supervising some men flaking down some ropes.

'Yes, Mr Grant, we surely could, but the Cap'n is *lettin'* them catch us, see? There's a difference between them catching us in a stern chase and us allowing 'em to catch up.'

Grant ran his hand over his chin. 'Well, I suppose then Sir Giles has somethin' up 'is sleeve then!'

Smith smiled grimly.' I'm sure of that Mr Grant. Now, time for a wet!'

Courtenay saw the men chatting and could almost hear what they were saying. He turned to pass a comment to Cressy, then suddenly realised his First-Lieutenant was no longer with him, and was saddened. St Clair was standing imperiously where Cressy would have been. That was where all similarity ended. St Clair, unfortunately, was not in the same class as Simon Cressy, and were it not for the fact he had no choice in the matter, Courtenay knew St Clair would never have been the ship's senior. Frobisher was the next one down the ladder, and he was still more or less an unknown entity when it came to combat, and the fury of a broadside battle. He had been in command of the lower gundeck, but he was now in charge of the upper batteries, with Jeffrey's friend Percy Wedderburn to assist him. Jeffery was now in charge of the lower batteries, with the sixth Lieutenant, Ralston as his assistant.

Courtenay mentally shook his head. He knew, even if no-one else on the ship apart from Alex Trafford did, that the two Frenchies coming up astern were intent on preventing *Hercules* reaching a British held port. He could have done with Cressy's steadiness now.

'Sir, those French ships have gained some more.' Midshipman Harvey Cook was shouting down from is position aloft.

'Very well Mr Cook, thank you. Come down and return to your normal duties now.'

Courtenay beckoned to the signals Midshipman, McMasters. 'Is there another Midshipman you would entrust the signals to, Mr McMasters? Mr Wright, perhaps?'

'Mr Fulford would have been eminently suitable sir, because I have been teaching him, but he is…'

'Yes, I know Mr McMasters.' Courtenay said gently. 'And I miss Mr Cressy being here as well, but the Navy is a hard school, and you learn fast or not at all. Mr Wright?'

'Aye sir.'

'Very well, you will take on the duties of acting sixth Lieutenant. I think Mr Jeffrey and Mr Ralston could do with your help on the lower gundeck.'

'Aye aye sir.'

He turned his back on McMasters giving instructions to young Arthur Wright, fifteen years old and about to become Signals Midshipman, not that there was anyone to signal in any event. He walked to the poop, climbed up and levelled his glass on the two French ships, which as Cook had stated, were gaining. He smiled, snapped the glass shut and returned to the quarterdeck.

'Leading frog wears a Commodore's Broad Pendant.' he said to St Clair.

'Does it by jove sir. Well, we'll give them a hammering today if they dare open fire on us!'

'I believe that is their intention, but since there are two of them, we will have to be that much cleverer.'

He left St Clair alone with his thoughts, which were no doubt that one day this might his quarterdeck and went to the larboard nettings.

Trafford joined him. 'We goin' to fight, Sir Giles?'

'They do not want us to get back to Antigua and report one of their ships has sunk *Spur*. They only way they can do that is to sink or capture us, but even if they do the latter, they run the risk of one of our patrols seeing the French with a prize.'

'So they will sink us, sir.'

'Not if I have anything to do with it, they will not.'

'I see you have a plan as usual, Sir Giles!' smiled Trafford

'I may have. Pass the word for the Master, Alex.'

Wetherby arrived a few moments later.

'Sir?'

'Would you say the wind is holding, Mr Wetherby?'

'Aye sir, from the nor'east.'

'Good.'

'If the frogs keep coming as they are, sir, they will have the advantage.'

'Yes Mr Wetherby. I am of course aware of that, which is why they are not going to get what they want! This is what we will do.....'

After a few moments, Wetherby smiled then rubbed an eyebrow. 'The only problem with that, sir, is that we are at peace with France. Supposing they don't open fire?'

'They will, Mr Wetherby. The trick is to make sure they open fire first. We then have every right to defend ourselves, would you not agree?'

The smile grew broader. 'Aye sir, reckon we would!'

It was the middle of a bright, sunny morning. The sun was not as yet as its full height where it would be overhead. Perfect for what Courtenay had in mind.

The French ships continued to close. It was clear they were intent on catching the British ship from the press of sale they were displaying, whereas *Hercules* was almost ambling along, with only the courses and topsails set. If the French Commodore was at all suspicious of this British ship apparently at ease with two French ships bearing down on it, he did not show it, because his ships came on without any slackening in speed.

Courtenay was studying the ships astern, then closed the glass with a snap and ran down to the poop ladder. St Clair turned to him expectantly.

'I think you may clear for action Mr St Clair, although quietly. No drums or fifes, no whistles. Just send the hands to quarters. Load, but do not run out. I intend we shall use the starboard battery, so ensure all guns are double-shotted and loaded with grape.'

'Do you think the French will dare to attack us sir? We are not at war with them!'

'Not yet Mr St Clair, at least not in Europe. We have however been waging our own little war with them ever since we arrived in the Caribbean! Yes, Mr St Clair I think they intend to attack us, and if you care to look astern, you will see why!'

St Clair went unhurriedly to the weather side and looked back at the French. Something was different from the last time he looked, but he could not pinpoint it. Courtenay joined him.

'Do you notice anything different, Mr St Clair?'

'Er, no sir, I do not.....they're stripping down to fighting sails sir! They have taken in their royals and I can see they are beginning to clew up their courses.'

'And I fancy the look-out would be able to tell you he can see their crew clearing for action as well. In a moment, I fancy you will see their gunports open, and if I were a wagering man, I would say the Commodore intends to get within hailing distance and then invite us to surrender in the face of what to them are overwhelming odds.'

'I see sir.' St Clair did not appear worried, but Courtenay was not deceived. He wished again he had Simon Cressy next to him. 'But will that not be seen as an act of war in any case, sir?'

'I very much doubt their Commodore honestly believes we will do him a favour and surrender, Mr St Clair!' Courtenay's voice was sharp, deliberately so. 'Even if we did, he takes everyone off, and sinks the ship. Then we are taken back to France, to be put in a prison where we will be left to rot, or abandoned on some god-forsaken island where we will all go mad from thirst and the sun!'

'I will clear and send the men to quarters, sir. Any other orders?'

'Not for the present.' Courtenay nodded his dismissal.

He waited for St Clair to walk away and start rapping out his orders than strolled over to the wheel where the Master stood looking keenly at the sails.

'In a moment Mr Wetherby, I intend that we shall change course three degrees to larboard. We shall keep to that for a few moments, then revert to our original course.'

'You going to get the frogs on our starboard side, is that it sir?'

'Just so. Then when they get closer, we will go about and cross the leading ship's hawse. Then we shall see what he does, Mr Wetherby.'

'His gunners will have the sun in their eyes, but the wind will blow the smoke our way, sir.'

'Yes, but more important is the fact we will catch him by surprise. How far apart would you say the two ships are?'

'About three cables, sir.'

'After sailing down the starboard side of the Commodore's ship, we will break their line, sail between them and rake them both. How does that sound?'

'Dangerous, Sir Giles!' He thought for a moment. 'Suppose they don't open fire?'

'Then neither will we. I am not going to provoke a war Mr Wetherby, they are!'

Hercules heeled to larboard as the helm went over. The French did not change course, which is what Courtenay expected, and now, they were on his ship's starboard side. They grew closer and closer. Courtenay watched as the French clewed up their courses and he fancied he saw a larboard gunport start to move.

'Very well, Mr Wetherby, put the ship about if you please.'

Wetherby bellowed his orders even as the ship's company completed clearing for action. A squad of Marines tailed onto the mizenyard and helped to drag it round. To the French it must have appeared that they were going to collide because *Hercules,* still with her main and fore courses set, suddenly altered course across their line of advance and, with the wind almost directly behind them, surged across. Almost immediately,. the helm went over again, and the British liner completed her turn across the leading French ship's bows to run down her starboard side.

Courtenay could almost hear the flurry of activity on the other ship then in a ragged wave, the starboard gunports on the French Commodore's ship opened. Guns poked through, just as *Hercules'* starboard ports also opened, but as one. The double line of guns ran out. Courtenay knew he was going to have to take some punishment first because he dare not open fire before the French did, but he need not have worried because there was a puff of smoke from a gun and a ball, followed by more in a ragged line, fanned across the water. There were thuds as some struck home, but most were aimed at masts and yards and missed.

Courtenay was at the rail, sword held high, Trafford next to him. The sword flashed down and the whole starboard battery fired as one. A double line of orange flames ran down the side of the British ship, and all their balls went home. Courtenay was watching the French ship, and saw wood flying in all directions as his gunners found their mark. There were more shots from the French ship and more thuds from below, and cordage and a block bounced on the nets which had been rigged above the gunners.

Hercules fired again, another well-timed broadside, and again, all their iron slammed into the French ship. There were marks on the side where grape had thudded home, and in two places on the upper deck there were gaps where should have been timber between gunports.

'Mr Wetherby, ' Courtenay said calmly,' stand by to change course three points to starboard.'

Wetherby nodded, seeing the gap opening up between the two French ships. The second one had its starboard artillery run out, ready to engage, but he knew they would be impotent.

'Now, if you please.' Courtenay said, and Wetherby rapped out his orders and threw his weight on the wheel as the helmsmen spun the spokes. *Hercules* was suddenly surging through the gap between the ships, and with a roar, the starboard carronade slammed back on its slide and its 32-pounder ball was on its way to the leading ship's stern. Courtenay just had time to see the name *Justine* before it disappeared under the impact.

'Run out the larboard battery!' ordered St Clair, just as the larboard carronade added its weight by firing at the second French ship. The range was a little too long and the ball barely reached the other ship, but in an instant the larboard battery was run out, and then Courtenay was ordering a change of course that would bring them broadside to broadside with it.

'Fire as you bear!' ordered St Clair. Frobisher, commanding the forrard division of guns on the upper gundeck was at least experienced enough to know a little better, and Courtenay noticed him through the smoke giving orders to fire division by division. The first of the larboard guns roared as he dropped his sword, and the French, caught by surprise barely had anything to reply with. Here and there, guns poked through their ports and opened fire and balls were striking *Hercules*. Courtenay watched as the other ship came more level, and several guns fired at the same moment. His ship fired a broadside in reply and then there was a larger amount of firing from the French, who had finally got all their guns out and were now firing back. Thud after thud sounded from between decks, and he could hear men screaming as evidence of the fact they were being hit hard. They had time for one more broadside before they were clear, but this one took away the French ship's mizenmast. The whole mast came down and fell over the larboard side.

'Mr Wetherby, wear ship if you please. We will cross his stern, raking him as we do so and then run down again on the French Commodore!'

Hercules turned across the ship's stern, and this time the larboard carronade was well within range. The huge ball took out all the sternlights and then exploded inside the stern cabin. Musket balls fanned the length of the ship.

Merrilees' Marines were adding to the mayhem by firing volleys into the smoke, and there were French sailors lying in the fighting tops as evidence of their marksmanship. There was a blast of canister close by, and several pieces of wood stood up in the planking not a foot from where Trafford and Courtenay were standing. Trafford cursed and spun round, clutching his arm. Courtenay turned to him straight away, hardly hearing St Clair rapping out orders for a broadside as they passed down the starboard side of the French ship.

A splinter had taken the cox'n in the arm, and he was swaying on his feet. Courtenay held him, and then Midshipman Cook ran across. Courtenay ripped Trafford's shirt and saw the depth the splinter was embedded.

Trafford took a breath and smiled. 'Don't look too bad, Sir Giles. Cut it out and bind it. I'll be all right.'

He slipped down against the side and looked away as Courtenay took his knife and very gently cut near the splinter. Trafford groaned but then Courtenay was pulling the splinter out. Cook handed to him a large and very clean handkerchief which Courtenay bound around the wound.

'Get him down to the orlop, Mr Cook. Get a proper bandage on that arm.'

'I'm staying with you, sir!' Trafford muttered, trying to get to his feet and choking on the smoke funnelling in over the side as yet another broadside ripped into the French ship.

'That's an order. Get below and have the Surgeon bind that properly!' Then Courtenay was turning back to see his ship surging ahead of their opponents. The side of the French ship was battered. The foremast was tottering, and there were large holes in the tumblehome. Blood was running down the side even as he watched. One or two guns were firing, but not many.

He looked ahead, trying to locate the French Commodore. He saw him, not coming to the aid of his compatriot and obviously waiting to see what the British ship intended. He looked down at the main gundeck as the target fell away and saw Frobisher lying by one of the guns, blood all around him. His stomach had been split open by a metal splinter. Wedderburn was there, trying hard not to vomit as he saw Frobisher's remains.

'Mr Wright!' Courtenay called to the Midshipman near the signals halliards. 'Find Mr Mallory. My compliments to him and I require him to assist the Fifth Lieutenant on the upper gundeck.'

'Aye aye sir!'

Courtenay felt, rather than saw the mizen topsail flapping and looked up. He turned to Wetherby. 'Wind is veering, Mr Wetherby!'

One last salvo was fired at the battered French ship from the after division of guns and then *Hercules* was ahead.

The Master was urging men to the braces as the sails were re-trimmed.

'Aye sir, course east sou-east, wind's veering to the north!'

'When I give the word Mr Wetherby, I want you to turn the ship three points larboard.'

'If you are going to try and cross that frog's stern, sir, he'll never allow it. He'll start turning with us and......' He stopped, suddenly thinking ahead and realising what his young Captain was intending. 'You aren't going to try to cross his stern to larboard, are you sir? It's a feint!'

Courtenay smiled grimly. 'Exactly Mr Wetherby. We will turn to larboard, and Mr Frenchman will see us, guess we are intending to cross his stern and come round with us, although how far he can turn is open to doubt, because he'll be in irons if he goes too far. Before he knows what we are up to, we will come back to starboard and cross his stern as we do so.'

'Bold plan if I may make so bold, sir. Supposing he guesses what we are up to?'

'Then we will have a fight on our hands!'

Hercules was gaining on the French ship. Courtenay levelled his glass at her and read out the name on the transom. *Provence.* A part of France, to the south. He watched as his ship gained rapidly on the French Commodore's flagship, realising the Frenchman had deliberately reduced sail to allow this impudent representative of the perfidious Albion to catch up and be given a stern lesson.

Wetherby held his breath as they grew closer and closer.

Courtenay spoke very calmly. 'Mr St Clair, run out the starboard battery again if you please.'

St Clair had of course heard his Captain's intentions and turned to stare at him. 'But sir, if....'

'If we were intending to attempt to cross his stern, Mr St Clair, we would have out starboard batteries run out, would we not? Yes, well in that case, kindly attend to my orders.'

There was the rumble of gun trucks as the starboard battery ran out. Anyone on the French ship would wonder what was happening, but there would be no doubts very soon. Wetherby swore *Hercules'* bowsprit was about to pass the French ship's taffrail, although it was of course an illusion.

Courtenay turned to him. 'You may alter course three points to larboard Mr Wetherby, and have the sails re-trimmed.'

Wetherby barked commands, the wheel went over, and the bowsprit started to move across the French ship's stern until it was pointing to the larboard quarter. Further still, with Courtenay anxiously watching to see what the French Commodore would do. He could not turn the ship much further otherwise they would lose the wind. He smiled as he saw the French ship edging round to larboard so that she would not present her stern to him. Further round, with the French crew obviously dragging on the yards.

'Very well, Mr Wetherby, alter course to starboard, four points.'

The wheel went over again, the men on the yards dragged hard on their braces, and *Hercules* abruptly started swinging back the other way. The French ship was committed to its turn, and although, through his glass, Courtenay could see feverish activity on the ship's decks, he knew they could not arrest the movement of the ship in time.

Courtenay looked round for a Midshipman, and realised they were all engaged elsewhere, two of them were on the main gundeck helping Percy Wedderburn, and the others, apart from Wright on signals were on the lower deck.

'Mr Wright. You are not needed on signals at this moment, so I would be pleased if you would go forrard and instruct the larboard carronade crew to aim for the Frenchie's steering.'

'Aye aye sir.'

Hercules was completing her turn back to starboard and gathering the wind in her fighting sails. She seemed to leap forward as she started to cross the stern of the ship named *Provence* and then just as Trafford came back onto the quarterdeck with a bandage wrapped round his arm, and which was already showing red from blood seeping from his wound, the larboard carronade crashed. There was a bright flash as it struck the French ship on the transom and part of the ship's stern simply caved in under the onslaught.

Smith looked up his Captain, his shirt and breeches covered in smoke and powder stains. 'She's lost her steering, sir!'

The French ship's sails were flapping as the crew desperately tried to turn their ship to follow *Hercules* as she swung back to starboard, but the carronade ball had smashed against the rudder head, and it had disappeared, together with all the windows above it.

Hercules' gunners needed no orders as their ship passed the enemy. Wedderburn, conscious of his new responsibility watched carefully as the Frenchman appeared through the first of the gunports, and ran down the line of guns roaring '*Fire!*' at the top of his voice. McMasters was there, hat gone, holding a sword in his hand rather than his dirk, and screaming at the gunners to keep to their timing. Division by division, the two gundecks fired their weapons at the French ship. waterspouts rose all around the stern as some balls missed, but others were hitting home.

The wind was pushing the French ship round helping the crew who were dragging the yards round, but she was in a bad way. Not so bad they could not manage to reply, though and Courtenay watched coldly as a double ripple of orange flashes ran down the side. He waited for the impact and felt the deck jarring as the French iron struck home. Some balls whistled between the masts, and there were screams from two men as they fell from the yards and into the sea. When Courtenay looked, all masts and yards were intact, then the larboard batteries fired a full broadside. *Hercules* was pushed slightly over to starboard, Wedderburn ordering the gunners to fire on the uproll and the force of the broadside pushed her over a little further. Some more French iron slammed into the lower hull and Smith's men needed no orders from him to get below and check the damage. Heeled over to starboard, those balls could have hit 'twixt wind and water.

The last broadside from *Hercules* caused a lot of damage aloft. The foretop went, then the maintop, and finally, the driver boom was hit by a stray 24-pounder and was blasted away, so she now had no driver.

'Hit 'em again, Mr Wedderburn!' screamed St Clair, then he spun round clutching his arm, looking stupidly at the blood running down his immaculate uniform and onto the decking. Trafford and another seaman ran to him, but he was already pulling out a large handkerchief and binding his arm.

'I'm alright thank you. Get back to your posts!' He swayed for a moment then held onto the rail as another broadside crashed out and more smoke funnelled inboard.

Trafford looked at Courtenay and shrugged, then held his own arm where he had been hurt. The bandage was covered in blood.

'Are you alright Alex?' asked Courtenay.

'Sure, Sir Giles. You got all the splinter is out and the Surgeon reckons he will put some stitches in when this is all over. Are you planning to go alongside the bugger!'

'No, not if I can help it. We are hitting her hard, and I want her to surrender. If we board, we'll lose a lot of the lads. And this is supposed to be a peacetime cruise!'

Yet another broadside crashed and Courtenay noticed there were only a few balls coming from the French ship now. Whole sections of planking had been blasted away and there were parts of the ship's side where the wood between gunports had disappeared. He could see there were guns overturned.

Wright had returned from up forrard, his young face set against what he had seen.

'Mr Wright, would you take a glass, climb up to the poop, and tell me what that other ship is doing?' Courtenay said gently. He could see the terror on the lad's face.

A few moments later Wright came back to report the French ship was still where they had left it.

Courtenay smiled to the others. 'Clearly he doesn't relish the odds!'

More broadsides and Courtenay was certain he could see the French ship listing to starboard. She wasn't under command and the wind was gradually pushing her closer to the British ship. The Tricolour still flew. He thought sadly that perhaps there was no-one left on the quarterdeck to strike it.

Wetherby had a hard look through a glass. 'She's going down, sir. That list won't get better, at least not without all hands to the pumps!'

The mainmast on the French ship came down, almost in slow motion and lay over to starboard. The list was growing more pronounced and now he could see men throwing things overboard and then following. They were abandoning.

'Mr St Clair. Avast firing.'

The gun crews of the *Hercules* stood back and cheered as they realised the fight was over. There was still the other ship, but she was making no effort to join in and Courtenay assumed she was still trying to put herself to rights. In the meantime, the French ship named *Provence* was doomed. Her list was growing more and more obvious. More and more men were abandoning and some boats had been got into the water. Hatchcovers were thrown into the sea, anything which would float and someone could climb onto.

The other French ship finally managed to get repairs effected and got under way again but Courtenay noted she had run her guns in, and she was moving very slowly.

'Mr Wetherby, I suggest you make all sail conformable with weather and lay off a course for Antigua. I think we can leave the Commodore's friend to pick up survivors. It might be a little embarrassing to have French prisoners on board when we return to the Admiral!

St Clair heard the exchange and smiled tiredly. His arm hurt like hell, and was bleeding, although not too badly. He knew the ball was still in there, from some French marksman who had probably been shot dead by one of their own Marine sharpshooters and wasn't looking forward to their Surgeon's ministrations, but he had survived and had not left the quarterdeck, or his duty. When he looked up again, Courtenay was standing in front of him.

'I think you should go below, Mr St Clair. Have the Surgeon take a look at that arm. Mr Wedderburn will be here soon and Mr Jeffery.' Courtenay held out his hand 'Well done Mr St Clair.'

St Clair took his Captain's hand and shook it warmly. 'If it is in order with you, Sir Giles, I will remain here until at least Mr Wedderburn can take over.'

'So be it Mr St Clair.' He turned to seek out Trafford 'Alex, if you are not too troubled by your wound, would you ask that rascal of a servant of mine to make some coffee? I am sure Mr St Clair and myself could manage a mug or two.'

St Clair smiled and nodded.

THIRTEEN

Hercules started to bear away, turning onto the course which would take them to Antigua when a seaman on the quarterdeck coiling a rope suddenly turned to Courtenay.

'Captain sir, there's one o'them frog boats heading our way.'

'We will leave them to their compatriots, Baker, I am certain they will be taken care of by their own.'

The seaman looked at the boat again and said 'That's very strange, sir!'

Courtenay followed his gaze and saw the boat altering course away, but there was someone in the water, swimming towards them, and every so often, stopping and shouting. 'What the devil...'

'Just as I looked again, sir, he jumped into the water!'

Courtenay opened a glass and looked at the figure in the water which was now again waving and screaming. Trafford, holding his injured arm and thinking now everything was over he could go below and have a couple of tots 'medicine' saw his Captain's lips start to twitch, and then his mouth gave a thin smile.

He said without lowering the glass to the Sailing Master, 'I think we had best heave-to Mr Wetherby, if you please. It appears Commander Spencer-White is wishing to join us!'

Hercules came to a stop and Courtenay watched with interest as Spencer-White swam towards them. A rope was lowered over the side which he eventually reached and he was hauled up with very little ceremony. He climbed over the side and Courtenay, watching from the quarterdeck rail with his hands behind his back, saw the man looking this way and that. He suddenly realised Spencer-White was looking for the side-party, and the thought made his smile again.

Marmaduke Spencer-White stormed up the larboard ladder to the quarterdeck, and stood dripping in front of Courtenay. St Clair moved away a little although not so far away he could not hear the exchange.

'You could have killed me, you damn fool! I was on that damn frog, and you opened fire on it and sunk it! I could have gone down with it if I hadn't the presence of mind to bribe some French sailors to let me into their boat! What the devil do you think you were doing firing on a French ship anyway? We are supposed to be at peace with them. By God, Captain, if you have started another war, my Uncle will have something to say about it! Then, when you do allow me aboard, there was no side party. I would remind you, Captain Courtenay, that I am Captain of a ship, and I *will* have the rights I am entitled to!'

He puffed him up to his full height, which was a good three inches less than Courtenay and dripped sea-water all over the decking.

'Have you quite finished *Commander* Spencer-White? Then let me tell you this. How dare you speak to me in the fashion you have, on my own quarterdeck, when you are one of my junior officers! Damn you sir, I have a mind to place you under arrest and have you subjected to a Court-martial when we get to Antigua! As to firing on that French ship, do you know what happened to *Spur?* No, I don't suppose you do, and I suspect you care even less. We cut her out, Commander, cut her out from under the noses of the frogs who had set a trap for us. I sent her off ahead of us under Lieutenant Cressy and Midshipman Fulford, with some of my lads. A French frigate comes along and sinks her, leaving only one survivor. We discover the wreckage and then two French liners turn up, and open fire on us. We are entitled to defend ourselves and we did. I did not know you were on board *Commander* and even if I had, on being attacked, my duty was clear. And do not talk to me about side parties, since you have no command, and, I would remind you, your rank has yet to be confirmed. If I have my way, Spencer-White, it never will be! Now, get off my quarterdeck before we are all afloat!'

He disappeared.

Lord Crompton had a good chuckle as Courtenay recounted the tale as he was performing their ritual of pouring claret.

'Damned cheek of the young puppy! Wish I had been there, Giles. I would have thrown him in the brig and then Court-martialled him for losing his ship. He would have been out of the service for good! As it is, although he will of course face the usual Court-martial, his Uncle will see he gets off. Mind you, I doubt his Uncle will be able to save the fact he will be back on the beach for the time being, as a Lieutenant.'

'Well, My Lord, half-pay is not likely to worry that one!'

'I suppose not. How is Jessica? I was very disturbed to find after you left that she was with child again. I would not have sent you my boy, you know that, had I been aware.'

'I know sir, and so did Jessica, which is why she said nought to stop me going.'

'She's a wife to be proud of Giles, but then I am sure you know that. How long is it now before the confinement?'

'Not very long at all. I was relieved that Vice-admiral Tarnworth did not try to hold me in Antigua for his own purposes. At least I have been able to get home in time.'

'Yes, I am very relieved too. It would not have sat well on my conscience if you had been away. Well Giles, you may have a decent leave now. I have to say I doubt this Peace will last very long, and I will then want you back again. We all know that Boney is just using the time to re-arm and re-equip and it won't be long before he is up to his old tricks again. We have already had some intelligence about invasion craft being constructed, some quite a way from the coast.'

'Colonel Tandy been fishing around again has he?'

'I am sure he is in the thick of it somewhere.'

'What is to happen to my ship, sir?'

'I am hoping to keep her in commission, although I have to appoint a temporary Captain. I gather you have none of your more senior officers left?'

'That is correct sir. Mr Cressy went down with the *Spur,* and Lieutenant Frobisher was killed in action.'

'What about Mr St Clair?'

'He performed well in combat sir, but I regret that he needs a lot more experience before he is ready for any kind of command.'

'Very well. Your old friend James Fenwick is about to report back for duty. I do not have anything for him at the moment, but I will promote him Captain and place him in command for the time being. When War is declared again, I will find something for him.'

'At least I will know my ship is in good hands, sir.'

'Good, now pour another Giles, and tell me again how you cut *Spur* out. There will be no trouble, by the way. This has been quite an embarrassment to the French, and they would want to forget it.'

'Just as well, sir.'

Crompton's Secretary, waiting outside the double doors, heard the laughter. He looked at the tall clock beside him and then at a long bench seat full of officers waiting to see the Admiral.

'I fear, gentlemen, you may be in for a long wait...'

THE   END

But keep a weather eye open for Giles Courtenay in his next swash-buckling adventure – The Return of the Warrior

CPSIA information can be obtained
at www.ICGtesting.com
Printed in the USA
FSHW021955100321
79392FS